DEATH ON THE AISLE

AN ANNABELLE ARCHER WEDDING PLANNER MYSTERY

LAURA DURHAM

BROADMOOR BOOKS

CHAPTER 1

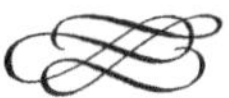

"What do you mean the pandit isn't ready?" I asked my assistant Kate over the muffled sounds of booming drums and cheering wedding guests.

"He said to wait and he'll come when he's done." Kate shrugged and ran a hand through her bouncy, blond bob. "It looked like he was in the middle of a ritual of some sort."

"Wait?" I said, trying to keep the hysteria from my voice. "Is he kidding?"

"He's a Hindu priest, Annabelle. I don't think he does 'kidding.'"

I knew Kate was right. I groaned and tried to think fast.

Thinking fast was a skill I'd developed over the five plus years I'd owned Wedding Belles, Washington DC's most up-and-coming wedding planning firm. That and the ability to stay calm even when I was running a wedding for over five hundred guests and the priest had no intention of following my detailed schedule.

I stood at the entrance door to the Mellon Auditorium with the bride's family and friends on the inside and the groom and all of his family coming down Constitution Avenue to meet them at the front. When they met at the door, the pandit and the bride's mother would greet the groom and lead him inside to the ceremony. To complicate matters, the groom was riding on an elephant surrounded by a troop of half a dozen drummers leading the crowd in exuberant dancing and singing. The entire process was called the Baraat, and every Indian wedding started with one. Not every one had an elephant, a fact for which I was grateful considering the laborious permitting process we'd gone through to make it legal for the massive animal to parade down the middle of the city.

"Can we slow down the groom?" I asked, putting a hand to my auburn hair tucked tight into a high bun and feeling glad that every hair seemed in place despite the late summer humidity.

"If you want to jump in front of an elephant, be my guest," Kate said. "But I'm not getting anywhere near it. These shoes are Louboutins and they don't take very well to elephant dung."

I glanced at Kate's spike heels and fought the urge to roll my eyes. It was a miracle Kate could still walk considering the inappropriate footwear she wore to work. I stuck to black flats on wedding days and only switched into heels when I needed to mingle with guests.

I stepped outside and craned my neck around the corner to check the progress of the Baraat. The procession of the groom to a Hindu ceremony was one of my favorite parts of an Indian wedding. I loved the energy of the drums and the joy of the family as they danced and cheered. This was the way to enter a wedding, I thought. After a Baraat, all my other ceremony processionals seemed downright sleepy.

"Almost here," I said to myself, as the colorful crowd advanced. The women's saris were a riot of crimson, turquoise, fuchsia, tangerine, and purple, adorned with beads and jewels, and each was more stunning than the last. No sedate black dresses here. Kate and I loved to play "pick the sari" to see which of us could find the most beautiful design of the day. I glanced down at my black crepe suit. Indian weddings were the only time my standard black wedding planner "uniform" didn't blend with the crowd, but I couldn't do my job in a sari.

I walked back inside and smiled at the mother of the bride, who stood inside the doors. She adjusted the top of her magenta and gold sari and looked around her. Her dark hair was swept back from her face and held up with jeweled hairpins. With flawless skin and pale eyes, she was as strikingly beautiful as her daughter and didn't look remotely old enough be a mother of the bride, or as those of us in the wedding biz refer to her, the MOB.

"Where is the priest, Annabelle? He should be standing next to me when the groom's procession reaches the door."

"On his way," I assured her with more confidence than I felt.

I crossed the lobby of the building, my black flats making virtually no noise on the marble floor, and peeked inside the grand hall where the ceremony would take place. The mandap was set up on the built-in stage at the far end of the room, and even though the stage was at least thirty feet wide, the mandap dominated the space. The bride had wanted a ceremony structure that made a statement, and the ornate towering mandap draped in iridescent gold fabric certainly did that. Even the lights illuminating the ceiling were gold, giving the room the appearance of being bathed in the precious metal.

The only thing not entirely gold on the stage was the tiny Hindu priest, dressed in modest white robes and crouching over what would soon be the ceremonial fire in front of the bride's and groom's chairs. I didn't want to bother him again in case he was in the middle of a pre-ceremony ritual and because, despite his hobbit-like stature, I was a bit intimidated by him. He must have heard the heavy door open, though, because he turned toward me and held up a finger.

"They will wait." He smiled at me and went back to his work.

I nodded and backed out, closing the huge wooden door behind me. I was sure they would wait since they had no choice. I could hear the drums and cheering getting louder. The bride's family craned to see out the glass doors, but luckily, the elephant hadn't reached the front of the building yet, so it was still obscured by the pillars in front. As I put on my most comforting face to reassure the mother of the bride that the pandit was on his way, and as I mentally convinced myself white lies were harmless, my phone rang in my jacket pocket. I pushed the talk button.

"Wedding Belles, this is Anna . . ."

"This is a catastrophe of biblical proportions. I just don't know if I can work under this level of duress."

I heard a muffled sob. Richard. He was arguably the city's best caterer and had also been my best friend since I'd move to DC and opened a wedding planning business several years ago. He claimed to have found my youth and inexperience charming, and had taken it upon himself to teach me everything he knew about weddings and navigating the DC social scene. I credited his mentorship for my rapid rise through the ranks of society wedding planners. Considering how crazy some of my clients had been, I was more grateful for this on some days than others.

One of the main drawbacks of my job was having to juggle so many weddings at once. Even when I was on-site at one wedding, it wasn't unusual to get calls about an upcoming one. I knew Richard was down at the District Marina preparing for next weekend's wedding so his call didn't completely shock me. Especially since the wedding was being held on a ship, which brought its own set of challenges.

I'd done a few weddings on boats before; garish paddle wheelers that got rented out for the afternoon. But nothing like the 164 foot luxury yacht *Mystic Maven*. Technically speaking, a superyacht, which was boat speak for a yacht big enough to have a helicopter pad on the top.

Despite the size of the yacht, it didn't have a catering kitchen, so Richard was concerned about the space on the dock for the makeshift kitchen he needed to create. "Okay, take a breath and tell me what's going on."

"As if it wasn't bad enough to work under a tent with a ten-foot drop into the water on three sides, I just don't have waterproof couture." He took a breath."And now the filming crew wants to use the galley kitchen on board to store their production equipment. Annabelle, you know I need that galley kitchen for plating."

"Filming crew? What filming crew? Are you sure you're on the right boat?"

A deep sigh from Richard. "Ship, Annabelle. When it's this big, it's called a ship. And of course I'm on the right one. How could I miss it? It takes up half the marina."

"Okay, okay," I said. "But what film crew?"

"The one from the *Diamond Weddings* TV show. You know, the reality show profiling the weddings of the rich and the richer."

I knew the show. Opulence meets excess times fifty. "Well, what are they doing there?"

"How should I know? I thought you had arranged for it. And what's all that screaming in the background, anyway?"

I rubbed my temples. "Dhol drummers. The groom's arriving on an elephant." I rocked onto the back of my heels. "Has the bride seen the crew yet?"

"I don't think so. At least I haven't seen her around today. An elephant? Is that why I couldn't get through Constitution earlier?"

I ignored Richard's question. "Good. That gives me some time to figure this out."

"You don't think the bride knows her wedding is going to be filmed by *Diamond Weddings*?

I thought about the sweet yoga-teacher bride who only agreed to wear crystals in her hair if they were healing crystals. "No way. That isn't her style."

"I have news for you, doll. This whole yacht isn't her style."

I raised an eyebrow. Richard had a point. "She wants to make her father happy, and he loves his boat. He always envisioned her wedding on it."

"Do you think he called *Diamond Weddings*?" Richard asked.

"No." I caught myself biting my lower lip. "This has the stepmother's name written all over it."

"Babs Barbery." Richard sucked in his breath. "Good luck with that."

Between the impending elephant and the domineering stepmother, I was going to need it.

CHAPTER 2

"Did the ceremony start?" Fern's voice startled me from behind as I stood peeking into the main hall at the Mellon Auditorium. "The bride wanted me to touch up her hair after the ceremony."

Fern, short for Fernando and a result of his mother being an Abba groupie, was the city's most sought-after wedding hairstylist and part of my wedding dream team. I booked Fern as soon as the brides set their wedding date, because no one could calm and entertain nervous brides as well as he could. Usually he did it with a patented mix of dirty jokes and slightly veiled insults to their virtue, but every client seemed to love it and him.

"It just began," I said.

To my great relief, the pandit had indeed made it to the doors to greet the groom by the time the elephant arrived at the front of the building. The groom's guests had danced into the building and taken seats in the main hall. After a few words from the pandit, we'd sent the bride down the aisle with her uncle, and the groom was about to be revealed as she reached the mandap. I closed the door as quietly as I could and turned around. "They're just about to do the reveal and . . . What are you wearing?"

"A sari, of course." Fern's dark hair in a low ponytail was the only thing not creamsicle orange about him. The mango-colored sari had beautiful gold beading along the edges, and it might have been a candidate for my favorite one of the evening if my male hairdresser hadn't been wearing it. I heard a faint jingle.

"Are those bells?" I hissed.

Fern picked up the hem of the sari and revealed a pair of tiny gold bells sewn in. "I couldn't resist."

"Couldn't you?" I looked around the foyer, grateful no one was there. "Has the bride seen you?"

"Of course." Fern gave me a look. "This is one of hers."

My mouth dropped. "You're wearing one of the bride's saris?"

Fern ran a hand over the gossamer fabric. "Well, I am a perfect size six." He sized me up. "You should try it on later. It would probably fit you, too. Wedding season stress has been good for your figure, sweetie."

"You have got to be joking." Kate's voice echoed in the marble foyer as she came around the corner. I put my finger to my lips to shush her.

"Thank you," I whispered, glad my occasionally superficial assistant was on the side of reason for once.

Kate ignored me and glared at Fern. "I can't believe she let you wear that and not me."

"This color wouldn't look good on a blonde." Fern patted Kate on the arm. "It would wash you out, darling."

"I'll have you know I look fabulous in orange." Kate flipped a strand of pale hair off her face.

Fern raised an eyebrow. "Well, this is more tangerine than true orange."

I groaned. "Will you two stop arguing over color palettes? We have much bigger problems to deal with."

"Well, you don't have to worry about the elephant," Kate said, giving Fern a final glare. "His trainer is packing him up as we speak."

"That's one down." I was glad the animal was on his way out. Livestock that large made me nervous. "Did either of you know about *Diamond Weddings* filming next weekend's wedding?"

"The reality TV show?" Kate asked. "Why didn't you tell me you called them?"

"*I* didn't call them," I said.

"The bride's stepmother did," Fern said. "I thought you knew, Annabelle."

I put my hands on my hips. "No, I didn't know. How did you know?"

"The stepmother's stylist. The one they flew in from Paris. I met him yesterday when I went down to do the bride's hair trial." Fern lowered his voice and leaned closer to us, as if there were people around to overhear. "He told me the stepmother has been telling everyone the TV show begged her to let them film the wedding, but she actually called them."

"Why?" Kate asked.

"She's wild for the publicity and she'll do anything to upstage her stepdaughter. From what I understand, she's a bit jealous that her husband dotes on his daughter."

"Nice," I said. The bride's descriptions of her stepmother had been less than flattering, but I got the idea she might have been playing down the mean.

"You should see what she's wearing to the wedding. Her gowns for the wedding cost more than the bride's. And her jewelry!" Fern whistled and the sound echoed off the marble floor and walls.

"Gowns?" I asked. "As in plural?"

Fern nodded. "Mmm-hmmm. And one of them is cream. With beading."

"What? No veil?" I rubbed my temples at the thought of the bride's stepmother wearing a beaded almost-white gown. "How are we going to break this to the bride? She'll hate the idea of all this publicity."

"Not to mention her stepmother wearing white," Kate muttered, pulling her trademark bag of gummy bears out of her pocket and offering them around.

I gratefully took a few sticky bears, only slightly warm from being in Kate's pocket all day. I needed the sugar rush since the wedding day was slated to last over fourteen hours, and I'd gone through my bag of gummies already. Nibbling on the sugary sweet candy throughout a wedding day was one habit I was glad to have picked up from my assistant.

"Cream, darling," Fern said, waving off the offer of gummies. "Huge difference. And the bride already knows."

My head snapped up. "About what?"

"The reality TV crew. She found out yesterday while I was there."

I was almost afraid to ask. "Did she take it well?"

Fern wrinkled his nose and thought for a moment. "Only if you consider running off the boat and threatening to cancel the wedding to be 'taking it well.'"

I didn't.

"Does this mean we have a day off next weekend?" Kate looked hopeful.

"No," I said. "It means we have a lot of work to do to smooth things over so this wedding actually happens."

"How are we going to do that?" Fern asked. "Lock the stepmother in a closet until the wedding is over?"

I ignored Fern's suggestion, even though it didn't sound so bad. "We'll come up with something." I tried to sound more sure than I felt. "This wedding is going to happen. Trust me." I'd spent too many hours on dock permits and water safety plans to let this event fall apart at the last minute.

Fern rubbed his hands together, and the bells of his sari tinkled. "Let the games begin."

CHAPTER 3

"Can we please stop for coffee?" Kate rested her head against the passenger window of my car. Her hair covered most of her face, and she tried to shield the sun with her arm.

"I told you we were getting an early start this morning." I'd swung by Kate's apartment in upper Georgetown and coaxed her down after a mere three calls to her cell phone. "And it isn't that early, anyway. It's almost ten."

"We did have a wedding yesterday, remember? Whatever happened to having a day off? You know, Sunday fun day?"

"Whatever happened to not going out with the bridal party after the weddings?" I headed down Wisconsin Avenue passing the always-bustling hair salon, Dry Bar, where Kate frequently had her hair blown out. Traffic was light so far, but the city was still waking up.

I glanced up at the windows of Carine's Bridal Atelier knowing it wasn't yet open, but envisioning the racks filled with designer gowns. I loved having one of the chicest bridal gown salons so close to the Wedding Belles headquarters.

Kate peeked at me from under her arm. "Was that ever really a hard and fast rule?"

I tried to give her my best tough boss glare. "Well, it should be."

Kate, per usual, had made fast friends with the groomsmen at our wedding and had been invited to go out with the whole bridal party afterward. Since the dancing went on until the early hours of the morning, I knew Kate had been out late. Which made waking her up bright and early to go to the boat with me even sweeter.

My days of thinking going out after a wedding was a fun idea were long over. After being on my feet for twelve hours or more, all I wanted to do was go home, take a hot shower, and crawl into bed.

"I thought Ian was back from tour and taking you out," Kate said. "Shouldn't you be tired too?"

Ian was the leader of the eighties cover band called The Breakfast Club. He had spiky blond hair, tattoos, and a Scottish accent. Truth be told, he was much more Kate's type than mine. She liked guys who looked dangerous. I liked men with steady jobs. But DC's dating scene was notoriously bad, so I'd loosened my rules for Ian. The fact that he was very cute also played a part.

"We didn't go out." I rolled down my window to enjoy the late summer air before it got stifling. Shops were starting to set out sidewalk signs, and a few people sat at the umbrella-topped tables outside Marvelous Market. "He just stopped by at the end of the wedding since his bar mitzvah at the W Hotel ended early and he was right around the corner."

"Nice to have a hot boyfriend with an equally weird work schedule."

"He's not my boyfriend," I said a little too quickly. "As a matter of fact, we decided to cool things off."

Kate's head snapped toward me. "Cool things off? How can you cool things off when you never heated things up?"

"I guess not according to your definition," I said.

Kate leaned her head against the window. "Not according to anyone's definition."

I raised my voice to talk over her muttering. "Anyway, we both have really crazy schedules. It's hard to connect, so we're going to be friends."

"Does this have anything to do with the detective?" Kate asked. "And can you roll up the window? It's cold in here."

"Reese?" I started to roll up the window then stopped. "How can you be cold? It's June." I looked at Kate's melon-colored sleeveless sheath, which ended at midthigh. That explained it.

Kate sighed. "Yes, Reese. The steamy detective we can't seem to stop running into. I definitely noticed sparks the last time we saw him."

When we stopped at the light at M Street, I reached in the backseat with one hand and grabbed a black cotton cardigan. "Here, put this on."

Kate sat up and slipped her arms into the sweater. "So? Did you dump Ian for Reese?"

"I didn't dump anyone. It was mutual," I said, making the left onto M Street. I didn't mention Reese had asked me out the last time I'd seen him. I didn't mention it because then I'd have to explain how our first date got cancelled when he got called in to a big homicide case right after he'd arrived at my apartment to pick me up.

She shrugged. "You know how they say a bird in the hand is worth two bushes?"

"No," I said. "They don't say that."

"All I'm saying is maybe you shouldn't have dropped Ian until you were sure about Cutie Cop."

I shot her a sideways glance. "Cutie Cop?"

"He needs a nickname." She motioned up ahead. "Now can we please get some coffee? Baked and Wired is only one block away. I'll run in so you don't have to park the car."

"Fine. Get me anything with mocha." I swerved over to a semi-legal street parking space so Kate could hop out.

"Have I told you lately you're the best boss ever?" She blew me a kiss and ran down Thomas Jefferson Avenue. Impressive, considering the sidewalk jutted up in places and she wore heels. Her navigating skill in stilettos had always impressed me, and these were, by far, the lowest shoes I'd ever seen her wear. Two and a half inches, tops. Flats were simply not in her repertoire. She hurried over the canal bridge and then disappeared into the little bakery with the bright pink bicycle leaning out front.

Kate had a point. Why had I dropped Ian when things with Mike Reese had barely gotten off the ground? Maybe it had something to do with the fact that I never understood why Ian was into me. Guys in bands usually had girlfriends who were equally cool and tattooed. I spent my life picking table linens and writing wedding timelines, had a collection of tasteful black suits, almost always wore my long auburn hair in a ponytail or bun, and had never even considered getting a tattoo. It felt like we didn't match and, call it the wedding planner in me, but I was big into things matching.

I couldn't say Detective Reese was exactly like me, either, but at least he didn't go on tour every few months and have a closet filled with kilts and leather. And I had to admit his dark hair and hazel eyes were a particular weakness of mine. My stomach did flips just thinking about him.

Kate threw open the car door and handed a bag across to me. "I got you a Smurfette and a mocha."

"A what?"

"A Smurfette—blueberries and lemon. Sounded amazing, and I know you love lemon. I got the birthday cake one."

I peered into the white paper bag. "Cupcakes? You got cupcakes for breakfast?"

"First of all, it's not breakfast. It's after 10 am, which means it's practically lunch," Kate said. "Second, cupcakes are just like muffins with icing, and everyone is fine with muffins in the morning. It's really unfair to cupcakes, if you ask me. And these are not just *any* cupcakes. These are hands down the best in the city. Trust me. I've tried them all."

I believed her. If there was one thing Kate loved above men (and maybe shoes), it was sugar. Cookies, cupcakes, brownies—she loved it all. It amazed me she stayed so thin. The only thing I could figure was dating and running in heels burned an awful lot of calories. I relied on wedding stress to keep me fitting into my size six jeans.

She pulled out her chocolate cupcake topped with swirls of vanilla frosting and began to peel off the wax paper wrapper. "I figured we needed some serious energy to deal with the Ship of the Damned."

She made a good point. I put my coffee in the cup holder next to me and held my cupcake in one hand as I merged back into Georgetown traffic. I wanted to get down to the docks and do some damage control with the bride before it got too late.

"So what's our strategy here?" Kate asked. "Take out the step-mom? Sweet-talk the dad? Throw the TV crew overboard?"

"I'm hoping we won't have to 'take out' anyone," I said. "I just want to find the bride, calm her down, and sort out this mess with the TV crew."

"Oh, is that all? You know," Kate said through a mouthful of cupcake, "our job always sounds easier than it actually is."

For once, I completely agreed with Kate.

CHAPTER 4

"Wow." Even though Kate wore sunglasses, she still shielded her eyes as she looked up at the ship that was to hold our upcoming wedding. We stood on the dock next to the yacht waiting to be let on board, and I glanced around me at the District Marina. Our floating wedding venue was so massive it made the other boats look like toys bobbing in a bathtub.

"I told you it was big," I said.

The ship was technically a superyacht and spanned over 160 feet from bow to stern. It rose three stories above us with each level getting progressively smaller, much like a tiered wedding cake. I knew the helicopter pad, which would be our dance floor, and the hot tub, which we were covering to use for the ceremony, were on the top.

The sides of the ship gleamed white with only the boat's name, *Mystic Maven,* swirling in black script across the pristine surface. What wasn't white on the boat was shining chrome. I could only imagine how much effort it took to keep all of it polished and was glad that wasn't my job, although as a wedding planner I'd had to do far worse tasks before.

"Welcome aboard," a voice called to us from above. "You must be the wedding planners."

"Yes," I called back, even though I couldn't see where the voice came from. "Annabelle and Kate."

"I'm Mandy, the chief stew." A tall, leggy woman with straight brown hair appeared at the top of the gangway leading onto the ship. A woman who could have passed for her slightly shorter and less leggy twin stood next to her. "This is Caren, one of the crew. Leave your shoes in the basket, put on some slippers, and come on up."

She motioned to a pair of baskets at the bottom of the gangway: one empty and one filled with leather slippers. Kate and I both exchanged our shoes for black leather slide-on slippers with the boat's name embossed on the top.

"Maybe I should get the name of my apartment building put on my slippers," Kate said under her breath. "It's a nice touch."

I elbowed her in the side. "Oh, be quiet."

We walked up the wooden bridge linking the ship to the dock and met Mandy and Caren at the walkway that ran along the outside. I noticed they both wore a black uniform with *Mystic Maven* embroidered on the left side in the same script used on the slippers and the side of the ship. These people clearly understood branding.

"I've been looking forward to meeting you," Mandy said, giving us each a quick handshake. "Mrs. Barbery wanted me to get you settled before she joined you."

We shook both women's hands. I reminded myself Mrs. Barbery was the stepmother of the bride and not even the first one.

"So what exactly is a chief stew?" Kate asked. Sometimes I was glad Kate was direct because it saved me from asking so many questions.

"I oversee what goes on inside the boat, from making sure the owners get their breakfast on time, to ordering new uniforms, to managing the inside staff." Mandy waved for us to follow her. "I only came on a few months ago, but all the staff has talked about is this wedding."

"It's pretty unusual to have a party for over a hundred guests on a yacht," Caren said. "We're used to the owners having dinner parties for six to eight friends."

"How many are on staff?" I asked.

Mandy thought for a moment before answering. "Fourteen including the captain."

"Fourteen?" Kate's mouth gaped. "Where do you all sleep?"

"The crew quarters are downstairs. The ship also can sleep up to twelve guests in addition to the family, but we rarely have that many people stay on board." Mandy led us into a casual dining room that held a tufted beige banquette curved around the wall and a polished wood table. Papers were spread across the table.

Kate whistled. "This is some boat."

"Don't forget Kristie is expecting one hundred fifty wedding guests," I said. "It has to be."

"And this is some wedding," Mandy said. "I don't know how you do this for a living."

"When we aren't planning weddings, we're solving crimes." Kate winked at the two women. "Sometimes I think the crimes are easier."

I jabbed Kate with my elbow. I knew she meant it to be a joke, but it was too close to reality to be funny to me.

"Seriously?" Caren asked, her dark eyebrows disappearing under her bangs.

"Not really," I said, giving Kate a look that forbid her to add anything. "I mean, we have ended up solving a few cases but our involvement was accidental."

Both women nodded but seemed taken aback. Perfect. The last thing I needed was for the crew to be whispering about our bad habit of falling into crime investigations. I did not want that information getting back to our client. I'd found that brides did not like crime to mentioned in the same breath as their wedding planners.

"We were hoping to talk to Kristie this morning," I said. "Is she around?"

Mandy motioned for us to take seats at the table and started stacking the papers into piles. "She's doing yoga downstairs in the gym. We're not supposed to disturb her until she's done. Imbalances her energy or something. But she should be finished pretty soon." She tapped Caren on the arm. "Can you go check without disturbing her?"

"Of course." Caren disappeared through another door in the room.

Kate's eyebrows popped up. "There's a gym on board?"

"Oh, it's small," Mandy said. "Like a big closet attached to the steam room."

Kate looked at me. "Steam room?"

Mandy gave a half smile. "Helps Mrs. Barbery with her stress. And after all the things that have been happening, that's a good thing, believe me."

"What do you mean?" I asked. "The TV crew?"

"Oh, no." Mandy moved a silver tray with glasses and a pitcher of water from the sideboard to the table. "Mrs. Barbery loves publicity. What she doesn't love are accidents. Mr. Barbery, the bride's father, is crazy about this boat, and if anything happens to it he goes nuts. And when Mr. Barbery goes nuts, his wife practically lives in her steam room."

"So what's been going on?" I asked.

Mandy shrugged as she poured out three glasses of ice water. "Nothing major. Just some little things. A rail on the stairs came loose, the tender fell from where it hangs at the back of the ship, and the doorknob to the pantry jammed and locked our chef inside for a couple of hours."

"That doesn't sound so bad." Kate took her water from Mandy and inspected the glass etched with the name of the ship. "Wait. What's the tender?"

"It's the smaller boat we have hanging from the stern," Mandy explained. "But it's still a sizable motor boat."

"Yikes," Kate said.

"Exactly. The hull of the tender cracked so no one is happy about that." Mandy lowered her voice. "Kristie thinks the boat has bad energy and all these things are a sign she shouldn't get married here."

"What does Mrs. Barbery think?" I asked.

"She's not happy about all the glitches, but she's also been planning on having a wedding on this ship for months. The invitations went out weeks ago, and her friends are starting to fly in from all over the world." Mandy took a long drink from one of the glasses. "There is no way she's canceling this wedding. I think she'd have it even if the bride didn't show up."

"That would be different," Kate said. "I wouldn't mind a bride-free wedding."

I shot Kate a look then turned back to Mandy. "So then it's not the TV crew that Kristie's upset about?"

"Well, it didn't make her happy, that's for sure." Mandy's voice got even lower, as though she expected the bride to be crouching outside the door. "But I think it was just the icing on the cake. She'd been getting worked up for the past few days. Every time something would happen, she'd become more convinced the boat has bad energy. When the TV crew came aboard, she just lost it and started yelling about moving the wedding."

I knew Kristie was very attuned to energy vibrations, as she put it. We'd even chosen the wedding colors, pale blue and silver, based on their positive vibrations.

I leaned close to Mandy. "Do you think Kristie is serious about not getting married on the ship?"

"Well, she seemed to calm down after talking to her father,"

Mandy said. "Between you and me, I think he's trying to keep them both happy at the same time, but owes it to his new wife to keep her more happy."

"What do you mean?" Kate asked.

"Well, Mrs. Barbery loves entertaining on the ship, but she won't be doing that for the next three months because her husband gave the bride and groom the ship for a round-the-world honeymoon cruise."

"By themselves?" I asked.

"Well, with the crew," Mandy said. "But not Mr. and Mrs. Barbery."

Kate's eyes widened and she looked at me. "Did you know about this?"

I shook my head. "No idea."

Kate wagged a finger at me. "You never find out where couples are going for their honeymoons."

Now it made sense. "So he's making it up to his wife by letting *Diamond Weddings* film her hosting a big society wedding on board."

"That's what we all think," Mandy said. "So in an ideal world, the daughter gets her trip around the world, the wife gets her appearance on national TV, and everyone's happy. So long as Kristie gets enough peace and quiet to forget about the TV crew, we should be okay."

Kate looked around. "The ship does seem quiet."

The door to the dining room swung open, and a tall man strode in. His blond hair swept back from his face in a perfect wave, and he stared down at us over his slightly upturned nose. He wore a navy suit with a pink tie widely knotted at his throat and carried an armful of blue cloths, which he dumped onto the table in front of us.

"Someone had better start explaining this mess or I am out of here." He folded his arms and glared at all of us.

Mandy gave me an apologetic look. "Meet Jeremy Johns, Mrs. Barbery's designer from New York."

So much for peace and quiet.

CHAPTER 5

Jeremy Johns looked me up and down and then did the same to Kate. One eyebrow arched in obvious disapproval. I wasn't sure if it was my khaki casual look or Kate's just-tumbled-out-of-bed hair that elicited the near grimace. "And you would be?"

"I'm Annabelle Archer, and this is my assistant, Kate." I put out my hand for him to shake. "We're from Wedding Belles."

His face remained blank.

"They're the wedding planners," Mandy added.

"Oh." He gave me a perfunctory handshake. "Then maybe you can explain these miserable blue linens." He pointed at the pile of pale blue tablecloths like he was accusing a murderer from the witness stand.

"These must be what Richard sent over for the bride to pick from." I ran a hand through the pile. Aside from one unfortunate shiny number and a too-heavy brocade, the linens weren't bad. They were exactly what Kristie had requested: pale blue with some texture. I especially liked a powder blue silk that looked like it was covered with fluttery petals.

Jeremy Johns put up his palms. "Maybe there's been a misunderstanding. You see, I've been given complete artistic control over this event and these linens do not fit into my vision."

"Since when do you have control over this wedding?" Kate asked. "We've been working on this for five months."

Jeremy folded his arms across his chest. "Since Mrs. Barbery called me in. This wedding is going to be on national television." Again with the arching eyebrow. "You didn't think she'd leave the design up to you two, did you?"

Mandy gave a nervous laugh. "Why don't we all talk this—"

"It isn't just the two of them." Richard walked through the sliding door behind us, and I saw it led to a galley kitchen.

I breathed a sigh of relief. I rarely had this reaction when Richard joined a tense situation, but it was good to have a diva on our side too.

"You're with them?" Jeremy sized up Richard, but didn't make a face. It helped that Richard wore a flawless polished cotton shirt in peacock blue with crisp tailored white pants and looked every bit the nautical aristocrat. Even his short, dark hair was perfectly coifed.

"Richard Gerard of Richard Gerard Catering." He didn't extend his hand. "And, yes, I'm with them."

"And I'll have you know we've designed some very fancy weddings," Kate said. She'd made it from drowsy to defensive.

Jeremy's voice became syrupy sweet. "I'm sure you have, sweetie, but this is a whole other league. Trust me, I've designed Mrs. Barbery's house in the Hamptons and her flat in London."

"Decorating a house and designing a wedding are two entirely different things," Richard said. "So unless the client wants new drapes, why don't you run along and let us do our jobs?"

Jeremy clenched his fists, and Mandy groaned.

"Mrs. Barbery flew me down to put my signature style on this wedding." His voice was nearly a hiss. "All the properties I've designed for her have a distinct style, and so will this wedding."

"I'm almost afraid to ask," Richard said. "What is the signature style?"

Jeremy fanned his hands out in front of us like he was pulling back curtains to a stage. "South Beach meets the South of France."

Everyone was silent for a moment.

"You must be out of your mind," Richard finally said.

Jeremy sniffed. "Mrs. Barbery likes to mix the vintage with modern. It's eclectic."

"I know I'm still half awake," Kate muttered to me, "but I don't even get it. How do those two things even go together?"

Jeremy's face reddened. "I don't expect you to understand what we're doing up in New York. You people in Washington are still wearing red power ties."

Richard sucked in air. "You take that back."

"This is insane." Kate turned to me. "First a TV crew and now a neon-rustic theme?"

I broke in. "Aren't you all forgetting something?"

"I doubt it," said Jeremy and Richard together, then they glared at each other.

"What about what the bride wants?" I asked. "This is her wedding, after all."

"Thank you, Annabelle." Kristie pushed into the room behind Jeremy with Caren close behind her. This was getting absurd. Any more people and we'd be nose-to-nose.

Kristie still wore black yoga pants and a formfitting batik-print tank top from her practice. Her ash blond hair was pulled up in a high ponytail giving her an extra inch or so, which she desperately needed. Everything about Kristie was tiny and delicate down to her soft voice.

Jeremy turned around and smiled at the bride. "We were just discussing your wedding," he gushed. "And how it's going to be a fairytale come to life."

Kate made a gagging noise and I dug an elbow into her side.

"My stepmother may have flown you here, Jeremy, but this is not her wedding."

Jeremy opened and closed his mouth like a fish.

Kristie smiled at the rest of us. "But since my father and stepmother are hosting this wedding, and since Jeremy is here, I hope we can all work together."

Richard started to say something, but Kristie continued. "Because if we can't, then I'm perfectly willing to call this whole thing off."

She spun on her heel and left the room. Caren followed the bride, a worried look on her face.

"Well, I guess that settles it." Mandy clapped her hands together, clearly glad to have the confrontation over with.

"Hardly," Jeremy said. "That girl is not in charge. I'm going to talk to Mrs. Barbery."

"Come on, boys." I looked from Jeremy to Richard. "I'm sure we can find a compromise."

Jeremy turned and pushed through the door. "Over my dead body."

"That can be arranged," Richard called after him.

"You are not helping," I said to Richard.

"What?" he asked in his most innocent voice. "You're always telling me to be more accommodating."

CHAPTER 6

"I'd say that went well," Kate said, as we listened to Jeremy Johns storm off to find the bride's stepmother.

"Do you want me to go after him?" Richard asked, not making a move toward the door.

"And do what?" I asked. "Catch him and stuff him in a closet?"

Richard's face brightened. "Now you're talking. Sometimes I believe we share the same brain, Annabelle."

I groaned.

"I hope he doesn't agitate Mrs. Barbery." Mandy wrung her hands in front of her. "She's much easier to work with when she's not upset. The last time she got worked up she decided to change the staff uniform design and made me redo the menus for the week. The chef wanted to kill me."

Kate looked at Mandy's worried expression and touched her arm. "Have you ever considered a different line of work? Because your job is starting to make our job look like fun."

Mandy gave a weak laugh, but still looked worried.

I clapped my hands together to rally my troops. "Okay, I think we should find where Kristie ran off to. We can talk her off the ledge and then worry about Jeremy. I'm sure he's more bark than bite, anyway." I turned to Mandy. "Now let's go find the bride."

"Follow me." Mandy led everyone from the casual dining room into a huge main salon. "I'll give you a tour of the ship. We're bound to run into her along the way."

The room was done in almost all white with accents of black and silver. Pristine cream-colored carpet (which explained the mandatory slippers), curved ecru couches, metal and glass coffee tables, and what looked like James Bond memorabilia displayed in glass cases along one wall. It didn't look like South of France meets South Beach yet, so I figured this must be more the father of the bride's style. This boat was his baby, after all, and he'd had it long before the new Mrs. Barbery entered the picture. I wondered how Jeremy Johns planned to work his mash-up theme around this look.

"The ship has five levels. On the main level is the bridge, the galley, the casual dining area, and the main salon. All the bedrooms are below. There's a staircase along the outside of the ship in the back, another on each side, and two inside the ship. One that goes through the kitchen at the other end and one here." Mandy pointed to the ornate gold staircase in the center of the main salon that led down into the ship. She walked us through the room to a set of glass doors that led outside. "This is the way to the transom and the wide staircase leading to the main salon. It's how Mrs. Barbery wants guests to enter. Has the most wow factor."

"The transom?" I asked.

"Sorry," Mandy said. "That's boat speak for the wide, flat area at the back end of the ship."

"Got it. So we're putting a couple of highboy tables here?" I looked out and saw the large wooden floor of the extended transom at the base of the wide staircase. Even though the ship was huge, we'd need all the extra space we could get for a hundred and fifty guests plus the staff to wait on them.

Two blond boys in white shorts and black shirts identical to Mandy's were polishing the metal stair railings. They looked barely out of their teens, but I assumed they were part of the staff.

"Who are they?" Kate asked, watching the tanned boys work.

"Deckhands," Mandy said. "They have a lot to do before next weekend."

"Too bad," Kate said so only I could hear her. "They're cute. I'd be willing to show them the DC sights if they got some time off."

"They're children," I said. "Hands off."

Kate made a pouty face, which I ignored.

"Let's go upstairs, so you can see where Mrs. Barbery thought we'd put the ice bar." Mandy walked outside and around to a set of spiral stairs.

We all followed her and came out on an upper deck with a covered lounge area that held a large half-moon table.

"We thought it could go against this wall," Mandy said, motioning to a wall with another set of glass double doors in the center.

"What is this?" I pushed open one of the glass doors and peered into a room that looked more like it belonged in an English gentleman's club than on an über-modern yacht. A pair of beige leather couches flanked a dark wood desk, and three of the four walls were floor-to-ceiling bookshelves.

"This is Mr. Barbery's study," Mandy said. "He'd prefer we not use it for the wedding."

"Understandable." Kate walked over to one of the walls of shelves and gestured to a display of ancient-looking coins. "It looks like he's a collector."

"Those are all things he recovered while he was an underwater treasure hunter," Mandy said.

Richard raised his index finger. "I beg your pardon?"

Mandy laughed. "Did you all not know that's how he made his millions?"

I shook my head. I'd yet to find an appropriate way to ask brides how their parents became loaded.

Kate looked at me. "We have got to start Googling our clients."

"Mr. Barbery was one of the most successful salvage divers in his day," Mandy said. "He's been retired for years after finding chests of gold coins off the coast of Africa."

"Treasure hunting, gold, diving." Kate touched one of the coins on display. "It sounds so exciting."

"The reality isn't quite so romantic, I assure you," a deep voice said from the doorway. "Freezing water, pirates, and hostile governments are more common."

"Mr. Barbery," Mandy stammered. "I'm so sorry. I was just showing the wedding planners and caterer around. We'll get out of your office."

The barrel-chested man laughed and waved his hands. "Don't worry. It's not every day I have such lovely ladies in my office."

Kate giggled and blushed. The bride's father wasn't tall, but he looked every bit the treasure hunter with bronzed skin and dark hair and a matching beard shot through with silver. He wore a white button down shirt rolled up to expose his thick forearms and a pair of gray cargo pants.

"We were admiring your finds," I said.

Mr. Barbery nodded. "Just a few mementos. Most of my discoveries were sold to museums."

"I think it's probably best that we don't use this room for the wedding," I said as I scanned the coins, antique guns, and leather-bound books on the shelves. "We should have enough space throughout the rest of the ship."

Mr. Barbery smiled at me, and the skin around his blue eyes crinkled. "I want my Kristie to have anything she wants for this wedding, so if you need anything, just let me know."

"Thank you, sir," Richard and I said in unison.

"I'd better go check on my wife." Mr. Barbery winked at us. "I have to keep both of my girls happy."

We watched as he left the room.

Kate shook her head. "He seems so much nicer than—"

"Most of our fathers." I cut off Kate so she couldn't finish her sentence, which I was sure would have been an insult about Mrs. Barbery.

"Good save," Richard whispered to me.

Mandy held open the glass doors and we all returned to the covered deck.

"So we won't use Mr. Barbery's office but we will have the ice bar out here?" Kate asked.

Richard cast his eyes over the space. "How on earth am I supposed to get the bar up here? A huge block of ice will never make it up that narrow staircase."

"You can use my crane." A tall, broad-shouldered man with brown hair and a slightly sunburned face came up the stairs behind us in a white uniform as spotless as everything else on the ship. Next to him stood a man who matched him in height but was as lean as the other was broad with white blond hair cut short. The broad man smiled and extended his hand. "Captain Frank Hammer at your service. And this is my first mate, Jan." He pronounced the *J* like a *Y*.

"Annabelle Archer." I shook both men's hands first, and everyone else followed suit. "It's nice to meet you. You have a lovely ship." I didn't know if this was what you were supposed to say to a captain, but he seemed pleased.

"She's a beauty, isn't she?" he said. "Let me tell you, this ship is a vast upgrade compared to other ships I've sailed on with Mr. Barbery."

"You were with him when he was a salvage diver?" I asked.

The captain grinned. "We go way back."

Kate put her hand on the first mate's arm. "Jan? That's an interesting name. Where are you from?"

The first mate didn't return Kate's smile. "Norway."

"Our crew is from all over the world," the captain said. "Norway, Scotland, Australia, the US."

Kate dropped her hand from the first mate's arm when he didn't respond to her fluttering eyelashes. She caught my eye and pantomimed shivering.

"We were just taking a look at where Mrs. Barbery wants everything for the wedding," Mandy said, her voice jumpy. "Are we in your way?"

The captain gave a dismissive wave of his hand. "Of course not. I'm at your disposal. If there's any way I can help, let me know."

"You mentioned a crane?" Richard said. I know he was as worried about getting the giant ice block on board as I was.

"Of course. We have a crane to get large things onto the ship. I'm sure we can use it for your ice. Right, Jan?"

The first mate gave an almost imperceptible nod.

"That would be perfect. Thank you." I breathed a sigh of relief. One more thing checked off my to-worry-about list.

"We'll get out of your way." Mandy motioned us back to the stairs as a scream came from below.

We all hurried down to the lower deck and saw one of the deckhands lying on the floor of the transom. He clutched his ankle as the other boy knelt over him.

Mandy rushed over to them. "What happened?"

"He slipped on a slick patch on the steps," the uninjured boy said.

I went over to the steps and scraped at a patch on the steps that looked shinier than the rest. I examined the white residue under my fingernail. "Someone must have spilled some wax and forgotten to clean it up."

Captain Hammer pushed past us and knelt over the boy, prodding his puffy ankle. "Probably just a sprain. Let's get him inside."

"I don't understand how this happened." Mandy looked on the

verge of tears. “I can’t tell Mrs. Barbery there’s been another accident.”

“I don’t think you’ll have to.” Richard pointed above, where a woman with long, unnaturally red hair stood glowering down at us. She wore a black fur-trimmed silk robe that whipped around her bare legs in the breeze.

“Unless I’m mistaken . . .” Richard began.

Mandy lost all color in her face. “That’s Mrs. Barbery.”

I cringed. This could not be good.

CHAPTER 7

"I'm telling you, this ship is cursed," Richard said as we stood on the dock switching out our boat-approved slippers for shoes.

"Be quiet," I whispered to him as I peeked up at the ship. Mandy stood two levels above us on the rear deck, so I gave her a final wave and she waved back. "Someone might hear you."

"I'm with Richard." Kate slipped her heels back on. "This boat gives me the creeps."

"It's not the ship that's the problem," Richard said. "It's that awful stepmother and her Guy Friday."

I looked up again at Mandy, hoping she was the only one who'd heard that, but she was too engrossed in a conversation with Captain Hammer and the first mate to notice us. It looked like the captain wasn't too pleased. Jan looked as surly as he had before, so he wasn't a good indicator. I hoped we hadn't caused problems for Mandy since she'd been one of the few people on board who'd been nice to us, but I guessed he was more upset about the injured deckhand and the recurring accidents.

"Well, we're going to have to deal with both of them," I said. "You heard what Mrs. Barbery said."

Our audience with the bride's stepmother had been brief and chilly. With Jeremy Johns standing behind her and grinning like the Cheshire cat, Mrs. Barbery had announced we were to incorporate his vision into the wedding, because Kristie was too young to know what she really wanted.

"*Diamond Weddings* doesn't feature weddings that are simple and elegant," she'd informed us in a slightly nasal voice that occasionally veered into a British accent. "And they don't care if a color has positive vibrations." She'd used air quotes on this, as if we had any doubt what she thought of her stepdaughter's ideas.

"Now I'm going to go back and finish my massage before someone else falls down a flight of stairs or breaks something and I have to fire everyone on board." She'd flounced back to her stateroom before we could argue, and Jeremy had blown us a kiss as he slammed the door behind them.

"I heard her," Richard said. "But what are we going to tell Kristie?"

"You mean if we ever find her?" Kate started walking down the dock, still looking over her shoulder.

"Watch where you're go—" I called out as Kate walked smack into a guy who might've stepped out of a Ralph Lauren ad. She really did have all the luck.

The man held Kate by the shoulders to keep her from falling over. "Are you okay?"

She nodded as she looked up at him, but she didn't seem able to speak. I'd seen Kate look at a guy like that a few dozen times before, and it was never good.

I couldn't exactly blame her though. The guy was gorgeous. Sandy blond hair that fell over his face just a little, muscled arms with enough of a tan to indicate he wasn't from DC, and eyes blue enough for me to notice from a few feet away. I fought the urge to knock Kate into the water and take him for myself.

"Did she seriously just meet someone on the docks?" Richard said to me under his breath.

"You're just jealous," I whispered back.

Richard raised an eyebrow. "Aren't you?"

I felt my cheeks flush. I hated that Richard knew me so well.

"Did I hear you say you're looking for a bride?" the man asked. When none of us did anything but nod, he said, "I may be able to help you."

Kate's face fell. "Are you the groom?"

The man laughed. "No. I'm Kristie's brother. Well, technically stepbrother." He held out his hand. "I'm Brody."

Kate melted into a smile again. Richard and I both shook his hand while Kate just held onto his other arm.

"Do you know where we can find Kristie by any chance?" I asked, trying to catch Kate's eye and motion for her to detach from the bride's brother.

"I passed her when I was just pulling into the parking lot." Brody motioned over his shoulder. "She waved, but she didn't look happy. I guess she had another fight with my mom?"

Richard and I just looked at each other and didn't say anything. Kate continued to stare at Brody.

He waved a hand. "You don't have to worry about me. I know how crazy my mother can be. She's never really understood Kristie or me. That's probably why Kristie and I always got along so well. We've been like best friends since our parents married three years ago."

Despite his being prettier than me, I really liked this guy. It helped that he was nothing like his mother.

"You don't know where she might have been headed, do you?" I asked.

"No." He pulled a cell phone out of his pocket and punched a speed dial number. "But I know someone who might."

"Her fiancé?" I asked.

"No," Brody said. "My girlfriend."

Kate dropped her hand from his arm. "Your what?"

"Kristie and my girlfriend are good friends. Yasmine is actually one of the bridesmaids."

Yasmine. I remembered the name from the bridal party information Kristie had sent us. Just the name sounded exotic and gorgeous, and I knew Kate would despise her on sight.

Brody smiled at us. "If this wedding goes well, maybe you'll get to plan mine someday."

Kate looked at me and mouthed the words "I quit."

CHAPTER 8

"You can't quit, Kate." We sat on the floor of my living room assembling what were surely the world's most elaborate welcome gifts. Matte silver boxes with lids that each took a good five minutes to put together had seemed like a much better idea when I'd ordered them. Since these were something we'd planned months ago, they had escaped Mrs. Barbery and Jeremy Johns's restyling. They may not match the new wedding theme, but they would make our bride happy.

"Why not?" Kate asked, popping a box top into place.

I'd thought giving Kate the rest of Sunday off after her heart-breaking encounter with Brody would have cooled her down a bit, but she'd been just as close to quitting when she'd shown up at my apartment the next morning for a day of paperwork and box assembly. At least she'd shown up, I reminded myself. Granted, she'd shown up wearing short shorts, a halter top, and wedge heels, but since it was an "office work" day, I didn't quibble.

"I can give you a lot of reasons," I said. "First of all, we talked Kristie into going forward with the wedding."

Kate held up a finger. "I think her father was more persuasive than we were. Especially when he offered to send her to the

Mandarin spa to recharge. And she still might change her mind once the massage stupor has worn off."

"Okay." I pushed up the sleeves of my white button-down shirt and reached for an unassembled box. "But you love this job. Where else can you meet so many men?"

"Married men," Kate corrected, leaning back against the leg of my pale yellow overstuffed couch. "The good ones are always married. Or engaged. Or gay. The best ones are gay."

"Since when have you been looking for marriage material?" I brushed some beige carpet lint off my jeans and made a mental note to vacuum someday.

Kate shrugged. "It would be nice to have the option. Don't you want to be on the other side of things one day?"

This was something I tried not to think about. Planning other people's weddings took so much time I didn't know when I'd ever be able to focus on having a normal relationship of my own. Being busy every Friday and Saturday night didn't lend itself to a healthy dating life, and the wedding business didn't offer up great dating options. Ian was the only guy I'd met through work in ages, and with his erratic lifestyle and bad-boy persona, he hadn't been what anyone would call marriage material. I suppose I technically met Detective Reese through work, as well, but things with him were moving at a glacial pace. Who knew if it would end up going anywhere? Kate was right about one thing: Our business didn't offer up many straight, single men unless you counted intoxicated groomsmen, which I didn't.

"Right now I just want to be on the other side of this wedding." I stood up and stretched my legs. "We still have to fill these boxes and tie them with ribbon. Do you want something to drink?"

Kate picked up the empty Frappuccino bottle next to her and waved it. "Do you have any more of these?"

"Do you have to ask?" I walked from my living room into the kitchen that opened into it through a shuttered opening over the pass-through counter. I ignored the growing collection of dishes in the sink and opened the refrigerator, where I kept a supply of Diet Dr Pepper, bottled Mocha Frappuccinos, and leftover takeout Thai. I eyed the bottle of Champagne Richard had left in my refrigerator door the last time he'd been over, but I knew it was too early to start drinking.

"So why are you *not* quitting?" Kate called from the other room. "Don't tell me you like refereeing fights between Richard and Jeremy Johns or trying to calm down the bride for the hundredth time."

I opened two bottles of Mocha Frappuccino and tossed the lids in the metal trashcan in the corner. "If I quit every time something went wrong, I'd have to quit at least once during every wedding."

"Exactly," Kate said. "There has to be an easier job. One where people don't start hyperventilating over linen colors or insist on a South Beach meets the South of France mash-up motif."

"Not every wedding is like this," I reminded her as I walked back into the living room and passed her a bottle. I set my bottle on the edge of the glass coffee table we'd pushed over to the side of the room to make more floor space. The curtains were pulled back, and the morning light poured in from the large windows that took up almost an entire wall. I liked to keep my curtains open since I was on the fourth floor and didn't have to worry about Peeping Toms in Georgetown, where most buildings didn't go above three or four stories.

"You're right." Kate took a drink. "Not every wedding has silver boxes that take half a day to put together."

I made a face. "Then we'd better get back to work."

"Yoo-hoo!" A singsong voice came from the front door, and I saw a platinum blond head appear. Leatrice, my octogenarian downstairs neighbor, had a habit of dropping by unannounced. In a recent hair makeover by Fern, she'd gone from electric burgundy to Marilyn Monroe blond. I was still adjusting. Today she accented her unnaturally blond hair with a pink sequined headband that could have come from the Hello Kitty store.

"Didn't you lock the door?" Kate whispered.

"It doesn't matter," I said. "She has a key."

Kate's mouth fell open. "You gave her a key?"

I shook my head. "She made a key. You know how she's really into spy movies. I think she learned how to secretly copy a key on some show."

"Great. What we really need is a little more crazy in our lives."

"At least she isn't obsessed with computer hacking anymore," I reminded Kate.

"Only because her online hacker friends went underground or went to prison," Kate whispered so Leatrice wouldn't hear her.

"We don't know they went to prison," I whispered back. "We just suspect. And she's very touchy about it, so not a word."

Kate made a motion of locking up her lips and throwing away the key.

"Oh, there you are." Leatrice's face lit up when she saw me, and she bounded into the room. She didn't stand over five feet tall, but between her hair and her wardrobe selection, you could never miss her. Today she paired her pink headband with what appeared to be a sailor suit. The white pants flared into bell-bottoms, and the matching shirt had a sailor collar edged in blue and a loose red bow at the neck.

Kate openly gaped while I tried not to laugh. "Wow, Leatrice. That's quite an outfit."

She spun on the spot. "Do you like it? It's nautical."

"I can tell," I said. "But why are you wearing it?"

"I want to be ready," she said as she sat down on the couch.

"Ready for what?" I asked, almost afraid to hear the answer.

"In case you need me on the boat."

Kate spluttered and almost spit out a mouthful of Frappuccino. "What?"

I didn't even bother asking how Leatrice knew we were planning a wedding on a boat. She found out everything about my life from either snooping or stalking.

"I don't think we'll need any help with the wedding, Leatrice," I said. "But thanks."

"Maybe I could just drive." She rubbed her hands together. "You know, be your wheelman."

Kate wiped Frappuccino from her chin. "Why would we need a wheelman?"

"I figured you'd want to beat the police there," Leatrice said. "And I'm the fastest driver you know."

I felt a nervous flutter in my stomach. "What are you talking about?" I asked.

"I just heard it on my police scanner." Leatrice jerked her thumb in the direction of her apartment below. "Some accident on the big boat at the District Marina. They called for an ambulance. So, are you ready to go?"

I looked at Kate, whose face had lost a few shades of its tan. So much for a quiet day in the office.

CHAPTER 9

I swung my car into the parking lot by the marina and searched for a place to park. Leatrice clapped her hands together in the backseat. "Look at all these police cars. And two ambulances." She looked practically giddy.

I craned my neck around to glare at her. "I only allowed you to come with us because you promised to stay in the parking lot."

"That and she refused to get out of the car when we tried to leave Georgetown," Kate muttered next to me.

"Don't worry about me," Leatrice said. "This is clearly where the action is. Look at all the cops."

I turned back around and surveyed the scene in front of us. Two ambulances were parked unevenly near the entrance to the long dock leading to the ship, and at least half a dozen police cruisers with lights still flashing were pulled in around it. This didn't look good. I edged my car into what seemed to be the last open space and turned off the engine.

"Just stay out of trouble," I said. I didn't know if I should be telling that to Leatrice or Kate as I watched my assistant adjust her cleavage before stepping out of the car. To be fair, there were a lot of cute men in uniform and Kate had a weakness for the combination.

"Ten-four." Leatrice bounded out of the car behind Kate.

I groaned as I watched Kate teeter over to an officer in her wedge heels with Leatrice trailing behind her in a sailor suit. I wondered how long it would take them to notice if I just drove off. Probably hours. Before I could be tempted any further, a rap on my car window made me jump.

"Could you step out of the car, ma'am?" The deep voice was muffled through the glass, but I still recognized it. I opened the car door and stepped out.

"I figured as much." Detective Mike Reese stood with his hands on his waist, and I couldn't tell if he looked annoyed or amused.

Considering our history together, it could be either. Most of our past encounters included me stumbling into his cases while he tried to solve them and keep me out of trouble at the same time. And now our history included three minutes of what should have been a first date. I'd always gone a little weak in the knees over Reese. He was the quintessential tall, dark ,and handsome with a healthy dose of knight in shining armor mixed in. The combination was catnip to any girl who grew up hearing stories of princesses being rescued from towers. Even a girl like me who didn't like to think she needed rescuing. My stomach did a little flip when I saw him standing in front of me in a navy button-down shirt rolled up to the elbows and jeans that, as always, fit just right. I couldn't help thinking back to the quick but sweet kiss he gave me after our almost-date, and my stomach flipped some more.

"What are you doing here?" I asked, holding my hair back as the wind off the water blew it into my face.

"It's good to see you, too, Annabelle." He gave me a lopsided grin and brushed a strand of hair off my forehead. "I *am* a detective, you know. The better question is, why are you and your sidekicks here?"

"Leatrice is not my sidekick," I said, although watching Kate sit on the hood of a police cruiser with her long legs crossed chatting with a group of officers, I wasn't sure if I should claim her either. I couldn't see where Leatrice had gone, which was not a good thing. "We're supposed to have a wedding on this boat on Saturday. And since when is the District Marina your jurisdiction?"

"I heard on the scanner a wedding planner made the call to the police, and I assumed it was you."

Not a bad assumption considering our past encounters. "Well, it's nice to see you."

His green eyes locked with mine. "It's nice to see you too. Although what I'd really like to do is kiss you."

I put a hand on the car door so my knees wouldn't buckle. "You would?"

He nodded. "If the entire marina weren't watching."

I glanced behind him at the police cruisers. "You're out in force, aren't you? Leatrice heard on the scanner the police were called to the District Marina, but isn't this a bit much?"

He tilted his head at me. "You don't know what's going on?"

I felt the flutter in my stomach again, but this time it was nervousness about my disaster-prone wedding venue. "Was there another accident?"

Leatrice rushed up to me, wringing her hands. Reese's eyes widened as he looked at Leatrice's outfit.

She tugged on my sleeve. "Annabelle, you have to come with me."

"I'm in the middle of talking to Detective Reese," I said. "You remember the detective, don't you?" I knew she did. Leatrice never forgot an eligible bachelor and never tired of trying to set me up with them. In the past she'd held high hopes for the UPS man, her grandson, the balding pizza delivery guy, and our building's leasing agent, who wasn't even remotely straight.

Leatrice smiled and batted her eyes. "So nice of you to drop by, Detective." Leatrice began chatting as if we were all at a cocktail party that just happened to be in a grungy parking lot with the scent of the nearby fish market wafting through.

"The detective was just telling me what's going on," I interrupted, turning my attention back to Reese.

Leatrice gave a tiny yelp. "Oh, that's right. I need to tell you about Richard."

"What?" I asked. "Is he here too? Does everyone have a police scanner?"

Leatrice jerked her head in the direction of the boat.

"He's on board?" I groaned. "What is he doing on the boat?"

"That's what I'm trying to tell you," Leatrice said. "Richard is involved. The other officers told me."

"What do you mean 'involved'? With the accident on the ship?" I threw my hands into the air. "I told him not to go anywhere near Jeremy Johns unless I was around to play referee, and now look what happens."

"Actually," Reese said, "it wasn't just an accident. We're dealing with a fatality."

The butterflies in my stomach turned into a knot, and my knees finally gave way.

CHAPTER 10

"Just take deep breaths." Leatrice knelt over me and fanned my face, making a nice breeze, but not doing anything to help the fish smell that dominated the air.

I swatted her away. "I'm fine. I just slipped, that's all."

Reese pulled me up with one hand, so I ended up almost chest-to-chest with him. "Are you sure you're okay?"

I looked up at the concerned look in his eyes, but what I couldn't stop staring at were his lips, which were so close to mine I only needed to stand on tiptoe to touch them with my own. I felt my face flush and realized I was still holding his hand, so I dropped it and stepped back. "Absolutely."

"As I was about to say when you collapsed, Richard is fine," Leatrice said.

"Then who's dead?" I asked, wiping dirt off the seat of my jeans.

Reese cleared his throat. "The harbormaster was found in the water next to the ship. Dead. Richard called it in."

"But he couldn't have had anything to do with it," I said.

"Probably not," Reese agreed, "but questioning him is standard procedure."

I could only imagine how Richard was handling being interviewed by the police. Ever since an unfortunate accident that almost shut down his business a couple of years back, Richard had been overly sensitive about law enforcement.

"There's nothing you can do here," Reese said. "Why don't you head on home, and I'll give you a call when we release your friend?"

I didn't think that was such a bad idea and started scanning the crowd for Kate. I found her quickly enough by looking for the crowd of uniformed men. I waved to get her attention, but she was staring through her crowd of admirers to some commotion at the gate to the dock.

"You don't understand," the agitated male voice was saying to a pair of uniformed officers guarding the entrance to the dock. "My family is on there."

I recognized Brody even though he wore a baseball cap, ripped shorts, and a faded T-shirt and looked much less debonair than the day before when we'd met him.

Reese sighed. "I'd better go help the guys with security. All sorts of people have been trying to get a closer look."

"He's telling the truth," I said. "That's Brody, Kristie's brother. Well, stepbrother."

"Is he single?" Leatrice asked, looking him up and down.

"Nope. He's got a girlfriend," I said, then added, "I only know because Kate was interested."

Reese shot me a crooked grin then started off toward the dock. I followed behind, pulling Leatrice along with me so she couldn't run off and get in any trouble.

When Brody spotted me behind Reese, he snapped his fingers and pointed. "That's the wedding planner. She can tell you who I am."

"She already did." Reese gave his best stern cop look. "That doesn't mean we can let you on board. The boat is a secure crime scene."

Brody's face paled, and I wondered if his tan was real or fake. "What do you mean by 'crime scene'? What happened?"

"A body was found in the water next to your family's boat," Reese said.

"The harbormaster," I said quickly, so Brody wouldn't think it was any of his family members.

Reese shot me a look over his shoulder, which I ignored. "We need to determine if the harbormaster was on board before he ended up dead in the water," he said.

Kate came up next to me. "What's going on?"

"Brady just found out about the dead body," Leatrice said in a stage whisper.

"Brody," I corrected.

Leatrice cocked her head. "The victim's name is Brody?"

Kate's eyes grew wide. "Wait, did you say someone's dead?"

I raised an eyebrow at Kate. "What have you been doing over there for all this time with half of the police squad?"

Kate shrugged and crossed her arms. "The crime didn't come up."

"But you have to let me on," Brody continued to argue. "That's where I live."

"And as soon as we've searched the ship, we'll be happy to let you on," Reese said, taking Brody by the arm and steering him away from the dock. "But for now, you'll have to wait."

"But I really need to . . ."

I looked at Brody's anguished face. "Maybe we should help . . ."

Before I could finish my thought, Leatrice and Kate were pushing past each other to get to him. Leatrice beat Kate, which I credited to the fact that she was lower to the ground and not wearing heels.

Leatrice looped her arm through his. "It looks like you need a friend, young man."

Brody took one look at Leatrice's sailor suit and his face went from pained to confused. "Do you work on the docks?"

Leatrice slapped his arm and laughed. "Aren't you a stitch?"

Kate grabbed Brody's other arm and batted her eyelashes at him. "Run along, Leatrice. Don't you have some knots to tie or spinach to eat?"

Leatrice glared at Kate while Reese choked back a laugh. "Come to think of it, she does look like a smaller version of Popeye," he said, leaning close to me.

"Don't let Leatrice hear you," I said. "You don't want to be on her bad side. It's hard enough to be on her good side."

Reese laughed. "I've missed that."

"Leatrice?" I asked. I'd always gotten the idea Reese only tolerated her.

"No, definitely not Leatrice." He laughed again, then looked more serious.

Leatrice and Kate's squabbling faded into the background as I met Reese's eyes. He leaned close to me, and I wondered if he was really going to kiss me with all his colleagues around. Then I heard high-pitched screams coming from the boat.

"Let me off this instant or heads will roll!"

I'd know that hysterical voice anywhere. Richard.

CHAPTER 11

"It was awful." Richard had fought his way off the boat, and the police had given up trying to keep him quiet.

"We already questioned him," one of the officers said to Detective Reese when they let Richard off the gangway. "He's all yours."

Reese didn't look thrilled.

"Richard." I grabbed him by the shoulders. "What happened?"

Richard took out a lavender toile pocket square and dabbed his brow. "I went to the kitchen to talk to the chef about our kitchen space. That galley kitchen is much too small for us to cook out of, but I thought the ovens might be good for warming food. The equipment is top-of-the-line, you know. And have you seen the wine cellar?"

Reese cleared his throat and gave Richard a pointed look. "Is this going anywhere?"

Richard pursed his lips and turned away from Reese. "As I was saying, I talked to the chef about using his kitchen space, then he left in a huff. No idea why."

I had a pretty good idea why, but I let him continue.

"I left and was walking around the outside when I heard a

knocking sound against the side of the ship. I looked over the side and spotted the body floating in the water." Richard put a hand over his mouth. "It took me a moment to register what it was, then I called for help."

Reese flipped back a few pages in his leather notepad. "He screamed so loudly the police got calls from half a dozen nearby boats."

"You'd think someone would have come faster." Now it was Richard's turn to give Reese a pointed look. "I thought the DC response time had improved, but the captain was the first person on the scene and then Mandy. It was a good ten minutes before the police showed up. I had to help Mandy to her quarters before they even arrived because she became a bit hysterical."

I could only imagine what a mess Mandy had been if Richard classified her as hysterical. Richard didn't look so hot himself. His beige linen suit looked as if it had been slept in.

"Do you want me to take you home so you can change?" I asked.

"Change?"

"Well, your suit is all wrinkled," I said.

Richard looked at the creases in his pants and jacket. "This is linen, darling. They're money wrinkles."

"Wrinkles are wrinkles, if you ask me," Kate said, walking up to join us.

"I certainly didn't ask," Richard said, running a hand over his jacket sleeve.

"I thought you were helping Leatrice entertain Brody," I said. I looked across the parking lot to where Leatrice stood, her arm tightly linked to the stepbrother. Brody wasn't getting free from Leatrice anytime soon. I only hoped he enjoyed talking about *Matlock* or violent crime reports.

Kate threw up her arms in mock surrender. "I give up. A girlfriend I can handle. But a girlfriend and Leatrice? No thanks."

"It isn't like you to throw in the towel so easily," Richard said. "Especially when they're cute."

"Well, I'm already seeing a couple of people, and if I get too many, it just gets confusing," Kate said. "You know what they say: Two's company, three's too loud."

Richard gave her a snarky smile. "I'm sure it is."

I elbowed him and noticed Reese grinning at me. I gave him an apologetic smile. I just hoped my friends didn't scare him off.

Reese tapped his pen on his notepad and looked at Richard. "Do you mind if I ask you a few questions?"

Richard shrugged.

"Did you see the harbormaster on board the ship at any point?"

Richard paused to think. "The place has been hopping the past few days, so he very well may have been on board without me noticing. But I know Mandy knew him."

"How do you know that?" Reese asked.

"That's what she was babbling about when they took her to her quarters to rest," Richard said. "That she'd had a meeting with him, but although she saw him on board earlier in the day, he'd never shown up to their meeting."

Reese flipped his notebook closed. "Now we know why."

CHAPTER 12

"What do you mean you need to seal off the boat?" I tried not to let my voice sound as upset as I felt.

Detective Reese took my arm and pulled me away from the crowds gathered in the parking lot. "Keep your voice down. I don't want people to panic and start rumors."

"If you shut down my wedding, I'll be the one panicking." I held up a hand and started ticking off fingers. "Not to mention the bride, her stepmother, Richard . . ."

"Be reasonable, Annabelle," Reese said. "If this is a murder, we can't let you have a wedding on top of the crime scene."

"The wedding is still a few days away," I said. "Can't you get all the evidence you need before then? You don't know the murder happened on the ship."

Reese shifted from one leg to the other. "That's what we need to determine. I'd say the chances are slim an experienced harbormaster fell into the Potomac and drowned."

I had to give him that one.

"Once we determine the cause of death, we'll know what we're dealing with. But aren't you worried you might have a killer on board the ship?"

I sighed. "Give me something I haven't dealt with before."

Reese saw I was serious and laughed. "Are all wedding planners like you?"

"Definitely not," Richard said, joining the conversation. "She's one in a million." From his tone, I couldn't tell whether I'd just been complimented or insulted. But that was usually the way with Richard.

"What do I have to do so you won't seal off the boat?" I begged Reese.

He considered me for a moment. "Can you convince the family to pay for private security?"

I glanced at Richard and he nodded. "I'm sure they'd pay for anything to keep the wedding plans moving ahead. I'll have Mandy talk to Mr. Barbery."

Reese pulled out his cell phone. "If you think it will be a go, I'm going to call the best security company I know, all former law enforcement guys, and have them put a twenty-four-hour crew on board. That way we can make sure nothing else happens, and our officers can search the ship for evidence."

I breathed a sigh of relief. "That sounds fair."

Reese dialed with his thumb and then narrowed his gaze at Richard and me. "They'll be reporting straight to me, so both of you had better behave."

Richard put a hand on his chest. "I resent the implication I would do anything but help law enforcement to the best of my ability."

"Seriously?" I whispered to Richard, as Reese turned away and talked into his phone.

"Too much?" Richard asked.

"Well, considering you've operated your business against police orders before and seriously considered getting Leatrice falsely arrested on more than one occasion, it may be a touch insincere."

Richard tapped his chin. "You make some good points."

Leatrice walked up with Brody in tow as Reese slipped his cell phone back in his back jean pocket.

"We're all set with the security," Reese said. "They'll be here in an hour or so."

"Security?" Brody asked. "What's going on?"

"There's been a death, dear, remember?" Leatrice whispered loudly, patting his arm. She leaned over to me. "He's very distraught."

Reese looked like he was making an effort not to laugh. "In order to move forward with the wedding plans, we need to put some security on the boat."

"Like armed guards?" Brody asked.

"More like retired cops," Reese explained. "Just to keep an eye on things and make sure there aren't any more incidents, what with all the wedding preparations going on."

"I suppose that's necessary." Brody rubbed his forehead. "My stepsister is already pretty upset."

Reese shrugged. "It's necessary if she still wants to get married on board. Otherwise, we can remove everyone, seal off the ship, and lock it down entirely to investigate."

Brody made a pained face. Maybe he was imagining his mother's reaction.

"So, as long as we have the security team we can go ahead with the wedding as planned?" Richard asked.

"Once the forensics team is done."

"Forensics?" Brody looked up at *Mystic Maven*. "This is out of control."

I'd seen a lot of wedding craziness, but I had to agree with him. This wedding was not going as planned.

CHAPTER 13

"Well, I'd say that went really well," Kate said as I maneuvered my car through the city. "We're less than a week away from the wedding on the yacht, and we now have one dead body and a security crew camped out on board."

"It's not our smoothest wedding so far, I'll give you that," I said. "But at least we have a security team to make sure nothing else goes wrong."

"When were they getting to the boat?"

I looked at my watch. "Probably around now. Reese said it wouldn't be more than an hour."

"Speaking of Detective Reese . . ." Kate let her voice trail off.

"What?" I tried to sound normal, but my voice came out high and nervous.

"If I didn't know better, I'd say things are heating up," Kate said. "You looked pretty cozy to me."

"How did you notice anything while surrounded by all those attentive cops?"

Kate shrugged. "I have special radar for people being hit on."

"Reese was not hitting on me. Anyway, we're taking things slow."

Kate glanced at me then changed the subject. "Well, at least we're going to make it to our appointment on time. If we'd stayed much longer we'd never have been able to get the fish market smell off us."

"And we got rid of Leatrice," I said. We'd just dropped her off at my apartment building after practically dragging her away from the crime scene at the docks and convincing her there was nothing more she could do to help console Brody or to help Detective Reese.

Kate sighed. "We got rid of one crazy, and now we're going to meet two more."

"Debbie and Darla aren't crazy," I said.

Kate gave me a look that said she disagreed.

"You have to admit they're our most fun clients." Debbie and Darla Douglas, the mother-daughter duo from the Deep South, had been planning Debbie's wedding to Turner Grant III with us for what seemed like years, and had even moved the date once, but it was finally just a few weeks away. Debbie and Darla loved anything pink, anything preppy, and anything that came out of a cocktail shaker. They had even been known to carry full cocktail shakers around in their preppy pink purses.

"Of course they're fun," Kate said, "they're always drunk."

"They're not always drunk," I insisted. "We just see them when it's almost happy hour."

"The breakfast meeting we had at their house?"

I cringed. It was hard to explain away Bloody Marys at nine in the morning on a weekday. "But they're so much fun and they always send in their payments on time."

Kate shook her head. "You're a cheap date, Annabelle."

"Look who's talking."

Kate ignored my comment and motioned to a street parking space on Thirty-First Street right across from the glass-fronted flower shop called Lush. We were meeting Debbie and Darla for the final floral meeting before the wedding. Usually we did the final floral rundown over the phone, but they'd changed the look so many times we thought an in-person meeting would be a good idea.

The shop was called Lush, but the shop's floral designers, Buster and Mack, were known as the Mighty Morphin Flower Arrangers in the Christian biker world they were a part of—and I'd never been able to think of them as anything else.

As Kate and I stepped out of my car and started across the street, Mack opened the glass door of Lush and waved from under the pale green awning. To say Mack didn't fit the usual image of a florist would be an understatement. Although he didn't have any hair on top of his head, he sported a red goatee, a pierced eyebrow, and enough black leather to make a vegan weep. At slightly under six feet and topping three hundred pounds, he was the smaller of the two men.

"Come on in, girls," he said, hurrying us over in his gravely voice. "We just got an espresso machine for the shop, and I'm playing barista. Can I make you a cappuccino?"

"That would be perfect." I followed Mack into the shop and hopped up onto a metal stool. I normally only drank coffee that came Frappuccinoed, but after the morning at the docks, I needed something to get me back on track.

"Do you have skim milk?" Kate asked.

Mack put a hand on her arm. "Buster and I only drink skim nowadays." He patted his massive waist. "We're trying to cut back."

While Mack fiddled with the elaborate espresso machine in the back, I looked around the über-chic floral studio. Nothing frilly about Lush, just concrete floors and galvanized metal buckets of flowers on chrome racks lining the walls. I sat at the long, high metal table that ran through the center of the room, taking in the vivid hues of blooms lined up in square glass vases in front of me: pale blue hydrangea, fluttery pink roses with orange centers, crisp green orchids, buttery yellow ranunculus with hearts of celadon.

"Two skinny caps with just a touch of chocolate shavings," Mack said, balancing two bulbous white cups on their saucers as he walked toward us. He set them down on the table. "Do I sound like a barista?"

"Mmmm." Kate made an appreciative noise as she took a sip from her cup.

"Can you make me one?" Buster appeared from the back of the shop, where there was an entrance to their workroom. His deep voice reverberated off the concrete and metal. "I need some energy before this bride and MOB get here."

He came over and pecked us on the cheeks. Buster was the more imposing of the two men with an extra few inches and quite a few more pounds. His goatee was dark brown, he didn't have any piercings, he kept his motorcycle goggles perched on top of his head, and he shared Mack's penchant for black leather. The pair reminded me of overgrown teddy bears who'd gone rogue.

"Remind me why we're meeting *again*." Buster sank onto a metal stool next to me, and it groaned from the impact.

"Because they were too tipsy at the last meeting to remember what we discussed," I said, sipping at my cappuccino.

"Well, this time we can dry them out with coffee," Mack called from his post at the espresso machine.

"Unless you plan to make it Irish coffee, good luck getting them to drink it," Kate said.

I suspected Kate was right. Debbie and Darla had been on a "liquid diet" for the wedding since we'd started the wedding planning. They avoided anything that wasn't clear and served straight up. I think the only exception they made was for olives.

Buster sniffed the air. "Do I smell fish?"

Kate slapped me on the arm. "I told you we stayed at the docks too long. I'll have to rewash my hair for my date tonight."

Buster cocked an eyebrow. "What were you two doing on the docks?"

"We have a wedding on a yacht there this weekend," I said.

Mack brought Buster his coffee and then folded his arms over his chest, causing several of the metal chains to jingle together. "Who's doing the flowers?"

"The stepmother insisted on using her own New York designer. The bride tried to talk her out of it months ago but finally gave up," I said, hoping to mollify Mack. "It was out of our hands."

"He's a nightmare," Kate said. "Can you please come push him overboard and take over?"

Mack uncrossed his arms and gave Kate a playful push that almost knocked her off her stool. "You know we'd do it for you."

"He's dreadful," I agreed. "He's trying to do a South Beach meets South of France theme."

Mack wrinkled his nose as if he, too, had gotten a whiff of fish. "How perfectly awful."

"What's his name?" Buster asked. "We know some designers from New York."

I took a sip of my cappuccino and dabbed at my top lip. "Jeremy Johns."

Mack sucked in air. Buster's face darkened, and he muttered some words I'd never heard escape his pious lips.

"They do know him," Kate said.

"Consider yourself warned, girls," Buster said, as Mack fanned himself with a nearby palm frond. "Jeremy Johns is not to be trusted."

I was beginning to believe that about everyone involved in this wedding.

CHAPTER 14

"So what's the scoop on Jeremy Johns?" Kate leaned closer to Mack and Buster, ignoring the fact that both men had flushed red under their leather and piercings.

Buster fanned Mack with a legal pad, not noticing it was upside down and dangling yellow paper in Mack's face. "He's a thief and a liar."

Mack swatted the legal paper away from him and stood. "Not to mention, a talentless charlatan." He sank back onto a metal stool, looking spent.

"Wow," Kate whispered to me. " I didn't think it was possible for anyone to like Jeremy less than Richard does."

I put a hand on Mack's arm. "It sounds like you know him well."

"And personally," Kate added.

Before Buster and Mack could elaborate on how they knew so much about the despised floral designer, Debbie and Darla Douglas swept into the shop in a cloud of expensive perfume and top-shelf vodka.

"Darlings," Darla cried, running over on pink kitten heels to exchange air-kisses with everyone. Her daughter, Debbie, followed her, and I got a flash of red from the soles of her impossibly high Louboutin pumps. I'd always been impressed by their ability to balance on heels while maintaining a state of perpetual intoxication.

Buster and Mack perked up instantly, recharged by the sight of clients wearing expensive clothes and carrying big checkbooks. After we all kissed and hugged without actually touching, the mother and daughter duo settled in at the table, and I couldn't help thinking how at home they seemed on bar stools.

Buster opened the thick file he had on the Douglas–Grant wedding and clicked his pen. "So, are we ready to finalize details and quantities, ladies?"

"The wedding is only a few weeks away." Mack tapped his finger on his oversized black rubber watch and smiled.

Darla and Debbie exchanged conspiratorial looks and my heart sank. We'd changed their wedding look as often as they'd gotten their roots done, and I didn't know how much more indecision I could handle. I pulled my small blue wedding journal out of my bag. This was going to require notes.

"Well," Debbie began, "I'm just not sure if we've personalized the wedding enough."

"The wedding cake will be handpainted to match your antique floral china pattern, which was also replicated for your letterpress invitations," I said. Darla and Debbie were from the upper echelons of the Deep South, and their family's antique china pattern had been passed down from Southern belle to Southern belle and was central to the wedding design.

"And the wedding cake designer is coming over from Scotland just to do your cake," Kate reminded them.

"We've sourced the perfect heirloom flowers in the pattern, so your bouquets will be identical to the china." Mack held up the order from the flower grower it had taken him months to track down.

"Not to mention you have four signature cocktails and a bourbon tasting bar," Kate said.

Darla's face lit up. "Don't get us wrong, we love all of it."

"Especially the bourbon bar," Debbie said. "Turner's daddy is tickled pink about it." She leaned in and gave us all a wink like she was letting us into a big secret. "Grant men are bourbon men through and through."

"Then this *is* a match made in heaven," Kate muttered only loud enough for me to hear her.

"We're just worried we might have given up the magnolia leaves too easily," Darla said.

Buster flipped through the file, and I knew he was looking to see which revision had included the swags of magnolia leaves. Luckily, Buster and Mack were sticklers for keeping paperwork, so they tracked every revision we'd ever done. It was the sign of seasoned professionals and a team used to working with brides prone to changing their minds.

"Here it is." He produced a sheaf of papers from the massive stack. "Revision 7. Swags of magnolia leaves draped along the banisters and balcony of the museum with floral catch points."

"What about the wall of magnolias behind the bar?" Debbie asked. I was impressed she could remember details about something so many revisions ago since she was rarely coherent for the meetings.

"Which one?" I asked. "You're doing five bars."

"The bourbon bar," Darla and Debbie said in unison.

"And we should have two of those," Debbie added to me as I hurried to make notes about the bars.

"So we're adding the magnolia leaves back in," Buster said, one eyebrow raised as though he didn't quite trust the decisions were final. "But we're not removing any of the other floral décor, are we?" He eyed the specialty floral order waving in Mack's hand.

"Remove?" Darla laughed. "Of course not. We're going for a serious wow factor here."

Mack stopped waving the floral order and sighed. "As long as we aren't changing my heirloom rose order."

"Since you won't let us do the miniature ponies during cocktail hour," Debbie said, "we just want to make sure the wedding is special enough."

I wasn't sure who Debbie was accusing of nixing the concept of livestock as décor, but I was happy to take the blame for what I confidently felt was the worst wedding idea ever. It was tricky enough getting a permit for an elephant to walk down Constitution Avenue. I was not going back to try to get one so miniature livestock could saunter around inside a museum.

"Don't worry." I looked up from my notes. Six bars, four signature cocktails, two magnolia leaf walls, several hundred feet of garland, a five-tiered handpainted cake created by a designer we were flying in just for the occasion, and letterpress invitations so thick we'd had to mail them in individual boxes. "I think you've got serious wow."

"What about vintage furniture groupings?" Debbie asked. "To go with the vintage look of the bars? Can we do that?"

"Of course." I wrote a note to myself to call Primrose and Poppy, the company we used for all vintage rentals, and add furniture groupings to the order.

Darla put her hand over her daughter's hand and squeezed it. "My friends are just going to die."

"So are those the only changes?" Buster held his pen over revision twelve, where he had added back in the magnolia leaves.

Debbie slipped off her bar stool and smoothed the front of her Lilly Pulitzer print dress. "That was it, wasn't it, Mother?"

"That's it." Darla looked at her diamond-encrusted watch as she stood up. "My word. We don't want to be late for drinks at The St. Regis with Turner."

Kate glanced at the metal clock on the wall and shot me a look. I knew without a glance at the clock it wasn't even close to happy hour. After another flurry of air-kisses, Debbie and

Darla were out the door and well on their way to afternoon cocktails.

Mack put a hand to his heart. "What just happened?"

"They just doubled the cost of their proposal is what happened," Buster said.

"Better that way than the other," Kate said.

Mack winked at us. "Isn't that the truth?"

I took out my iPhone. "I need to call Richard and tell him about the extra bar."

"Do you think he's back at the office by now?" Kate asked. "He wouldn't still be on the boat, would he?"

Buster looked up. "Richard's working with you on the yacht?"

I nodded. "Unfortunately for him. He and Jeremy Johns are about to kill each other."

"Well, if he needs help killing Jeremy, tell him to give us a call," Mack said, his expression dark again.

"Okay, spill it," Kate said. "What did Jeremy do to you?"

"He ruined us." His words came out more like a growl.

Buster patted Mack on the shoulder. "We used to have a shop up in New York."

Kate looked at me and I shook my head. This was news to me. As long as I'd known Buster and Mack, they'd only been running Lush in Georgetown.

"When did you work in New York?" I asked.

"Over ten years ago," Mack said. "Before you came onto the scene."

"Before Jeremy Johns ruined our business and ran us out of town," Buster said, one fist clenched by his side. "He told everyone we spray-painted our flowers."

Mack muttered what sounded like a curse under his breath, even though the boys had a hard and fast rule against cursing. Then again, being accused of spray-painting flowers would be enough to make any florist let fly a few profanities—even the Christian biker ones.

"He's a liar who will do anything to get ahead," Mack said. "Don't ever trust that man."

I rubbed my head. "Richard's problems with him seem pretty small compared to yours."

"Trust me," Mack said. "No one hates Jeremy Johns as much as we do."

Kate looked at me with wide eyes. "The 'I hate Jeremy Johns club' seems to be getting bigger by the moment."

My iPhone vibrated, and I read the text message that had just come in. "And so do our problems with the wedding," I said.

CHAPTER 15

"So what exactly did Fern say in his text yesterday?" Kate asked the next morning as I let her in. The morning sun streamed in through my windows and highlighted the dust on my hardwood floors. After this wedding was over, I needed to do some serious housecleaning.

"I already told you, remember?"

"Tell me again," Kate said. "I was distracted by Mack and Buster. And I'm pretty sure those cappuccinos were Irish."

"Just that he's with Kristie at her hideout. You know how attached he gets to some of his brides."

Kate scratched her head. "I didn't know she had a hideout."

"Wouldn't you want a hideout if you had a stepmother like Babs Barbery?"

Kate dropped her purse on the floor and sank onto my couch, throwing her feet up onto the coffee table and knocking a pile of papers off the side. "I'd leave the country."

"Well, Kristie doesn't want to be anywhere near her or the boat until the negative energy has been cleared out," I said.

"So now we're supposed to clear negative energy too?" Kate sighed. "Just add that to the weird list of things people ask us to do." She snapped her fingers. "Remember that awful bride who got married at Belle Haven Country Club? What was her name . . . Angel? Angie?"

"The one who ordered us to clean her kitchen and take out her trash?" I asked, sitting down next to Kate.

"Could you believe that? She didn't even ask nicely." Kate folded her arms over her chest. "I'd like to tell her where she could put those rubber gloves."

"It wasn't as bad as having to give her grandmother a pedicure."

Kate made a face. "Please, don't remind me. Grandma Hammertoes ruined feet for me forever."

"Not all of our clients are like that," I reminded her. "Some of them we love."

"You're right," Kate said. "But it's the evil ones who seem to be seared into my brain forever."

I pulled my hair out of its ponytail and ran my fingers through it. "At least this bride is sweet. Remember the thank you cookies she sent us after we talked the printer into rushing her invitations?"

"Sure, but she has a stepmother from hell. I think we're going to need a lot more cookies."

"You can't win them all," I said, pulling my hair up into a high ponytail. "What should we do for lunch?" I knew the answer would have to be takeout considering the perpetually sad state of my fridge. "It's almost one o'clock."

"Annabelle?" A deep voice came from the doorway as Mike Reese poked his head inside.

I yelped and put a hand to my heart.

The detective stepped into the room. "Did I scare you? Leatrice let me in downstairs."

Of course she did. And no doubt Kate didn't pull the door all the way closed when she came in.

Kate let out a breath. "You're lucky I didn't have a weapon."

I knew Kate would never carry a gun until they came out with a designer version that coordinated with a Kate Spade clutch, and I breathed a sigh of relief knowing that day was a long way off. If the world was lucky, it would never arrive.

Mike held up his hands. "Sorry. I didn't mean to startle you." He smiled at me and raised his eyebrows. "I thought I might catch you alone."

I felt my pulse quicken a bit. "Well, it is a workday. Is this about the case?"

Reese closed the distance between us. "Not really. I thought you might be free for lunch. To make up for me having to leave our date before it started."

I glanced at Kate who'd picked up a magazine from the floor and was pretending to be engrossed by it. I could tell from her smirk she was listening to every word, and I knew I would have plenty of explaining to do later.

"I should be working," I said. "We still have a big wedding this weekend and a security team encamped at the venue."

He grinned as he reached back and pulled my ponytail so it spilled over my shoulder. "Touché."

I touched his arm and looked up at him, hoping he couldn't hear the hammering in my chest. "A girl does have to eat though."

"A girl does." His voice wasn't more than a whisper.

Kate cleared her throat. "Maybe I should run out for coffee?" She scooped her purse off the floor and batted her eyelashes at me. "Can I get you anything? Frappuccino? Muffin? Hose?"

I shot her a look, but she just smiled and blew me a kiss. My iPhone trilled inside my purse and we all stopped.

"Ignore it," Kate said.

I cringed. "I can't ignore it. Let's hope it's nothing."

"Then I'll check it," Kate said, lunging for my bag. She pulled it out and read the screen. I saw her eyes grow wide, and then she rolled them.

I held my hand out for the phone. "What? Who is it?"

"Richard," Kate sighed. "Apparently the bride didn't stay in her hideout. She and Fern just showed up on the boat with a space healer." She read more. "They're trying to remove anything with negative vibrations."

I imagined Jeremy Johns and Mrs. Barbery being carried out and put on the dock by a spiritual healer dressed in flowing purple robes. This I had to see.

Reese cocked an eyebrow. "A space healer? What kind of wedding is this?"

"The insane kind," I said, running a hand through my hair. "Is there any other?"

CHAPTER 16

We could hear the shrieks before we reached the end of the dock, and I swallowed hard and shifted from a walk into a run.

"That doesn't sound good," Kate said, her heels clip-clopping behind me.

Even though both voices were high pitched and verging on hysterical, it didn't narrow down the list of possible shriekers. I ran though options in my head: Richard, Fern, Kristie, Jeremy Johns, Mrs. Barbery, the unnamed space healer I still imagined wearing dramatic robes. I just hoped it wasn't Richard or Fern.

We reached the ship and I ran up the wooden gangway, not stopping until I reached the top and remembered the hard-and-fast rule about not wearing shoes on board.

I smacked my forehead. "Shoes," I said, hopping on one foot to take them off as Kate nearly ran into me from behind. She muttered something but took hers off as well, and we followed the sounds of chaos.

The voices seemed to be coming from one of the top decks, so we ran up a narrow flight of steps on the back of the boat. As we rounded the corner to the rear outdoor lounge, I stopped short.

Two women stood nose-to-nose screaming, and I didn't recognize either of them. One wore a white T-shirt and black cargo pants and had her pale hair pulled back in a messy ponytail, while the other had lots of dark, wavy hair cascading loose down her back and across the straps of her white tank dress. Caren stood next to them in her *Mystic Maven* uniform. From her hand gestures it looked like she was trying to calm them down, but her words were drowned out by the shouting.

Kate looked around her. "Who are these people? Are we on the right boat?"

Before either of us could check the side of the boat for the name, Fern appeared around the corner. He looked impeccable in a slim, dark suit and seafoam green shirt with a matching pocket square folded perfectly into the breast pocket. I took a moment to admire his folding skills since I'd had more than one battle with a groomsman's pocket square in the past.

"Annabelle! Kate!" He beamed as he ignored the catfight in front of him and rushed to us for air-kisses.

"What's going on?" I asked, after Fern stepped back from our pseudo embraces.

Fern raised an eyebrow and then started twisting the gargantuan amethyst ring on his finger. "Oh, yes." He darted a glance at the women, who had stopped screaming and were glaring at each other and breathing heavily. "This is Sonia Romanov-Feinstein, the space healer." He gestured to the woman in the dress and dropped his voice. "She may be descended from the last Russian tsar, but now she lives in Hoboken."

"Oh, boy," Kate said.

"And I'm Janet Evans." The other woman turned from the spiritualist-cum-Russian-tsarina and held out her hand. "The producer for *Diamond Weddings*."

"Nice to meet you," I said, shaking her hand. This explained a lot. "Why are you on board? I thought you already scoped out the ship the other day." I couldn't help but remember Kristie's first reaction to the film crew coming aboard and had hoped they wouldn't be making regular appearances before the wedding day.

Janet took a breath and seemed to be picking her words carefully. "We were requested to come on board."

"As was I," Sonia said, her fists planted on her hips. "Kristie brought me on for the sole purpose of ridding her wedding venue of negative energy. And all these cameras are throwing the energy out of balance." She pushed a loose strand of hair off her face. For a space healer, she was giving off some pretty hostile vibes.

I held up my hands. "Okay, okay." I turned to Janet. "Who asked you to come back?" I tried to sound sympathetic but firm. "You know Kristie has an issue with all this media coverage."

Caren nodded. "She's very upset."

Janet rolled her eyes. "Believe me, I didn't drag my guys down to the docks for fun. Mrs. Barbery requested we film her first session with her stylist."

"Jeremy Johns?" Kate asked. "But he's been here for days."

Janet shook her head. "No, her personal hair and makeup stylist. The one from Paris."

I'd forgotten she had a stylist from Paris. Why was I surprised? I glanced at Fern to see how he was handling the competition.

Fern bobbed his head up and down. "Damian. He's divine. He's been giving me all the scoop on Babs and her friends and their jewelry."

There wasn't much Fern loved more than enormous jewelry and juicy gossip. The combination was his personal Valhalla.

"So if you were with Damian, where's the bride?" I asked Fern.

He gave me a blank look. "I thought she was with Sonia. The last I knew, they were clearing the negative energy from the main foyer when Damian came in with the film crew headed up to Mrs. Barbery's suite. Damian admired my ring and we started talking about jewels and the time just flew by and the next thing I knew, I heard screaming." Fern fluttered a hand to sum up his story, and I tried hard not to let out a sigh of exasperation.

"I can't wait to meet this Damian guy," Kate whispered to me. "Since when have you seen Fern like this?"

I had to agree. It was unusual for Fern to be impressed by anyone.

"They ruined our ritual, so Kristie went to talk to her stepmother," Sonia said. Her voice had become much calmer now and she seemed to be returning to her spiritualist persona. "I insisted this woman remove her invasive technology from the ship, but she refused."

Janet shrugged. "I have to get the shots. This is a big wedding."

"Can you shoot in Mrs. Barbery's suite and avoid the rest of the boat while Ms. Feinstein performs her rituals?" I asked.

"That's Romanov-Feinstein," the spiritualist corrected me.

I ignored Kate's suppressed giggle as I turned to Sonia. "Does that work for you? You can clear the rest of the boat, but just don't touch Mrs. Barbery's room."

Sonia sniffed and gave the smallest nod of her head. "Space healing wouldn't work in there anyway. I'd need a whole fleet of healers."

I tended to agree with her. It would take a team of exorcists to tackle Babs Barbery and more time than we had until the wedding.

"Well, I'd better get back to Damian," Fern said, bouncing on the balls of his feet. He motioned to Janet. "I'll take you to the suite."

Fern led Janet away, Sonia disappeared inside the boat ringing her finger cymbals as she went, and Caren mouthed a 'thank you' to me as she hurried out of the room.

I let out a breath. "Problem solved."

"Not exactly." The woman's voice from behind made me jump.

Mandy descended the stairs from above with a tall man I'd never seen before following closely behind her. He wore a black polo shirt tucked into a pair of black slacks, and since there was no monogram on his chest, I knew he wasn't affiliated with the ship. From the ever-so-slight gray peppering his brown hair, I could tell he was about a decade older than most of the staff aboard. I also noticed he lacked a suntan.

"We need to have a word," the mystery man said, his expression stony.

"This doesn't look good," Kate said.

I gulped. When Kate was right, she was right.

CHAPTER 17

"I'm Reese." The man in black extended his hand to me.

"I'm sorry," I said. "You're who?"

Kate shook her head as if she was trying to loosen something. "We already have a Reese."

The man smiled, his hazel eyes crinkling at the corners, and I felt a stirring of familiarity. This guy looked a lot like Detective Reese, only about ten years older.

"This is the head of the private security team that Mr. Barbery authorized," Mandy said. "Daniel Reese."

"The security team is made up of retired law enforcement, right?" I took the man's hand and shook it, locking eyes with him. "You wouldn't happen to have a brother who's a DC police detective, would you?"

His smiled widened. "You know Mike then."

Kate's eyes grew wide. "You're Reese's brother?" She gave him a noticeable once-over and nodded in appreciation. "Talk about good genes."

The man in front of us was probably fifteen years older than Kate and was just as tall and broad as his brother, the scattered gray in his dark hair only making him look more distinguished. As Kate stepped closer to him, her eyes seemed to glaze over.

He let go of my hand. "Older brother. And call me Daniel. You must be the wedding planners Mike told me about."

"I'm Annabelle, and this is my assistant, Kate."

Kate held out her hand and fluttered her eyelashes. "I'm really more of an associate."

I wanted to ask Daniel what his brother had said about me, but I caught the phrase "wedding planners" in the plural, so chances were good we'd just been mentioned as part of the ongoing case.

"I was showing Daniel around the ship and giving him the rundown of the accidents," Mandy said. "He's got three other guys with him, but he'll be our point person."

"Three more retired cops?" Kate asked, putting a hand on Daniel's arm. "Are all of them as good-looking as you?"

Mandy gave me a look and we both shook our heads. Kate's age window for acceptable men was generous, especially when they looked like Daniel Reese.

I stepped on Kate's foot, and she yelped a little and released Daniel's arm. "What can we do to help you, Daniel?"

"You can tell me why there are so many people on board."

As if on cue, we heard voices coming from the deck below us. Two deckhands were discussing where the paint needed to be touched up.

"Most of the people are temporary," Mandy explained. "The only people living aboard are the staff, the owners, and Kristie."

Daniel Reese pulled a small flip notebook out of his back pocket and scribbled some notes with what looked like a golf pencil.

"Jeremy Johns and Damian aren't staying here?" I asked.

Mandy snapped her fingers. "I forgot about them. The designer and stylist also have rooms."

Daniel raised one eyebrow, but nodded and continued writing.

"What about Brody?" Kate asked, leaning close to Daniel. "He's the bride's stepbrother."

"He has a room," Mandy said. "But he's also got one at the Mandarin Hotel with his girlfriend."

Kate twitched at the word 'girlfriend.' A smaller boat passed by and gave a tap of its horn. Mandy waved to them out of habit then continued.

"The space healer is a one-time visitor and should be leaving soon, and the TV crew just comes aboard to tape segments. And then there are Annabelle and Kate and Richard. He's the caterer, but they're all with the wedding, so they just come and go."

Daniel shook his head. "That's a lot of traffic."

"This wedding is a big deal," Kate said.

"And a bit of a circus," I said, lowering my voice so it wouldn't travel far. I was well aware we were on an open deck, and Mrs. Barbery seemed to have ears everywhere.

Daniel looked up from his notes and grinned at me, and I saw the flash of his brother's smile again.

"So does Reese, I mean *Mike*, bring you in to help on his cases often?" I asked.

Daniel pressed his lips together as if considering what to say. "Mike isn't the kind of man to ask for help a lot."

That sounded about right. I had a hard time imagining Reese calling in reinforcements for anything.

"He only calls us in for special cases. But since I'm twelve years older than my brother, he grew up watching me on the force. I like to think I taught him everything he knows."

"Were you a detective, too?" Kate asked.

Daniel nodded. "Vice and Homicide."

"How thrilling. You must have tons of stories." Kate took a step closer to Daniel and out of the reach of my kick.

"So you said your brother only brings you in on special cases," I said, more for Kate's benefit. "What makes this case different?"

I thought I caught him giving me a knowing look, but then he cleared his throat and flipped his notebook closed.

"Well, the death of the harbormaster. Accidents on a boat are one thing. A harbormaster's murder is another."

"He was definitely murdered?" I asked. "It wasn't an accident?"

Daniel Reese shook his head, his mouth set in a grim line. "He was dead before he went in the water. Blunt force trauma to the head."

Mandy raised a hand to her mouth. Even though we'd thought there was foul play, it was sobering to hear it confirmed. I felt a jolt of shock, as well. Mandy moved over to one of the banquettes that ran the edge of the deck and sank down onto the blue-and-white-striped cushion.

"Are you all right?" Daniel asked.

Mandy gave a quick bob of her head. "I'm fine. It's just that I spoke with the harbormaster the day he died. He seemed like a nice guy."

"Why don't you let Kate get you some water?" I shot a look at Kate who, for once, was paying attention and hurried off to the kitchen.

"I'm fine." Mandy managed a weak smile.

I sat next to Mandy. "Do you remember anything else about that day? Anyone who may have been around him?"

"It wasn't unusual for the harbormaster to come aboard," she said. "Usually there was paperwork to fill out so he met with the captain or the first mate."

"Did you see him with either of those men on the day of the murder?" I asked.

Mandy looked up at me and then at Daniel. "Not that I remember. I already told the police that I was supposed to meet with the harbormaster but didn't see him after he left Mr. Barbery's study."

Daniel cleared his throat but I ignored him. "He was in the father's study? Why?"

Mandy shrugged. "I think he'd heard about Mr. Barbery's history as a treasure hunter. He's pretty well known in certain circles."

"So Mr. Barbery was with him the day he died?" I asked.

Mandy nodded then her eyes widened. "You don't think that Mr. Barbery had anything to do with it, do you?"

"Mr. Barbery is not a suspect," Daniel said before I could answer, and he gave me a look that told me to keep quiet. "The police don't have any suspects yet, although Detective Reese does have a theory regarding the escalation of the accidents and the murder."

I leaned back against the banquette. "What do you mean?"

"There's a pattern," Daniel said, his face somber. "The accidents have been getting more serious. And now someone's been killed. It's an escalation."

I felt my stomach clench. "Reese thinks the same person who killed the harbormaster is responsible for the accidents?"

Daniel's eyes held mine, and I noticed they'd darkened. "He thinks all of this is the work of a violent and dangerous person."

CHAPTER 18

I lobbed my keys into the bowl by my front door and dropped my purse on the floor. I let the door shut behind me and reveled in the silence. I'd dropped Kate off at her place and managed to tiptoe upstairs so Leatrice wouldn't know I was back. After the drama of the past few days, it was nice to be alone in my apartment even if it was a bit of a mess. I ignored the stack of files on my coffee table as I kicked off my shoes and sank onto my couch, letting my head roll back and my eyes close. I took a few deep breaths and almost instantly felt calmer.

I felt my shoulders relax and I tried not to think about the wedding and the murder, but questions kept flitting through my mind. Who on board *Mystic Maven* wanted the harbormaster dead? What did they gain with him out of the way? Had he seen something he wasn't supposed to? And if Reese was right, how were the accidents tied into the death?

I shook the chaotic thoughts from my head and tried to remember the meditation techniques I'd learned in yoga class to clear my mind of all noise. No use. I reminded myself that even when the yoga teacher had explained the mind-clearing technique, I'd been thinking about my wedding to-do list. A different wedding at the time, but it was clear I'd become obsessive about my job.

"Great," I whispered to no one but myself. "I'm a workaholic who can't seem to plan a wedding without someone getting killed."

I felt tears pricking the backs of my eyes and the stress of the past few days washing over me. Now that the adrenaline was wearing off and I wasn't running around trying to talk people down or smooth things over, I realized how much I'd internalized all of the drama. I let a few tears snake down my cheeks.

Richard had warned me not to get so emotionally involved with my clients when I'd first started in the wedding business. He'd been catering weddings for over ten years before I'd come on the scene, so he spoke from experience.

"Never forget you're the hired help, Annabelle. As close to these families as you may feel, you're still being paid to do a job. The wedding will end and they'll move on. If you let weddings become your entire life, you won't be left with anything in the end but a few thank-you notes and a stack of old ceremony programs."

He'd been right, of course. Most of the time I was happy to let clients move on, but I became so involved with some of the families it felt like a breakup when the wedding was over. And since I gave my all to my job, I didn't have any time or energy left over for much else. When I let myself think about it, I realized the years were flying past me, and I was rushing from wedding season to wedding season always trying to get through the one or two high-maintenance or overly elaborate weddings on the horizon. But there was always another big wedding coming around the corner, and Richard's warning echoed in my head. Was I missing having a real life because I was so caught up planning other people's weddings?

I wiped the tears from my face and let my eyes flutter open. I was well past thirty years old, and I'd never gotten a marriage proposal or even come close. My only friends were people I worked with, and almost all the men I hung out with were far from being eligible. My life was filled with cake tastings and Champagne, but not many personal celebrations. The realization almost made me start crying again. A knock on the door snapped me out of my pity party.

"Coming," I called as I touched my cheeks to make sure I'd wiped away all the tears. I opened the door and stared. "Detective Reese?"

The detective wore broken-in jeans and an untucked dark green T-shirt matching his eyes. He wasn't wearing a blazer like he usually did when on duty, and he had a day's worth of scruff, making him look even more attractive. I felt my pulse quicken.

"Is this a bad time?" He shifted from foot to foot and looked over my shoulder into my living room. "Do you have company?"

"Actually, no." I stepped aside and held open the door. "Come on in."

He walked inside, and I closed the door behind him. "How did you get past without my neighbor seeing you and escorting you up?"

He shrugged. "I may have jimmied the front lock and tiptoed past her door."

"Jimmied the lock?" I tilted my head as I studied him. "That doesn't sound very cop-like."

Reese winked at me. "I wasn't always a cop."

I motioned for him to sit. "Interesting. Your brother said you followed him into law enforcement. It seems like following the straight and narrow is a family tradition, but now you're confessing to breaking into my building. What gives, Detective?"

I didn't know why he'd felt compelled to confess this secret to me, but I enjoyed having something to tease him about. I also enjoyed the fact that, for once, he was the one turning red.

He gave a nervous laugh as he sank onto one end of my couch. "What he didn't tell you was I was a bit wild when I was younger. Very unlike my big brother. Daniel was the one to set me down and tell me to pick which side of the law I wanted to end up on."

"And you picked the right side." I took the other end of the couch, tucking my legs underneath me as I sat.

Reese grinned. "I like to think so."

"I'd have to agree with you," I said. "You're a really good cop."

He cleared his throat, the flush spreading up his neck to his cheeks. "How did we get on this topic?"

It was my turn to grin. "You confessed to breaking into my apartment building. I can only assume you had a really good reason. Aside from wanting to avoid an exhausting encounter with Leatrice."

He straightened up, twisting around to face me. "I wanted to talk with you about the situation on the ship."

"Your brother already spoke to us," I said, then snapped my fingers. "Where are my manners? Can I get you something to drink?"

"Sure," he said. "Whatever you're having."

I pushed myself up and headed for the kitchen. "Keep talking. I'm listening."

"Did you ever see the harbormaster on the *Mystic Maven*? Or see anyone from the *Mystic Maven* talking with him?"

"No, but Mandy told me he spoke to Mr. Barbery the day he was killed." I opened the refrigerator and scanned the contents. I didn't think the detective was up for flat Diet Dr Pepper, so I pulled the bottle of Champagne from the door, saying a silent thanks to Richard for bringing it with him the last time he'd come over. According to Richard, a girl should always have a bottle of bubbly chilling. "Are you sure his death was connected to the *Mystic Maven*?"

"We have statements from two other neighboring boaters who saw him go on board not long before he was found floating in the Potomac."

I shivered as I thought of a body bobbing in the water. I

pulled the foil wrapper off the bottle and unwound the wire cage holding the cork in place. I grabbed a dishtowel from the counter and placed it over the cork while I twisted the bottle away from me. I caught the cork in the towel as it flew out of the bottle with a muffled pop. Another advantage of being a wedding planner: I was very adept at popping bottles of Champagne.

"I just got a report back from the coroner with some strange details," Reese said.

I pulled two Champagne flutes down from a top shelf and inspected them for dust before pouring. "Strange in what way?"

"Flakes of rust in the head wound."

"Rust?" I asked, as I walked back into the living room holding two flutes of Champagne. "That's odd. The last word I'd use to describe anything on board *Mystic Maven* is rusty. Maybe that proves that the murder weapon didn't come from the ship."

"Maybe." The detective raised his eyebrows. "Champagne?"

I paused as I handed him a glass. "You do drink Champagne, don't you?"

"Sure, why not?" He took the flute from me. "But I thought you once assured me wedding planning isn't a glamorous job."

I sat back down on the couch. "It's not, but Richard left this bottle in my fridge and your other option is Diet Dr Pepper with no fizz."

Reese raised his glass. "Then cheers to Champagne on a weeknight."

I clinked his glass and took a sip. "Weeknights are my weekends anyway."

"How so?"

I took another drink then set my glass on the coffee table. "Well, I work almost every weekend and all my friends work every weekend, so instead of going out on a Saturday, we go out during the week. While everyone else in the world is saying TGIF, we're bracing for another marathon starting on Friday."

"I never thought of it that way. So asking you out for a Saturday night isn't going to get me very far."

I felt my pulse flutter. "I thought you were here to ask me about the harbormaster."

He set down his flute on the coffee table and slid closer to me. "That's part of the reason. I did want to tell you to be careful. I don't have a good feeling about some of the people on that ship. And, I'm technically off duty, so this isn't a purely official visit."

I ran a finger down his cheek. "Hence the scruff?"

He shrugged. "It was a long day."

"Don't apologize. I like it."

Reese narrowed his eyes at me. "Really?"

Now it was my turn to shrug. "Makes you look a little dangerous."

He leaned in and ran a finger along my jawline. "And that's a good thing?"

"I'm learning to appreciate it."

He reached an arm around my back and pulled me to him so our bodies were flush. I inhaled sharply. He raised his hands to my face and dragged a thumb across my lips. It took every ounce of self-control not to moan as he lowered his lips to mine, kissing me softly, then more urgently. I lifted my hands, brushing my fingers over the stubble on his cheeks then raking them through his hair.

When he pulled back, I realized I'd stopped breathing, and I felt dazed.

"I'm so sorry," he said as he pulled his phone out of his back pocket, "but that's my brother's ringtone."

I placed a hand behind me on the couch cushion to keep from collapsing. I hadn't even heard his phone ring. I felt myself pulled back to reality as I watched Reese's face darken. "Bad news?"

He clicked off his phone and sighed. "There's been a fire on the ship."

Good feeling gone.

CHAPTER 19

"I thought we'd be riding in a police cruiser," I said as I slid into the leather passenger seat of a black Chevy Tahoe that still smelled like new car.

"I don't drive a cruiser," Detective Reese explained as he got in beside me. "Especially when I'm off duty."

I ran my fingers over the spotless dashboard. "I guess I've never noticed your car before. And we didn't make it this far the last time you picked me up."

The keys jingled as Mike put them in the ignition. He twisted to face me. "I'm really sorry. I promise our next date will not happen on the night of a triple homicide."

I waved him off. "It's fine. I understand." I paused. "Our next date? You don't consider this our first date, do you?"

He grinned at me as he started the car and pulled out onto P Street. "Well, it was something. And the night's not over."

I tried not to blush, but I could feel my face reddening. "I don't know about you, but I don't consider going to the scene of a fire a great date. It's right up there with the triple homicide."

Reese weaved through Georgetown traffic, veering around double-parked cars and taxis unloading passengers. Since

Georgetown didn't have a metro stop nearby, cars filled the streets at all times of the day and night.

I nibbled my lower lip. "Did your brother say if the fire was out or how much of the ship was damaged?"

Reese gunned it to make it through a yellow light. "It was out, but the fire department was trying to determine how it started. He didn't say anything about damage."

I wondered how many more things could go wrong before we threw in the towel on this wedding. Between the accidents, the personality conflicts, the dead harbormaster, and now the fire, it seemed as if the wedding gods really did not want this to happen. Or Reese was right and there was somebody desperate on board and getting more desperate every day. But desperate for what?

My mind went to Kristie. I couldn't help worrying about how she was handling the latest disaster. If we were lucky, no one had told her, although the space healer would have her work cut out for her now. No amount of essential oils could mask the scent of smoke damage.

I leaned my head back against the car seat and let myself take in the lights of the city as we skirted the Potomac River and passed by the iconic curves of the newly renovated Watergate Hotel. I watched the lights from the hotel reflected in the water as we sped underneath the Kennedy Center underpass and approached the Lincoln Memorial from behind. We passed the Washington Monument, illuminated and surrounded by a ring of American flags, and then shot by the Smithsonian Castle and the modern Air and Space Museum before turning to go under the highway, and emerging next to the Potomac again.

Reese swung into the parking lot for the District Marina. Two fire trucks with lights flashing sat closest to the entrance to the long dock leading to *Mystic Maven*. The neon lights from the nearby fish market added their light to the parking lot and illuminated the men in heavy uniforms, their helmets in hand, milling about the trucks. I leaned forward and stared at the massive white yacht at the end of the darkened dock. No signs of billowing smoke or charred outer hull. That was a good thing.

"Can you please let me take the lead on this?" Reese asked, putting a hand on my arm as I reached for the door handle. "I wasn't even supposed to bring you with me."

"Of course," I said. Maybe the kissing on my couch had mellowed me out, but I wasn't feeling my usual need to argue with the detective.

He released my arm then reached for it again. "And no calling your friends. I do not want this to become even more of a scene than it already is."

I felt my defenses kick in. "Hey, now. My friends can behave themselves."

Reese raised an eyebrow. "Name one."

I sighed as I thought of how Richard, Fern, and Kate usually reacted in a crisis. "Fine. Mum's the word." I held up a finger. "For tonight, at least."

I followed him past the fire trucks and squad cars gathered around the entrance to the dock. A few officers slapped Mike on the back as we passed, but none said anything about me. He put a hand on my back as we walked the uneven wooden slats of the dock toward the looming yacht. We exchanged our shoes for slippers, then he held my hand as we walked up the wooden gangway. I liked the solid feel of his hand, and I didn't mind the extra balance on the narrow ramp, either.

When we reached the deck, he dropped my hand and held the glass door open for me. As we stepped into the casual dining area, I smelled smoke but didn't see any. I pushed the door to the main salon open and instantly knew this was where the fire had taken place.

I put a hand over my mouth and coughed. The scent of char and chemicals hung in the air. "It's in here," I said to the detective as he came in behind me.

I spotted Mr. Barbery and the captain talking with their heads together while Daniel Reese talked to a group of firefighters. Mike's brother spotted us and crossed the room in a few long strides. He greeted me and gave his brother a questioning look.

Mike cleared his throat. "I was questioning Miss Archer when you called. I didn't think it would be a problem if she tagged along."

Questioning me? Tagged along? I tried to suppress the irritation I felt at being dismissed as a hanger-on. Not to mention how he obviously didn't want his brother to know there was anything going on between us. I reminded myself this was his work, and I shouldn't overreact.

I crossed my arms. "This is my wedding venue, after all. I need to see how much damage we're talking."

Daniel motioned for us to follow him across the room to where a pair of firefighters stood in full gear along with Mandy and the captain. "It's not bad. No structural damage."

"I'm so glad you're here," Mandy said once we'd walked up. "Maybe you can help me figure out how to fix this before the wedding."

My eyes fell on the burned section of sofa spanning the length of the room. Only two of the silk segments looked damaged, but the fire had reduced the cushions to ash and blackened the fabric on the back of the sofa. Even the walls showed evidence of contact with the flames.

"What happened?" I asked.

She shook her head, her eyes wide. "I have no idea. I was checking the casual dining room—making sure it was set for breakfast tomorrow—when I smelled smoke. I followed the smell and saw the cushions on fire, so I grabbed the kitchen's fire extinguisher. The flames were pretty high already, but I managed to put them out. By that time, the fire alarms had gone off and the fire department was on the way."

"The fire alarms didn't go off before you put out the fire?" I asked.

"The one in this room never went off." She lowered her voice. "It was only when the smoke reached the galley kitchen I heard an alarm."

My eyes scanned the ceiling of the room until I located the fire alarm near the center. The plastic casing had been removed, and wires spilled out from inside.

Mandy followed my gaze. "I told the fire department and they checked it out. No batteries and the wires were cut."

"That's not good," I said more to myself than anyone.

The Reese brothers talked with the firefighters while I stood with Mandy, but I heard one of the firefighters use the words "accelerator" and "tampering" and wished I could hear all of what was being said.

"I think this classifies as going above and beyond the call of duty," Mr. Barbery said when he spotted me and walked over.

I laughed it off. "We're a full-service wedding planning company."

He met my eyes. "I appreciate you coming down here at night. I thought my daughter was exaggerating when she talked about you and your colleague, but I can see that you're as impressive as she says you are."

I felt my cheeks flush. "Thank you. Kristie has been wonderful to work with."

Mr. Barbery reached out and squeezed my hand, meeting my eyes with his brilliant blue ones. "Remember, anything you need." He turned back to talk to the captain, then the two men left the room.

"What are we going to do about this?" Mandy waved a hand at the burned sofa. "Mrs. Barbery refuses to consider moving the wedding even after I told her I can't find one of my girls."

"Even after this?" I asked. "Wait. What do you mean you can't find one of your girls?"

"One of the girls who works under me hasn't been seen since this afternoon. I told Mrs. Barbery, but she doesn't care. She claims Caren couldn't handle hard work and must've ditched the job." Mandy rubbed her forehead. "I know Caren, and she wasn't afraid of working hard."

I remembered Caren. She'd reminded me of a smaller version of Mandy and had seemed very attentive to Kristie. "Maybe she left because she was afraid of all the things happening on board," I said.

Mandy shrugged. "Maybe, but it doesn't seem like her to run off without saying something. And Mrs. Barbery only seems to care about being on that TV show."

"If this keeps up, we may end up on the evening news. Is that good enough for her?" I looked around me the second I said it to make sure Mr. Barbery hadn't come back in. "The only thing I can think of to do is repair and reupholster the couch and paint over the smoke stains on the wall."

"Is that possible in time for the wedding?"

"Anything's possible," I said, "but it won't be cheap."

"Don't worry. Mrs. Barbery will approve it." Mandy nudged me. "It's not like it's her money anyway."

Not all second and third wives were loose with their husband's money, but Babs Barbery didn't strike me as the type to lose sleep over burning through her stepdaughter's inheritance.

"I'll have my fabric people come down in the morning," I said. "I'm assuming your deckhands can handle the painting."

"I have a feeling they'll be starting tonight," Mandy said. "It's not like any of the crew will be sleeping after a fire on board."

I didn't blame her for being nervous. If I had to sleep in the crew quarters in the bowels of the ship, I'd be terrified of being trapped in a fire, too.

"Listen." I leaned close to Mandy. "Can you talk to the crew? See if they saw anything about this or the murder? I'm sure they'll say things to you they never would to the police or to me."

She gave me a quizzical look. "Are you trying to solve the case or save the wedding?"

"Both," I said. "If we find out who's behind all of this, the wedding will be smooth sailing."

Mandy nodded. "Of course you're right. Sorry if I was rude. I'm just a bit stressed out. I'll see what I can do."

Mike came over to me and put a hand on my back as his brother left with the firefighters and captain. "You ready to go?"

"I'll talk to you tomorrow." I gave Mandy's hand a squeeze and felt bad when I saw the worried look on her face. Nothing more I could do about it, though. We already had extra security on board. Not that it had helped.

Mike steered me off the ship and we walked the length of the dock in silence, both of us absorbed in our own thoughts. When we got to his car, he opened the door for me and I couldn't help feeling pleased. It had been ages since a man opened a car door for me.

When he got in the car next to me, Detective Reese sat for a minute with the keys in the ignition before turning to me. "What do I have to do to get you to quit this wedding and get you off this ship?"

CHAPTER 20

"Are you alive?" Kate asked me when I finally answered my trilling cell phone.

I rubbed my eyes and focused on the old-fashioned chrome alarm clock on my nightstand. "Is it really almost ten?" The bright light seeping through the slats of my blinds confirmed the time for me.

"You sound like I woke you up, but that can't be possible. You don't even sleep this late after our weddings. What's going on?"

"Can't a girl catch up on sleep?" I swung my legs over the side of the bed. It seemed impossible I'd rushed down to the ship with Reese last night because a fire had been set on board. I cringed when I thought about Reese. He hadn't been very happy when he dropped me off. Mostly because I'd balked at quitting work on the wedding.

"Sure, but weren't we supposed to deliver hotel welcome boxes today?"

I groaned. I'd completely forgotten I'd told Kate I would pick her up so we could make the rounds of the guest hotels and deliver the elaborate boxes we'd assembled. "How did that slip my mind? And I told Mandy I'd get an upholsterer over this morning."

"An upholsterer?"

I arched my back to stretch. "There was some fire damage to the sofa in the main salon last night. We need to have someone fix it and make new cushions."

"I beg your pardon?" Kate said. "Fire? What fire?"

I rubbed my head, feeling too groggy to fully describe the previous night's events. I also wasn't sure I was ready to admit to Kate I'd been with the detective when he got the call. I'd have to answer more questions than I knew the answers to. "It wasn't major. Just the sofa in the main salon. Mandy put it out before it spread."

Kate gave a low whistle. "More accidents. That can't be good."

I didn't like to think about how bad it could have been. If I thought too hard about it I'd have an urge to quit the way Reese wanted me to. He'd been very persuasive last night when he'd told me the firefighters were convinced the fire had been started on purpose. Even with the acrid scent of ash and smoke, they could smell traces of an accelerant on the remains of the cushions. I wasn't surprised the small fire had been arson. It fit in with everything happening on board. But to me the fire seemed more like the petulant actions of someone trying to get their way than the dangerous actions of a killer.

He'd clasped both of my hands in his. "Annabelle, these things happening on the ship—a fire, a murder—aren't minor. And I'd bet my job they're being done by the same person. You can't go through with this wedding."

"And I'd bet my job that quitting a few days before a wedding won't do my business any favors."

"Your business doesn't matter if you end up hurt or killed."

I sighed. "Usually it's my friends who are the dramatic ones."

He pulled his hands away from mine. "I don't know if I've ever known anyone as pigheaded as you. Don't you see that I'm trying to keep you safe?"

Looking back at the conversation in the light of day, I did see that Reese just wanted to keep me from getting hurt. But the night before, it had felt like he was trying to tell me how to live my life, and I'd bristled at the thought. After I'd told him that I didn't need a man protecting me, he'd driven me back home in silence. Not exactly how I'd wanted our first pseudo-date to end.

"Why don't I hop in the shower and come get you in an hour?" I stood up and ran a hand through my hair. "We can still get the boxes out today."

Kate agreed, and I clicked off the phone. I grabbed my monogrammed terry cloth bathrobe from its hook on the back of the bedroom door and headed down the hall in my bare feet. I hoped I had at least one bottled Mocha Frappuccino in the fridge.

"Oh, Annabelle!" The voice came from outside my front door and was accompanied by a series of raps.

I froze in front of the refrigerator. Leatrice. Had she heard me or could I stay silent and hope she would give up? I didn't know if I was up to facing Leatrice this morning.

"I have something for you."

Knowing Leatrice, that could mean anything from the phone number of the single water delivery man to a batch of brownies she'd made with Ex-Lax because she'd run out of chocolate. I didn't move.

"It's a package someone dropped off last night. You didn't answer the door, so I offered to take it."

Now my curiosity was piqued. I wasn't expecting anything, but my usual calligrapher often dropped off finished place cards, and sometimes hotels or caterers delivered gifts. Usually they were for holidays, like heart-shaped cookies at Valentine's or Champagne at New Year's, and today was not a holiday. Still, it could be something from a client. Like a ten-foot long scroll outlining their demands.

"Hi, Leatrice." I opened the door, not wide enough for her to come inside.

She stood in the hallway in a lime green velour tracksuit so bright it almost hurt my eyes. She looked me up and down. "Did you just wake up?"

I sighed. Had no one ever seen me sleep in before? "I caught up on my sleep. Is that the package?" I asked, pointing to the flat manila envelope in her hands, eager to change the subject.

She handed it to me. My name was written in black Sharpie across the front, but there were no other identifying markers. "The woman buzzed your place a few times, so I offered to give it to you."

"Thanks for taking it for me." I hoped it was a signed contract and deposit check from one of the new brides I'd recently met. When brides were anxious to start working, they hand delivered the contract or sent it by FedEx so we could get going right away. This flat envelope felt like a new contract.

Leatrice tried to look past me into my apartment. "Is Kate here?"

"Nope. I'm actually just about to hop in the shower so I can pick her up."

Her eyes brightened. "Are you headed to the boat?"

"Not today," I said, glad I could be honest and dissuade her from trying to tag along at the same time. I felt incredibly lucky she had somehow missed the boat fire and wasn't chomping at the bit to see the damage. "We're just delivering welcome boxes to the hotels."

"Oh. Tell me the next time you go to the boat. The cruise wear I ordered just came yesterday and it really should be worn on a boat."

I tried not to visibly cringe as I imagined Leatrice's version of "cruise wear." "Absolutely," I said.

I closed the door before Leatrice could launch into a description of her new outfits. I put the envelope on the bookshelf by the door. The thrill of seeing a new deposit check would have to wait until I'd showered and dressed. For once, Kate was actually waiting on me and I didn't want to get stuck delivering the welcome bags in rush hour, which in DC could begin anytime after two o'clock.

I took the last Mocha Frappuccino from the door of my fridge and started down the hallway when I heard another knock on the door. What had Leatrice forgotten? She already knew I was home, so I couldn't ignore her. She'd stand out there knocking all day. Or, worst case scenario, she'd let herself in.

I marched back down the hall and opened the door. But instead of launching into an explanation to Leatrice of how much of a hurry I was in, my mouth fell open.

It wasn't Leatrice.

CHAPTER 21

"Surprise!" The woman pulled me into a hug then held me by the shoulders at arm's length. Her brown hair was cut in a stylish bob, and a pair of oversized sunglasses rested on the top of her head. She wore a black fitted sheath dress and a collection of delicate gold tassel necklaces dangling almost to her waist.

"Alexandra? I didn't know you were already here." Our favorite cake baker had moved to Scotland several months ago. She claimed to love the Scottish highlands, but Kate and I were convinced she'd been desperate to escape the increasingly demanding DC brides. She'd agreed to fly over and make the cakes for our most important clients as long as she didn't have to meet with them in person. Surprisingly, the brides had gone for it. The cachet of having a cake baker fly across the pond to do your cake had been like catnip to our upscale brides.

"I just dropped my bags off at the Ritz and had to come see you." She walked into my apartment and sank onto the sofa, trailing a cloud of expensive perfume. Most bakers smelled like sugar, but Alexandra always smelled like the inside of a Neiman Marcus catalog.

"So how is Scotland?"

"Well, not all the men look like they walked off the set of *Outlander*." Her slightly Eastern European accent had taken on a bit of a Scottish lilt. "Which is a real shame. I'd love to get my hands on a Sam Heughan look-alike."

I didn't have to ask who Sam Heughan was. I'd subscribed to the Starz channel for the sole purpose of watching the show *Outlander* and the smoking hot actor who played the lead. As an added bonus for viewers, he spent a decent amount of his on-screen time partly clothed or in a kilt. I thought about Ian, who wore a kilt onstage when he performed, and wondered if that had been part of his appeal.

"Did you expect them to?" I asked. I knew Alexandra was single and considered herself a connoisseur of men, but even I didn't think many Scots wore kilts on a daily basis.

She winked at me and shrugged. "A girl can dream. At least the brides are more laid back."

"You're doing wedding cakes over there? I thought you were tired of the cake business."

She crossed her legs and let one of her black peep-toe pumps fall to the floor. "It turns out I was just tired of type A brides. The girls getting married near my town are just delighted to get a pretty cake. I don't have to embed crystals in the icing or cover the entire bloody thing in gold dust. The pressure is off."

"Then you're not going to be thrilled about this weekend's wedding," I said.

She sat up straighter. "Did they change the design? I thought the bride wanted a pale blue cake with white lotus flowers."

I shook my head. "That hasn't changed. At least as far as I know. We're just having some issues on the boat."

"Like what kind of issues?"

"Accidents, fires, a dead body."

She waved a hand at me. "Well, that's not new. Don't all of your weddings have those now?"

I glared at her and tied my robe a little tighter. "No, they do not."

She glanced at her watch and looked me up and down for the first time. "Wait a second, Annabelle. What are you doing in a bathrobe at this time of day?"

"I slept in."

She narrowed her eyes at me. "You don't sleep in. You send me emails at six in the morning, even on weekends." Her eyes glanced down my hallway. "Is there a man here? Do you have a boyfriend you haven't mentioned?"

"There's no one here," I said.

She pointed a finger at me. "You didn't answer the second question."

"Don't you think you would have heard if I had a boyfriend?" I started down the hallway. I was not going to get into Reese and our fledgling relationship. Especially since he wasn't talking to me at the moment. "I need to get in the shower if I'm going to pick up Kate on time. We have to get these welcome boxes delivered."

"That's not an answer," she called after me. "But that's okay. I'll come with you to pick up Kate. She'll fill me in on everything."

I tried not to groan as I went into my bathroom and turned on the water in the shower. Kate would gladly fill Alexandra in on everything. Luckily, even Kate didn't know about my status with Reese. Come to think of it, even I wasn't sure where we stood after last night.

One thing I was sure of: This week was probably not the best time to make my personal life more complicated.

CHAPTER 22

"That's one massive boat," Alexandra said as we stood on the dock and looked up at the *Mystic Maven*.

The breeze was light, but it still felt several degrees cooler next to the water than it did downtown. I heard ships' flags snapping in the wind and looked up. I felt grateful the pungent fish market smells were being blown away from us, even though I wished I'd worn a jacket. I knew once the sun disappeared it would get chilly, and I felt goose bumps forming on my arms already.

I shaded my eyes from the reflection of sun bouncing off the gleaming hull of the ship. I spotted one of Daniel Reese's security guards decked out in head-to-toe black patrolling the outside of the ship. "They're pretty touchy about people calling it a boat."

"Apparently if it's this big, it's a ship," Kate said. She wore large white-rimmed sunglasses, so she didn't need to shade her eyes.

The three of us had spent the afternoon delivering welcome boxes to the hotels, and we'd decided to swing by the District Marina so Alexandra could see where she'd be setting up the wedding cake in a couple of days. From the outside, the ship looked quiet, though that was no guarantee drama and chaos weren't taking place on board.

"Can we scout out where I'll be setting up the cake?" Alexandra asked.

Kate's eyebrows popped over the rims of her sunglasses. "You sure you want to go on the Ship of the Damned?"

Alexandra laughed. We'd filled her in on all the happenings on the ship as we'd made our deliveries, and I'd spent an equal amount of time fending off her and Kate's questions about my love life. I'd managed to keep my pseudo-date with Reese under wraps, but only by distracting her with the wedding drama. Since designing cakes and delivering them before guests arrived removed her somewhat from a lot of the craziness we experienced, she was a sucker for hearing about it.

"I'll take my chances," she said as we slipped off our shoes and traded them for monogrammed slippers then started up the wooden gangway.

Kate and I followed behind, and I wished we'd both worn something other than jeans and button-downs. Our casual looks had been perfect for wedding errands, but I felt underdressed to be seeing a client.

"Where will the reception be?" Alexandra asked once we'd reached the deck.

"This way," I said, leading her into the main salon. The large oval dining table was surrounded by carved blond wood chairs and covered with bolts of tangerine, lime green, and turquoise fabric. It looked like Jeremy Johns had already started stocking up for his South Beach meets South of France look. Heavy on the South Beach.

At the far end of the room, a pair of men worked on the burned sofa. The affected sections of fabric had already been ripped off, and bolts of fabric surrounded the upholsterers. I glanced at the wall that had been burned and was impressed the deckhands had already covered the damage with paint. You'd never know someone had intentionally set a fire in the room a few hours before. Except for the smell. The air still held hints of a cookout gone wrong.

Kate sniffed. "That's not pretty. Remind me to bring some Febreeze next time."

"I could put the cake on this." Alexandra walked behind the dining table to the matching blond wood sideboard, which was flush with the salon's back wall and underneath a massive gilded mirror. "It would look nice in front of the mirror. Kristie doesn't want a huge cake, so I'm going to elevate it on a cake stand. Then the reflection will give it more impact."

"How many tiers?" I asked.

"Just three. And stacked on top of each other, so no separation or columns between them. It's a very tasteful design."

Alexandra had been emailing Kristie directly since we'd connected them. As long as I got a look at the final design, I felt comfortable skipping fifty emails about cake flavors and tier shapes.

Kate ran a hand over the shimmery turquoise fabric on the table. "Then your cake may be the only thing here that is."

"We're lucky the designer didn't have the couches reupholstered in that." My phone trilled and I pulled it out of my purse. Richard.

"Where are you?" he asked when I answered.

"On the ship," I said. "We brought Alexandra over to scout out cake placement."

"Perfect. I'm walking up the gangway now."

"Really? I thought you'd be avoiding the scene of the crime."

"I still have to cater this wedding, Annabelle. And that means seeing if there are any serving pieces I can use or if I need to rent everything. My final order has to go in first thing tomorrow morning."

"Well, we're in the main salon," I said.

"I can hear you," he said as he entered the room. When he saw me he hung up, dropped his phone in the pocket of his gray blazer, and shifted his black leather messenger bag. His face lit up when he saw Alexandra. "How is my favorite cake designer?"

"Darling!" She pulled him into a hug. "I see you're surviving without me."

"Barely," he said. "No one does sugar flowers like you do."

Alexandra beamed at him. "Stop it." She clearly didn't mean what she said. "And there isn't a caterer in all of the British Isles who can hold a candle to you."

Kate looked at me and rolled her eyes. "Do you think they'll be done anytime today?" she whispered so only I could hear her.

Richard held up a finger. "What do I smell?"

"There was a small fire last night," I said, pointing to his twitching bag. "What do I hear?"

Richard's face flushed as the top of his black bag popped open and a tiny Yorkie's head appeared.

Alexandra jumped back in surprise then put her hands to her cheeks. "He's adorable."

"You brought Butterscotch?" I asked, trying to keep the amusement out of my voice.

Richard sighed. "You know I prefer to call him Hermès." The frown on his face was a stark contrast to the happy grin of the little dog, whose pink tongue stuck out of his mouth.

"And I also know his owner, your significant other, named him Butterscotch," I said. "The bag is an Hermès."

"The bag and the dog have the same name?" Alexandra asked.

Kate nudged her. "You know Richard loves things to match."

Richard waved a hand at me, ignoring Kate and Alexandra as they fawned over the dog. "He's much more of an Hermès. And I had to bring him. He gets anxious when he's left alone."

Kate began to rub the dog's head. "And he'd rather be toted around in a satchel?"

Richard sucked in air and put a protective hand on the black leather. "It's called a man bag, and you know it. There's no such thing as a couture satchel."

Kate made a face at him and scratched the Yorkie under the chin. "Blink twice if you're being held against your will."

"Hilarious." He angled the bag so Hermès was out of Kate's reach before his eyes fell on the colorful fabrics. He staggered back a few steps. "Is this for the wedding? It's worse than I thought."

"You thought South Beach meets the South of France would be good?" I asked.

Richard arched an eyebrow. "It looks like South Beach ate the South of France and spit it out again." He leaned close to Alexandra. "Have they filled you in on the creative catastrophe?"

"A little." Alexandra's eyebrows pulled together in an intense furrow as she eyed the fabric. "But I thought the bride's colors were pale blue and silver. I designed an all-blue cake."

"They were, I mean are," I said. "But Kristie and her stepmother are having stylistic differences."

"She means the bride has a sense of style and the stepmother doesn't," Kate said.

"I don't even think the stepmom picked out these colors," I said.

Richard scrunched his nose and picked up a swatch of fabric, rubbing it between his fingers and cringing. "This is all Jeremy." Hermès gave a small yip, and I wondered if the dog had heard Richard rail about Jeremy before.

Alexandra's face registered shock. "Is Jeremy a new DC florist?"

"That's the only bit of good news." Kate flipped her blond hair off her face with one hand. "He's a designer from New York, so once this wedding is over we won't have to see him again."

"If we're very lucky," Richard said.

Alexandra pulled out one of the dining chairs and sat down. "What's his last name?"

"Jeremy's?" I asked. "Johns. Jeremy Johns."

"Doesn't it sound made up?" Kate asked. "His real name is probably Melvin Carbunckle and he changed it to sound posh."

"This is not good," Alexandra whispered. She'd pushed her sunglasses back on top of her head and slumped back in the chair.

"Of course it isn't good," Richard said. "Look at these colors. It's like a nuclear meltdown in a crayon factory."

"What's wrong, Alexandra?" I asked. I sat down next to her and put a hand on her arm. "You look like you've seen a ghost."

She laughed, but there was no joy in it. "Heard about a ghost is more accurate."

"I'm confused. Why are we talking about ghosts?" Kate asked.

Alexandra took her sunglasses off her head and ran a hand through her hair. "I wish he was a ghost. Unfortunately, he's my ex-husband."

"Who is?" Richard's eyes darted between me and Alexandra, and I could tell he sensed what was coming.

Alexandra cringed as she said the name. "Jeremy Johns."

CHAPTER 23

"Jeremy Johns is your husband?" Now Kate sat down with us. "How is that possible?"

Hermès yipped every time Jeremy's name was uttered, his black eyes alert and his brown furry head quivering with excitement. If I didn't know better, I would have guessed Richard had trained him. But I also knew dog training was not part of Richard's repertoire. I gave a nervous look around the room in the hope no one would hear the barking.

"Ex-husband." Alexandra wound a strand of long brown hair around her finger. "Emphasis on the 'ex.'"

"I don't understand," Richard said to himself, shaking his head as if trying to dislodge the idea. "Jeremy Johns had a wife?"

Yip.

"When were you married?" I asked. I'd known Alexandra for as long as I'd been planning weddings in DC, and she'd always been single. And she'd never identified herself as a divorcée. I understood why, of course. Newly engaged women didn't like to hear about divorce, so having a divorced cake designer might not appeal to some.

Alexandra kept her eyes down as she opened and closed her

sunglasses on the table. "It ended almost ten years ago. Before I came to Washington. We lived in New York together and when things fell apart, he stayed up there and I came down here. It seemed the best way never to run into each other again."

"So it wasn't an amicable split?" I asked.

Alexandra smiled weakly, her eyes darting up at me. "Not by a long shot."

"I still don't understand why Jeremy Johns would have gotten married," Kate said. "I mean, isn't he . . . ?"

Yip.

"It's all an act," Alexandra said.

Richard crossed his arms in front of his chest. "I could have told you that."

"You knew?" I asked him. "How?"

Richard shook his head at me like it was a ridiculous question. "I'm very highly attuned, Annabelle."

"So you're convinced the entire male cast of *Magic Mike* plays for your team, but not Jeremy Johns?" Kate asked.

Yip. Yip.

He shrugged. "I don't make the rules, darling."

I tried to ignore Richard and Kate as I turned back to Alexandra. "But why pretend?"

"When he first decided to break into the design world, he realized people would listen to his ideas more if he had a certain sensibility. As soon as he began dressing more flamboyantly, his business took off. The wealthy women of New York couldn't hire him fast enough."

"Is that why you split up?" I asked. I could imagine how a husband pretending to be flamboyant would put a crimp in a relationship.

Alexandra's face darkened. "No. Jeremy was good at living two different lives. I left him because he ruined my business."

Yip. Yip. Yip.

"Can we not say his name out loud?" I asked. "It seems to upset the dog."

"Fine by me," Richard said. "Clearly Hermès has a sixth sense about people."

I narrowed my eyes at him, not totally convinced he didn't have a part in the dog's reaction. The story about Jeremy was starting to sound familiar though. Buster and Mack had told us the exact same story, and neither was a stretch to believe considering how unpleasant we found Jeremy.

"But you're a cake designer," Kate said. "Why would he want to torpedo your business?"

Richard cocked his head to one side. "And I know he didn't want it for himself. He who must not be named is not the type to get his hands dirty in the kitchen."

I glared at Richard, who only shrugged and smiled sweetly at me. "What? You asked me not to say his name."

Alexandra stood up and started pacing the room as she talked. "I wasn't always a cake designer. In New York, I was a private chef for the über-wealthy. That's how he was able to weasel his way into the upper crust of the city. I recommended him and helped spread his name. At first, it was good for me, too. The more successful he became, the more income we had coming in and the less I had to worry about work."

"So why bring you down?" Kate asked.

Alexandra's shoulders twitched up then down again. "It took me a while to figure out what was happening. First, calls started dropping off and then parties I'd always catered went to other chefs. Finally, one of my longtime clients told me my husband was behind it. That he'd been spreading rumors about me and promoting another chef instead. My own husband! The man I'd helped get to where he was."

Richard shook his head in disgust. "I knew he was a snake from the second I laid eyes on him."

"Then you're smarter than I was," Alexandra said. She stopped her pacing in front of one of the upholstered beige armchairs and flopped down in it. "I never knew how threatened that man was by my success and stature in New York society until he stripped it away from me. He shot to the top by ripping me apart. The society women loved the gossip, and he got a reputation for making and breaking people. So other creatives both feared him and courted him."

"That's awful," Kate said.

"This guy is like an onion," I said. "But every layer we peel away is more rotten than the one before."

Alexandra raked both of her hands through her hair. "It was awful. So I left New York and came to DC and focused on baking wedding cakes. I thought since weddings are happy occasions, they would be less stressful."

I laughed. "So much for that theory, right?"

Alexandra smiled and held up two fingers as if measuring something tiny with them. "So I was a little off base. But I figured working in weddings down here would ensure I'd never run into my ex-husband again."

"If I'd had any idea, I never would have recommended you," I said. "And you flew all the way across the ocean too. I'll bet you thought you'd really escaped him in Scotland."

"It's not your fault," Alexandra said. "You had no way of knowing the dramatic interior designer was actually my ex-husband."

She had a point. It was hard to feel guilty about a scenario I wouldn't have dreamed up in my wildest nightmare.

"Who says you have to see him?" Kate said. "He has no idea you're doing the cake. It's not like we gave him a vendor list. Plus, you make the cake off-site anyway so we can just arrange for someone else to deliver it, and you'll never have to lay eyes on that rat again."

"Kate's right." Richard walked over and took Alexandra by the hand, pulling her out of the chair. "Let's sneak you out of here before that fink Jer—."

Richard interrupted himself and gestured to the Yorkie in his bag. "He who must not be named."

Alexandra's smile faded as she stared behind Richard. We all turned to see Jeremy Johns in the doorway, his hands on his hips and a characteristic sneer on his face. "Too late."

Richard flipped the flap over Hermès's head as the little dog let out a torrent of barks.

CHAPTER 24

"Well, look at what the cat dragged in." Jeremy sauntered into the room, eyeing Alexandra up and down. "I never thought I'd see you again."

He wore a bright pink and purple paisley shirt that fell open at the neck and exposed a few strands of chest hair, reminding me of a lounge lizard who'd wandered into a World Market sale. Even his cologne was too much, overpowering the smell of burned fabric and making my nose twitch. I'd never been a fan of heavy cologne on men, especially on a man as unappealing as Jeremy.

She took a small step backward then clenched her fists and squared her shoulders. "I hoped the next time I saw you, you'd be six feet under."

Jeremy arched a brow. "Kitty has claws."

Alexandra rolled her eyes. "Give up the act, Jeremy. I told them all about you and who you used to be."

A flash of anger and fear darted across his face, then he sneered. "Do I care what these two-bit amateurs think?"

"Hey," Richard said as his bag growled. "Who are you calling amateurs?"

I tried to send Richard a warning look to stay out of this

fight, but he wasn't focused on me. The last thing we needed was for Jeremy Johns, confidant and preferred designer of the stepmother, to run off and tell Mrs. Barbery we brought a dog on board the ship. Knowing how strict they were about shoes, I could only imagine how they'd feel about a dog.

Jeremy's eyes darted between Richard, Alexandra, and Richard's quivering bag. It seemed as if he couldn't decide which one to focus on first as he opened and closed his fists.

Richard waved a hand at the gaudy fabrics spread across the dining table. "Bold words from someone who picked out this horror of a color palette. Not to mention that shirt."

"The only taste he ever had was in his mouth," Alexandra said. She ran her eyes up and down her ex-husband and gave a dismissive sniff. "And even that he learned from me."

Jeremy's face flushed scarlet and he stamped his foot. "How dare you! I am a visionary."

Alexandra laughed. "Your only vision is of money and how much you can talk people out of. And if this is the best original idea you can come up with, I feel sorry for you."

Kate looked at me, her eyes wide. Neither of us had ever heard Alexandra go after someone like this. Even with the most difficult brides, she'd always managed to keep her cool and her somewhere-in-Europe sophisticated reserve. Clearly, Jeremy had a talent for making even the most unflappable people feel homicidal.

Jeremy glared at his ex-wife, his breathing heavy. "You'd better leave before I have you thrown off the ship. You should know by now what happens to people who cross me."

"You don't scare me anymore, Jeremy." Alexandra strode across the room until she was inches away from his face. "And you'd better be careful, or you may find yourself off this boat. Floating facedown in the Potomac."

Jeremy took a step back from her, and I could see he was startled. Even I was surprised she'd gone there since we had, in fact, recently found a body floating in the Potomac.

"Damn, girl," Kate muttered under her breath.

"Can I be of assistance?" Daniel Reese came into the room and put a hand on Jeremy's shoulder. Jeremy jumped and twisted around to face the retired police officer.

Several inches taller than Jeremy, Daniel wore gray cargo pants and a black button-down shirt he had rolled up to the elbows. He cleared his throat and looked around the room at all of us.

"Everything's fine." Jeremy shrugged Daniel's hand off his shoulder and tugged at the bottom of his shiny shirt to straighten it. "I need to get back to Mrs. Barbery." He shot a menacing glance at Alexandra and left the room, pushing past Fern and another man on his way out.

"What's going on?" Fern asked, pulling the other man into the room behind him. "We heard Jeremy screeching."

"It's nothing. Jeremy and Alexandra had a few words." I took a moment to absorb his outfit. "Do you mind if I ask what you're wearing?"

Fern touched a hand to his navy blazer with gold epaulets on the shoulders. "Don't you know dress blues when you see them?"

I rubbed my temples. "Please tell me that's not an actual Navy uniform."

Fern laughed and swatted me. "Of course not. Those jackets are cut too boxy. I had this one designed for me when I knew I'd be working on a boat. I kept the gold stripe down the sides of the pants but tapered them to elongate my legs. See?"

I nodded as I took in the slim-fit pants and matching tailored blazer embellished with gold braid and a colorful bar of fake commendations over the left pocket. I hoped no actual military officers ever laid eyes on this.

"I, for one, thought you were part of the ship's crew," Alexandra said.

Fern's eyes rested on the cake designer, and he clapped his hands together and ran to give her a hug. "You're here!"

"I didn't know you were on board," Alexandra said when Fern had released her.

"Officially I'm not here since Kristie isn't staying on the boat anymore," Fern said. "Damian and I were just gabbing downstairs. Everyone, this is Damian, Mrs. Barbery's hairstylist from Paris."

The man with Fern smiled at us. "*Bonjour*."

I could see Kate turn up the wattage on her smile when she heard his accent, and I tried not to groan out loud. Kate had a weakness for accents. Actually she had a weakness for most things having to do with men.

I had to admit he was striking. Tall with muscled arms the color of raw honey and dark dreadlocks that reached his shoulders. He wore a snug black T-shirt and dark wash jeans only a Frenchman could pull off. Everything about Damian was too cool to be from DC.

"So you can't stand Jeremy either?" Fern asked Alexandra, holding both of her hands in his.

Richard's bag yipped, and he coughed over it.

"She hates him even more than the rest of us," Kate said. "She used to be married to him."

Fern's face registered disbelief. "Jeremy Johns? You were married to Jeremy Johns?" He held her out at arm's length "Are you sure, darling?"

Kate, Richard, and I all coughed as Hermès let out a series of small barks. Fern, Damian, and Daniel looked around the room, so I did as well—shrugging after the yipping stopped. Daniel began walking toward Richard, and Richard edged away from him.

Alexandra laughed. "It's a long story."

Fern winked at her. "You know what I say, girl. The longer the better."

"*Oui*," Damian said, and he and Fern giggled.

Richard shook his head and shifted his bag behind him. "Oh, for the love of all that's holy."

I leaned closer to Kate. "Do you think Damian speaks any English?"

"When you look like that, who cares?" Kate whispered back.

"Is everything okay here?" Daniel asked. By this point he'd made a full circle of the room and so had Richard, so they remained on opposite sides of each other. Daniel's face told me he was more amused than concerned. "Jeremy Johns seems to have a lot of enemies on board."

This time when Hermès yipped, he leapt out of the bag and onto the floor. Damian's hand flew to his mouth as he screamed.

"How did that get in there?" Richard said, peering into his messenger bag and pretending to be startled.

Clearly thrilled to be out of the bag and in daylight, Hermès trotted around the group sniffing all of our feet.

Fern reached down and scooped him up in his arms. "Was that big, bad man keeping you inside his bag?" He shook one of the dog's tiny brown paws at Richard. "Naughty Richard."

Damian had recovered from his surprise and reached over to pet the Yorkie. "Adorable."

Daniel laughed. "So that's what you all were hiding?"

"Sorry." Kate batted her eyelashes at him and held out her wrists. "Do you need to lock us up?"

"I'm here to keep an eye out for danger, not dogs." He tousled the fur on top of Hermès's head. "Anyway, I like dogs."

"And I'm sorry I lost my temper," Alexandra said. "I let Jeremy get to me. But I promise I won't let this impact my work for this wedding."

"Don't worry," Richard said. "That toad is the master at pushing people's buttons. There have been plenty of times I would have liked to see him floating in the Potomac."

"I'm sure you don't mean that." I gave Richard a pointed look and hoped Daniel wasn't taking what he said seriously. "Have you met Daniel Reese? Detective Reese's brother and the head of the security team on board?"

"I'm sure I do mean it," he said, then glanced at Daniel. "And yes, I've met Big Brother. I told him he was even better looking than the detective in a silver fox kind of way, and I hoped not nearly as arrest happy."

I put a hand over my eyes. Between Richard threatening people on board, Hermès's surprise appearance, and Kate's flirting, we were making a great impression.

"He knows I would never really push Jeremy in the Potomac," Richard said.

Daniel rocked back on his heels. "Of course not."

"And he knows I mean silver fox as a compliment." Richard winked at Daniel.

"Anyone over twenty-five is not automatically a silver fox." I felt myself blushing for Daniel.

"I'm not criticizing." Richard spread his arms out in front of him. "I'm expanding my horizons."

Good heavens. I took Hermès from Fern and handed him back to Richard, then grabbed Kate by an arm. "Why don't we go? We've caused enough fun for one day." I glanced back at Alexandra, avoiding looking at Daniel. "You coming? I can drop you back at your hotel."

Alexandra put her sunglasses back on. "I'm with you. It would be smart to put some distance between me and my ex-husband."

I pushed my motley group out the door of the salon and through the informal dining room. As we were trading the *Mystic Maven* slippers for the shoes we'd left in the big basket, I heard my name being called from above. I glanced up and saw Mandy waving at me from one deck up.

"Hold on a second," she called down, and then disappeared from sight.

"We were so close," Kate said.

I handed my car keys to Kate. "You guys go ahead to the car. I'll wait for her."

Kate and Alexandra teetered down the ramp in their heels, and I hoped neither of them turned an ankle.

Mandy appeared at the bottom of the circular staircase at the other end of the deck and hurried toward me. "Sorry to stop you. I wanted to talk with you about Caren."

"She hasn't come back?"

Mandy darted a glance over her shoulder. "No. She didn't come to see you, did she?"

"Me? Why would she come to see me? I don't even think we ever spoke."

"I know." Mandy let out a breath. "But she knew you were with the wedding, so I thought maybe she'd reached out to you. I'm sorry. I'm grasping for straws."

I put a hand on her shoulder. "It's okay. I know you're worried about her."

The glass door to the informal dining room opened behind me, and the bride's stepbrother stepped outside. "Hey! The wedding planner, right?"

"You got it," I said. "Brody, right?"

He snapped his finger and grinned, the tanned skin around his blue eyes crinkling. He really was spectacular looking. I was glad Kate had already left the ship, or I knew I'd never get her off.

"My mother was looking for you, Mandy," he said.

"Thanks for the chat," Mandy said as she rushed toward the staircase.

Brody bestowed a wide smile on me as he snapped his fingers. "Actually, I have a question for you. Is it true that you've been involved in murder cases before?"

I cocked my head to the side. "Where did you hear that?"

Brody's shoulder twitched up in a hint of a shrug. "Your assistant might have let something slip."

Of course she did. "Maybe once or twice."

"So this is par for the course for you," Brody said, leaning against the ship's railing.

I brushed a strand of hair off my face that had escaped from my ponytail. "I wouldn't say that. Murder is never what I'd consider routine."

His face became serious. "Of course not."

"Anyway," I said. "Our focus is on Kristie's wedding, not the murder."

"Too bad." Brody winked at me. "You two are much easier on the eyes than the security guys or the cops."

Even though I knew he was just being friendly, I couldn't suppress a nervous laugh. "I'd better go."

Brody arched a brow at me and grinned. "Weddings to save?"

"Something like that." I walked down the gangway as fast as I could without breaking into a jog. I glanced back at the ship once and saw Brody watching me. I got the feeling he was standing guard. I just wished I knew if he was guarding against a threat on board or someone on land with me.

CHAPTER 25

"You didn't need to buy groceries," I said as I followed Richard up the stairs to my apartment, a heavy grocery bag in each arm. I stopped when we reached the third floor landing and shifted the weight of one of the reusable fabric bags onto my hip. A bag of tomatoes sat on top of one of the bags, and I inhaled the fresh vine-ripened scent. I hated to think how long it had been since a fresh tomato had passed through my doorway.

Alexandra and Kate had decided to have a single girls' night out looking for men, and Richard and I had decided that sounded like torture. But Richard also felt like takeout would be torture, so we'd swung by Whole Foods on our way back to my place.

Richard paused while I adjusted the bags. He had one grocery bag and his messenger bag with Hermès riding shotgun. "What are the chances you have anything decent to eat in your kitchen?"

"I have food," I said, knowing it was a lie the moment the words left my mouth.

"Beverages, Annabelle. You have beverages. That doesn't count as food." Richard started walking again, Hermès's tiny black and brown head bouncing with each step. "And takeout. I'm sure you have some old takeout in your refrigerator."

I followed behind him up the last flight of stairs. "Well, we could have ordered takeout. You don't have to cook."

"If you eat any more Chinese food you're going to start sneezing out sweet and sour sauce."

"Very funny," I said. "I don't eat that much Chinese."

We reached my landing and Richard stopped in front of my door. "What's the name of the delivery person?"

I started to tell him about Glen and the cool, retro superhero T-shirts he wore, then I saw Richard's smug look and glared at him.

"I think I've made my point," Richard said.

I set my bags down and groped inside my black Kate Spade purse for the keys. "Fine. I'll take a break from Dynasty Express."

"Which does not mean just shifting to Thai Palace to go," Richard said.

I made a face at him and mentally cursed how well he knew me.

Richard squeezed my arm. "I'm doing this for your own good, darling." Hermès yipped.

"Et, tu, Hermès?" I unlocked my door and held it so Richard could walk in, then I scooped up my bags and came in behind him. I turned on the overhead light and cringed a bit when I noticed the files still spread out on my glass coffee table, along with a couple of empty Diet Dr Pepper cans. I felt relieved that, since it was almost dark outside, the light wasn't spilling through my windows and highlighting the dust bunnies on my floor. I knew Richard would have something to say if he could see my mess illuminated by sunshine.

Richard dropped his messenger bag on my yellow twill sofa, and Hermès toppled out onto the cushions. We both put our grocery bags on the kitchen counter, then Richard shooed me out.

"I cook better alone. Anyway, there isn't room for two people working in this kitchen."

"What are you making?" I asked as I went back into the living room and dropped my purse on the floor by the couch.

"Something that doesn't have MSG or the words 'happy family' in it."

"Hilarious." I sat down on my couch next to the energetic Yorkie, attempting to rub his head as he scampered from one end of the couch to the other. I craned my neck to look at Richard through the chest-high open space in the wall between my kitchen and living room. I kept the slatted-wood accordion doors of the opening folded back to give the illusion of an open floor plan, and so Leatrice couldn't sneak up on me so easily when I was in the kitchen.

"So, do you want goat cheese on your salad or not?" Richard leaned his head across the open space, giving me a glimpse of the Santa Claus apron he'd dug out from my kitchen drawers. It was the only one I owned, and Richard was the only person who ever bothered to wear it.

"What? Oh, yes. Goat cheese is great." I leaned over the side of the couch and picked up my metal emergency kit, setting it gingerly on the glass coffee table in front of me.

Now was the perfect time to inventory my wedding supplies. There was little I hated more than discovering the bridesmaids from the last wedding had used up all the fashion tape or decided to keep my pocket-sized hair spray. I flipped open the double clasps and unfolded the levels of the multitier case, letting the compartments fan out like stairs leading down to one large space at the bottom where I stowed larger items.

I let Hermès inspect the contents and sniff diligently at the box of chalk and tin of breath mints. I took out each individual bag and packet and laid them on the glass surface. Straight pins and safety pins? Check. Shout wipes? Check. Floral tape? Check. Fake wedding rings? Check. I shook my mini bottles of static spray, hair spray, red wine remover, and deodorant to ensure they were full, then arranged my spools of white and black thread, needles, calligraphy pens, butane lighters, spare garters, clear nail polish, scissors, and white ribbon in the bottom of the box. I gathered up crumpled wrappers from breath mints and cough drops to throw away, returned all the items to my kit, and snapped it shut. Even if I couldn't control the crazy things happening on the ship, I could ensure I was well prepared. Though I doubted how much my emergency kit could do to stop a killer.

I dismissed thoughts of arson and murder from my mind, closed my eyes, and sank back on the couch, letting Hermès settle in my lap as I enjoyed the smells of cooking filling my apartment. If my nose was any indication, Richard was making his salmon with dill sauce and heating up the frozen yeast rolls he'd purchased at Whole Foods. My stomach growled as I tried to recall when I'd last eaten. I promised myself to stop skipping meals as soon as I survived this crazy wedding. If I survived, a little voice in my head reminded me.

I petted Hermès on the head. "Well, we're not going to think like that, are we?"

"Talking to yourself is the first sign of madness, Annabelle."

My eyes flew open. Richard, wearing an apron that made him look like a malnourished Santa, stood next to me with a whisk in hand.

"How many stages are there?" I asked. "I think I may be past the first stage."

"I think after this wedding we'll all be looking at the first few stages in the rearview mirror." Richard sighed and pulled off a red oven mitt.

"I wish we knew why all these crazy things have been happening," I said. "It just doesn't make any sense."

Richard sat down next to me, but Hermès didn't move from my lap. "Clearly, it's someone who wants to sabotage the wedding."

"But who would that be?" I asked. "Everyone has a separate agenda for wanting it to happen. Mrs. Barbery and Jeremy want to get on TV, Kristie wants to make her father happy and get married on the boat she's known for half her life, the crew wants to keep the father and stepmother happy . . ."

"And we want to get paid and live to tell the tale," Richard finished for me.

I twisted around so I faced Richard, and Hermès rearranged himself with a small yip. "And killing the harbormaster seems like an extreme way of preventing a wedding from happening."

"A much more efficient way would be to kill the bride or groom."

"Richard!"

He shrugged. "I'm not suggesting it. I'm just saying if shutting down the wedding was the reason someone killed the harbormaster, then it was a spectacular failure."

I tapped my chin. "You're right. The killer must have had a different reason for doing it. But what?"

A timer went off, and Richard popped up. "No clue. But luckily we have a police detective on the case and a security team on board the ship, so there's absolutely zero reason for you to worry about it."

"Except they haven't discovered a motive or any real suspects."

"Well if they can't, then we certainly don't stand a chance." Richard headed for the kitchen, talking as he walked.

"Maybe." I followed him into the narrow kitchen, holding Hermès under my arm. I hopped up on the counter, letting my legs swing from side to side. "But as long as things keep happening, I can't help but worry."

Richard slid a round tin of golden browned yeast rolls out of the oven and set them on the stove top, glaring at the dog who sat next to me. "Worry all you want, as long as you let the professionals do their job."

I inhaled the addictive aroma and reached for the tin, hoping to steal a bite. "You know I've gotten much better at letting other people be in charge."

Richard swatted at me with an oven mitt. "You'll burn yourself. Let them cool, Miss Instant Gratification. And since when have you been able to let go and let someone else fix things?"

I made a face at Richard but didn't make another attempt at the rolls. "Fine. I'm definitely working on it. At least I'm thinking about working on it."

"Before you even think about it, the dog can't eat human food," Richard said.

I nuzzled Hermès's furry head. "Sorry, bud. Herr Richard says no people food for you."

Hermès yipped as if he knew what I'd said, and Richard gave me a look that told me he wasn't amused.

"Hold on a second," I said. "I did let Reese take the lead when we went to the fire on the ship. It wasn't easy—"

"Wait," Richard interrupted me. "As in you went together?"

Damn. Leave it to Richard to pick up on the subtlest of verbal cues. "Yes, Detective Reese and I happened to be together when he got the call about the fire. It's really no big deal."

Richard tapped his foot on the tile floor. "Your flaming red cheeks tell me otherwise." He pushed the tin of rolls out of my reach. "You can either tell me what's going on between you and the detective or no rolls for you."

Just perfect. If I wasn't dealing with murder and arson on the ship, my friends were blackmailing me. I slid down from the counter, grabbed the Yorkie, and made for the living room. "I think you and I need to hang out with some new people, Hermès."

I paused at the bookshelf next to the front door. Now that I had a second to breathe, I thumbed through the mail I'd been piling on top. Mostly junk. I picked up the manila envelope Leatrice had delivered. A new client contract would be the perfect thing to raise my spirits, especially if a deposit check accompanied it.

I ripped open the envelope and pulled out a stack of papers. I flipped through them, recognizing that they were printouts of online purchases along with a handful of arrest records.

"What's that?" Richard asked, as he walked past me to put two dinner plates on the dining table.

"I assumed it was a new contract but it's a bunch of random papers and arrest records. It must have been delivered to me by mistake. I have no idea who these people are or what these printouts mean."

Richard came up and looked at them over my shoulder. "That one looks like an online receipt. Let me know if you're going to start reimbursing for expenses because I'd be happy to send you my receipts."

"You do know designer clothes are not a valid business expense, right?"

Richard sucked in a breath. "Bite your tongue, Annabelle. You clearly don't have the right accountant."

CHAPTER 26

"I can't believe you're just now telling me about Reese," Kate said, as we wound our way through midday traffic.

"Technically, I didn't tell you. Richard did." I'd known that Richard would rat on me the second he left my apartment if only to get support from Kate for his indignant outrage. "Did you even hear what I said about the odd receipts?"

"Yeah, yeah. Weird receipts. Big whoop." Kate twisted to face me. "I can't believe I had to hear about your date with Reese secondhand."

The light changed and I eased the car forward. We were headed down New York Avenue past modern office buildings wedged between hotels and the occasional historic house. I'd decided to avoid Georgetown traffic by taking the long way to the District Marina.

"Richard wasn't supposed to find out either," I said. "And it wasn't a date."

"Even worse." Kate turned to face forward in her seat. "If Richard hadn't found out, you never would have told us. I can't believe you'd keep something so big from me."

"I think you're blowing this out of proportion. It's not that big a deal. Like I said, it wasn't an official date." My mind flashed back to kissing Mike on my couch, and I couldn't help smiling at the memory. It may not have been a real date, but it had felt pretty amazing.

"It's kind of a big deal," Kate said. "You've liked him for a while now."

"How do you know?" I floored it to make a right turn in front of an oncoming line of traffic.

Kate braced her arms against my dashboard. "Please. The amount of tension between you two is nuts."

"I promise I'm not going to run off and get married," I said. "And the only reason I didn't tell you is I knew you'd make a big deal of it. At least you're better than Richard. He practically went into cardiac arrest."

I slowed as we approached a work crew set up in the middle of the street. No matter what time of the day or night you drove around DC, there always seemed to be road work. I looked in my rearview mirror before making a U-turn so I could detour around the work zone.

Kate shrugged and rolled down her window. "Well, can you blame him? It's hard to compete with someone who looks like Mike Reese."

"What do you mean compete?" I took a deep breath and inhaled the scent of hot dog from a nearby street vendor. "Richard and Reese aren't exactly playing for the same team."

Kate sighed. "Competing for your attention. Richard's been your best friend since you came to DC and you've been single for that entire time. Now a hot guy comes along and you fall for him. What's to say you won't start spending every weekend with Mike instead of Richard?"

I paused at a traffic light and eyed the gleaming white U.S. Capitol building in front of me. "That won't happen. For one, I work every weekend—usually with Richard."

"Richard's used to going up against temperamental chefs and

nutty brides, not unbridled masculinity and a great butt. You're going to need to give him time to adjust."

I eased the car forward as the light turned green. "He may not need to adjust. Reese hasn't called or texted since we ended up getting in an argument that night when he dropped me off."

"Give him time to cool off." Kate pulled her red patent leather purse onto her lap and began rummaging through it. "Anyway, making up is the best part."

I rapped my fingers on the steering wheel as I let a school tour group in matching green T-shirts cross in front of us. "We haven't reached the making up stage yet."

"Don't worry. He'll call you." Kate pulled out a black lipstick tube and flipped down the sun visor to access the mirror. "He's just playing it cool—someone has to."

I decided to ignore her obvious jab and listen to her advice. If anyone knew men, it was Kate. I waited until she'd applied her lipstick to accelerate the car and pass a slow-moving tour bus clearly searching for street parking.

My phone trilled from inside my purse, and I reached behind my seat with one hand to pull it out. I took my eyes off the road to glance at the caller ID, feeling a rush of pleasure when I saw Reese's name.

"Annabelle?" he said when I answered. "Are you on the ship?"

"Actually, I'm not, but I'm on my way." I could hear the flirtation in my voice, and I knew Kate would pick up on it.

"Then I'll see you when I get there." He sounded all business, and my warm feeling evaporated as I noticed the edge in his voice.

"What are you talking about? What's going on?"

There was a long pause. "We found the crew member Mandy reported missing."

I knew without asking this wasn't a good thing.

"She ran out into traffic in Georgetown last night and got hit by a car. They just identified her body."

Even though I knew the girl's accidental death couldn't have anything to do with what had been happening on the ship, it felt like another bad omen. I burned through a yellow light as I approached the marina.

"Whoa, there." Kate looked over at me as I swung one hand behind me and dropped my phone back in my purse. "Where's the fire? Wait, is there another fire?"

"I want to get to the ship before Reese does." I made a sharp right into the District Marina parking lot and picked the closest empty space to the dock leading to *Mystic Maven*. "One of the crew went missing last night, and Reese just told me she was hit by a car in Georgetown."

"That's awful." Kate shook her head. "Someone we knew?"

"Caren, the one we met with Mandy." I opened the car door and stepped out, smoothing my green floral wrap dress until it fell back to my knees.

Kate walked around the car to join me. I'd thought her pinstriped shirtdress had looked short because she was sitting in the car, but it was just as short now that she stood in front of me. "So why do we need to beat the detective here?"

"I'd like to get a few moments to talk to the crew before Reese tells them." I took the lead as we walked down the uneven wooden slats toward the ship. "As soon as they find out one of their own is dead, it may be tough to get information out of them."

Kate reached out and grabbed my elbow, causing me to slow down. "What information?"

I shrugged. "There have been a lot of odd things happening regarding this ship. Since neither the police nor the security team seem to be able to stop it or figure it out, it can't hurt for us to try."

"Here we go again." Kate sighed. "You know how thrilled Detective Reese will be when he finds out you're poking your nose into his investigation."

I stopped when we reached the wooden gangway at the back of the ship, dropped my nude flats in the shoe basket, and slipped on a pair of black *Mystic Maven* slippers. "I have no intention of interfering in his investigation. But I do think that you and I might find out more by talking to the crew than the police would."

Kate followed me up the gangway. "I am pretty good at sweet-talking men."

"You're the best," I said. "I'll bet you could find out what the deckhands or the captain really think about all of this."

If Kate knew I was buttering her up she didn't let on. "So while I'm charming information out of the men on board, who will you be talking to?"

I paused when we reached the ship's outer walkway. "There are women on board this ship, you know."

"Really?" Kate looked genuinely surprised. "Well, they must do a good job of being inconspicuous."

I thought it was more likely that Kate just didn't notice women as much as she did the men. "You want to take the front part of the ship, and I'll take the back?"

Kate patted my arm. "The bow and the stern, Annabelle." She cocked an eyebrow at the curious look I gave her. "What? I've dated a few sailors."

I knew Richard would have a zippy comeback about exactly how many sailors, but I let it slide as we parted ways. I walked around the outside of the ship to the lounge where we would soon have a massive ice bar filled with pricey vodka. No one in sight. I peered over the railing to the transom below. Also empty.

I squinted to look past my own reflection in the glass doors that led to Mr. Barbery's study. He appeared to be sitting at the desk, so I rapped my knuckles lightly on the doors then pulled one open a crack. "Do you mind if I come in for a moment?"

He looked up, a look of irritation replaced instantly with a smile when he recognized me. He stood and waved me inside. "Of course. Please come in."

I stepped into the room and let the door fall silently back into place. "I hope I'm not disturbing you."

"Not at all." Mr. Barbery gestured for me to take a seat on a beige leather couch. "Just going over the latest invoices for the wedding."

I cringed, knowing the amounts. "I'm sorry."

He laughed. "Oh, these particular bills don't have anything to do with you. They're for my wife's dresses. She had to have three of them for the wedding."

I'd had brides select two dresses for a wedding day—one for the ceremony and another for dancing—but never three. And never a stepmother. But I didn't put much past Mrs. Barbery.

"Are the plans going well?" He ran a hand over his close-cropped beard, his blue eyes focused intently on me.

"As well as possible considering the accidents, fire, and murder."

The bride's father leaned forward in his brown leather desk chair. "The police don't think they're accidents. What do you think? Do you think it's too dangerous to hold the wedding on board?"

"I'm not sure."

"I'll be honest, Miss Archer." He stood and began walking the length of the shelves behind his desk, passing the leather-bound books and encrusted artifacts I'd examined earlier. "I've seen my share of danger and gotten my share of threats, but I can't stand the idea of my family being in danger."

I was struck again by how much I liked this man and how different he was from his current wife. "Can you think of anyone who would have a reason to do these things? Maybe someone who has a grudge against you or one of the crew or another family member?" It seemed rude to suggest that there must be a thousand people who held a grudge against Mrs. Barbery.

He tapped a finger against his chin. "Competition in the treasure hunting world is intense, but most of my colleagues and I respected each other. And since we brought the ship over from

Europe, no one on board knows anyone in DC. Except Kristie, that is, and no one could get angry at Kristie."

I had to agree with him there. I didn't think the bride made enemies unless you counted her stepmother, and Mrs. Barbery wanted a successful wedding so she could appear as the glamorous hostess on *Diamond Weddings*. Back to square one.

I stood up. "I won't bother you any longer."

Mr. Barbery walked around the desk and took my hand. "If you find out anything that would put my daughter in danger, I want you to come straight to me. And you have my permission to talk to anyone on board to get to the bottom of this."

Was the bride's father asking me to investigate? "Of course, sir."

As he walked back around to sit at his desk, my eye caught a blank spot on the bookshelves behind his head. The clear stand that had held the antique pistol was now empty.

CHAPTER 27

"The gun is missing," I said when I found Kate in the hallway outside the gym. I could hear the hiss of the steam jets as I breathed in the faint smell of eucalyptus. I felt a momentary pang of jealousy toward the person relaxing inside the steam room.

"What gun?" Kate's eyes darted around me. "Has someone been shot?"

"No." I grasped both of her hands in mine. "The antique gun that was in Mr. Barbery's study. The really old one."

Kate narrowed her eyes at me. "I don't remember a gun."

I tapped my toe on the carpet. "Did you notice anything in the study aside from Kristie's father?"

"There's leather," she said, "and a desk."

I forced myself not to roll my eyes. "There are also several artifacts from Mr. Barbery's career as a wreck diver. One of them was an antique gun, and now it's missing."

"What does that mean?" Kate asked. "Should I be worried that someone's going to try to shoot us with an ancient gun?"

"I don't think that gun could fire it's so old and rusted, but it did look heavy. What if it was used to knock the harbormaster over the head?" I said. "Reese mentioned that flakes of rust were found in the harbormaster's wound."

Kate made a face. "So someone hit the guy over the head with a heavy old gun and then pushed him overboard?"

"It's the best explanation we have," I said, lowering my voice as I heard the door from the steam room open and the hissing of the steam grow louder. I tugged Kate by the arm as I made my way to the staircase at the end of the hall.

"Miss Archer!" The shrill voice stopped me in my tracks.

I slowly turned to find Mrs. Barbery standing in the hall, wrapped in a beige towel, her cleavage spilling over the top. The fragrant steam filled the narrow hall before evaporating into the air. I coughed and concentrated on keeping my eyes averted from her overflowing bosom. "Yes, Mrs. Barbery?"

"I am not happy that there's a security team on board this ship." She put a hand to the mass of red curls piled on top of her head.

"It's really for the protection of everyone on board—," I began.

Mrs. Barbery cut me off with a snap of her fingers. "It's an inconvenience and a nuisance, and it's the last thing I need during an already stressful time."

I swallowed hard. I wasn't sure why she was so stressed since it wasn't even her wedding. And if she was stressed by a few inconspicuous men patrolling the ship, she really wouldn't be happy when the cops arrived to question everyone about the dead crew member. "We're doing all we can to ensure that the wedding goes off without a hitch."

She took a step toward me. "Well, it's not enough."

"It's enough for me and they're my wedding planners." Kristie came down the staircase behind us.

I turned to see her wearing black yoga pants and a lavender T-shirt with a yin-yang symbol on the front. Her hair was swept up in a messy ponytail, and she held a black duffel bag in her hand.

Mrs. Barbery's lips curled up in a predatory smile. "When did you come back on board, dear?"

"Just now." Kristie put an arm around Kate's shoulders. "Since I'm going to spend the next six months on board for my honeymoon, I figured I should start stocking my room."

I glanced at the duffel bag in her hand and wondered if it was filled with crystals and scented candles.

Mrs. Barbery crossed her arms across her chest. "It's absurd that you're taking a six month honeymoon on my yacht."

Kristie gave her a sticky smile. "Don't you mean my father's yacht? Let me know if you need me to help you pack up your things, Babs."

Kate looked at me with wide eyes as Mrs. Barbery stamped one bare foot and huffed off to her room.

"Are you okay?" I asked Kristie once her stepmother was out of earshot.

She nodded. "I'm fine. It felt good to stand up to her for a change."

"Well, you sure did that." Kate laughed. "I thought her head was about to pop off."

Kristie leaned in to us. "No such luck, right?"

"So you're feeling better then?" I asked.

"You bet. Fern gave me a pep talk and a little liquid courage."

Now this was making sense. Fern had gotten her both whipped up and liquored up before she came over. Luckily, the combination seemed to work for Kristie.

"Do you need any help setting up your room?" Kate asked.

Kristie reached out and squeezed her hand. "I should be fine, but thanks. I'm finally getting excited about my wedding and honeymoon around the world."

"It's going to be fun, isn't it, Kris?" Brody came down the stairs at the far end of the hall wearing black gym shorts and white T-shirt.

"Absolutely," Kristie said, pulling him into a hug when he'd reached us. "It's a good thing you and Matt get along like brothers."

I reminded myself that Matt was the groom. Since he lived in California, we'd only met him once during the planning process.

Brody gave her a playful nudge. "Hopefully I won't be on board long enough to cramp your style."

Kristie laughed. "You could never cramp my style. Unlike some other people we know."

"At least your dad had your back on that one," Brody said. "It would not have been fun to have my mother along for the ride."

Kristine shuddered. "Talk about a long six months. I'd rather have walked the plank."

Brody put a finger over his lips as the two collapsed against each other in a fit of giggles. "Shhhh. She might hear us."

It was hard not to join in their contagious laughter. Seeing how excited the bride was for her wedding and honeymoon made me feel even more determined.

"That settles it," I said so only Kate could hear me. "We have got to figure out what's happening on this ship before it wrecks her wedding."

CHAPTER 28

"There you are." Detective Reese looked up from where he stood in close conversation with his brother on the transom. "I'd been wondering where you were hiding."

I rubbed my arms as Kate and I stepped fully into the open air. No matter how warm it was in downtown DC, there always seemed to be a breeze on the water.

I tried to make my laugh sound normal but it came out high and shrill. "I wasn't hiding. I was checking on a few details for the wedding, that's all."

I couldn't help noticing that while both brothers were tall, Daniel had about an inch on his younger brother and a bit more bulk.

Reese raised an eyebrow at me but I ignored him. "How's the security gig going?" I asked his older brother.

"Yes," Kate walked over to Daniel and rested a hand on his arm. "Are you working hard?"

"Not much to report," he said. "I was telling Mike that everything has been relatively quiet. Since the psychic left and the TV crew finished filming their establishing shots, it's been drama free."

"For one of your weddings, that is," Reese added.

I put my hands on my hips. "If you're going to keep making disparaging comments about my work, I may not share the information I just discovered."

Reese let out a breath. "Should I even ask how you came across this information?"

Kate patted him on the shoulder. "I wouldn't."

"Fine." Reese crossed his arms. "Spill."

"You know how the ship's owner, Mr. Barbery, used to be a treasure hunter, right?" I said.

Kate nodded and both men exchanged glances like this was new information to them.

I kept going. "Well, he has a few mementos of his underwater wreck diving days on display in his study. I was just up in his study, and I noticed the antique pistol is missing." I paused for a reaction but both men continued to stare at me as if waiting for the bombshell. "That's it. That's the information."

"You think . . ." Reese said, prompting me to finish his sentence.

I threw my hands in the air. "I think that the killer used the heavy, rusted-iron gun to bash the harbormaster over the head. You did say the coroner found flakes of rust in the head wound, right?"

Reese rocked back and forth on his heels. "I did say that."

Daniel looked at his brother. "It's possible, and it's the only lead we have."

"But you said the gun is missing," Reese said.

My shoulders sagged. "Unfortunately, yes."

"But now you know what to look for, right?" Kate asked, her voice eager.

"I guess that's the silver lining," Reese said. "Although chances are high that the gun, if it was used to kill the harbormaster, was tossed into the Potomac along with the body."

"Could we drag the river or send divers down to search for it?" I asked.

Reese grabbed me by the shoulders. "Do I need to remind you that there is no 'we' when it comes to investigating this murder?"

"I didn't mean 'we,'" I said, shrugging out of his grasp. "I meant you. I'm not chomping at the bit to do your job for you, despite what you may think."

Daniel coughed into his hand then left the hand over his mouth, and I wondered if he was attempting to cover up a grin.

Kate linked her arm through mine. "Well, we need to give you boys space to do your work." She tugged me toward the gangway. "Let's go, Annabelle."

When we got to the dock and had switched out of *Mystic Maven* slippers to our regular shoes, I glanced at Kate teetering on her heels. "You mind telling me why you rushed me off the ship?"

She put a finger to her lips and leaned on my arm as we headed down the dock. "Because I didn't want to tell them about the argument I overheard before we ran into each other down below deck."

"Argument?" I stopped as she bent over to free her heel from two warped slats of wood. "Who was arguing?"

Kate stepped out of her shoes then tugged the heel jammed in the dock with two hands before it popped loose. "Jeremy Johns and the captain."

"Might I suggest flats for the millionth time?" I said as Kate waved the suggestion off. "So what were they arguing about?"

"It was a little tough to hear." Kate continued barefoot down the dock. "I was standing outside the door to the casual dining area and they were inside, but I do know that it was about the captain giving him money."

"Was Jeremy extorting money?"

"I don't know. But it sounded like the captain was going along with it."

"But why?" I wondered aloud as we crossed the parking lot. "Is Jeremy blackmailing someone on board? Maybe Mrs. Barbery?"

"That would explain why she hired a talentless hack to design the wedding." Kate leaned against the hood of my car as she slipped her heels back on.

"Only one more day and we get to see the hack's design vision come to life," I reminded her.

Kate shuddered. "Why do I have the feeling that I won't be taking any photos of this wedding to post online?"

CHAPTER 29

"Thank heavens it's Friday and this hellish wedding is one day closer to being over." Richard met us at the bottom of the boat's gangway in a mint green tie and beige suit, one hand over his nose since the breeze carried the scent of the fish market. After so many trips to the dock, I'd become somewhat immune, although I knew it would be a long time until I got a craving for seafood again.

I sighed as I dropped my black flats in the shoe basket and slipped on a pair of *Mystic Maven* slippers. It felt like it had only been minutes since Kate and I had left the ship discussing clues, but it had been an entire day and we were no closer to figuring out any of it.

"What is she doing here?" Richard asked.

At least he was talking to me as he normally did and not in the wounded voice he'd adopted after I told him I'd kissed Reese. "What are you talking about? Kate's always at our rehearsals."

"Miss me already?" Kate blew him a kiss as she took off her heels.

"Not her." Richard pointed a finger behind us. "I meant *her*."

I looked to where Richard was motioning and did a double

take. What was my nutty neighbor doing here? She couldn't have followed me because I'd picked up Kate and then coffee before heading to the marina.

I gave Richard a push. "Get up to the ship. Maybe she won't see us."

We hurried up the gangway, crouching as we went. When I reached the top, I turned around and saw Leatrice throw both arms in the air and wave them wildly as if summoning a rescue from the top of a burning building.

Kate sighed. "I'm pretty sure she sees us."

"What in heaven's name is she wearing?" Richard asked.

"Well, that's always the million-dollar question, isn't it?" I said. It appeared Leatrice was wearing her version of cruise wear—a pair of white pedal pushers with navy blue anchors embroidered all over and a blue-checked shirt tied at her waist. It looked like Vineyard Vines had run smack into Mary Ann from *Gilligan's Island*. I couldn't tell from where I stood, but I hoped to goodness she wasn't showing midriff.

"Yoo-hoo! Annabelle!" She started up the gangway.

"Leatrice, what are you doing here?" I asked once she'd reached the top. I was relieved to see her shirt covered her stomach, but not relieved she was at the site of my wedding rehearsal.

"I tried calling you, but you didn't answer."

I pulled my phone out of my purse and saw it was on mute. I'd switched it to silent for our meeting with Alexandra and forgotten to switch it back on. "Sorry about that. What's going on?"

"A woman stopped by to see you and said it was about the wedding."

"This wedding?" I asked. I had about twenty weddings going on at the same time, all in different stages of planning, so it was entirely possible my visitor was a bride or vendor from another wedding. I tried to keep some separation between my business life and personal life and strongly discouraged clients from popping by my place.

Leatrice tapped a finger on her chin. "I think so. She said it was urgent."

Kate rolled her eyes. "That doesn't mean anything. Every client we have thinks everything about their wedding is urgent even if it's sixteen months away."

"Was she drunk?" I asked. Debbie and Darla had been known to pop by after their liquid lunches in Georgetown.

"I don't know about that but she seemed nervous." Leatrice put a hand to her Mary Tyler Moore hairdo, which was lacquered permanently in place. "She told me to tell you she'd come by and that you'd know why she came."

"How mysterious," Richard said. "Your brides are getting so cryptic, Annabelle."

"Did she give you her name?" I asked.

"Yes." Leatrice smiled at me. "And I wrote it down so I wouldn't forget."

I nodded, trying not to act too impatient. I'd noticed Leatrice had been forgetting little things lately, but we'd come to an unspoken agreement to pretend it wasn't happening. So she used more Post-it notes, and I fought the urge to get exasperated when it slipped her mind to give me a package for three days or to tell me the building's water would be shut off for an afternoon.

Her smile faded and she dropped her eyes. "And the Post-it note flew off the dashboard and out the window while I was driving here."

I took a deep breath. I really didn't have the time to deal with this. I had a rehearsal to run. Plus, I was still trying to shake off the news of Caren's death. Even though I hadn't known her, the thought of the girl escaping the danger of the ship just to be hit by a car had upset me. I patted Leatrice on the arm. "Don't worry about it. I'm sure it was just a nervous bride and she'll call me about whatever was bothering her anyway." I turned to Richard. "Have you seen Jeremy lately?"

"Do you hear bloodcurdling screams coming from my lips?" he asked.

I shot him a look. "I'll take that as a no. Have you seen Kristie?"

"The bride? Yes. She's in the main salon doing a final space clearing. I'm surprised we can't hear the bells from here."

"Bells?" Kate asked.

"The sound of bells removes negative energy," Richard said. "Come on, Kate. Get with the program."

Kate stuck her tongue out at Richard. "If that's true then I hope Kristie brought some really big bells."

I had to agree with Kate. With all the fights and fire and the murder that had taken place on board in the past week, I wasn't even sure if the Liberty Bell would do the trick. "Let's go see if we can convince her to stop ringing and start rehearsing."

"I'm with you," Kate said. "The sooner we're off this ship, the better."

"It will all be over soon," I reminded her. I couldn't remember the last time I was so thrilled to be closing in on the end of a wedding. In a little more than twenty-four hours, the wedding would be over and all of the drama would be a fading memory. I, for one, couldn't wait to break up with this wedding and especially with this stepmother of the bride.

Richard led the way through the glass door and into the casual dining room attached to the upstairs kitchen. Brody sat at the curved banquette with the ship's captain and first mate across from him. All three men looked up when we came in, although only Brody smiled at us.

"The wedding planners!"

"And caterer," Richard said. He didn't like being mistaken for a wedding planner any more than I liked it when people asked me if I catered weddings.

The captain and first mate stood. They nodded to us then

slipped through the back door leading to the bridge. The captain's friendly demeanor from earlier in the week had evaporated. I brushed it off because I knew he had his hands full running the ship and preparing for the six-month around-the-world honeymoon trip for the bride and groom. I also knew Reese had delivered the news about the dead crewmate earlier, so that had to be affecting him. The first mate had never seemed approachable to me, so this wasn't a change.

"We were discussing the ocean crossing after the wedding." Brody slid out from behind the table and stood.

"You're going with them?" I asked. "I thought it was just the bride and groom."

"I'm not going on the entire trip," he said. "I'll be with them across the Atlantic, and then I'll get off when we reach the coast of Africa. They'll continue around the Cape to the Seychelles while I go on a bit of a safari."

"Brody is the only family member Kristie says won't cramp her style," Mr. Barbery said as he walked in from the main salon. "My wife and I are being kicked out. Not that I enjoy ocean crossings. I've had my fill of pirates."

"Did you say pirates?" Richard asked.

Brody laughed. "I'd prefer pirates to rogue waves."

Mr. Barbery laughed along with him. "You and me both."

"Are you serious?" I looked from one man to the other.

"The chances are pretty slim," Mr. Barbery said. "But on a superyacht like this we have to be prepared for anything. That's why we have a full arsenal of guns downstairs."

I swallowed hard. "This ship has a storehold of guns?"

Mr. Barbery grinned at us. "All ships like this do. We carry so much valuable artwork on board we're a prime target for pirates."

Kate's eyes were big and this time I thought her shock was genuine. "I never thought about that."

"I don't mean to scare you." Mr. Barbery patted Kate on the shoulder. "You really don't need to worry about pirates while we're docked in DC. I was just on my way to talk to the captain about what he's been picking up on the radar." He disappeared into the doorway leading to the bridge, and Brody followed him.

"Suddenly working on this ship got even more dangerous," Richard whispered to me.

I had to concur. The idea of a ship filled with people who didn't get along and a bunch of guns was not a comforting fact.

CHAPTER 30

"Is it true?" Kristie asked me when we found her in the salon. She wore a pale blue sheath dress, and I was a bit surprised to see her in anything but yoga pants. A selection of small silver bells lay on a white marble coffee table, and she held one in each hand, alternating as she jingled them. I supposed with all the chaos on the ship, clearing the negative energy with bells was a constant process. I wondered if I should start carrying bells in my emergency kit to ring around my brides every time they got stressed.

"Is what true?" I asked. With so much going on, I honestly didn't know what she meant. The room still held the slight scents of scorched fabric and fresh paint. Not an appealing combination. I stifled a cough and hoped the flowers and food would mask the odors the next day.

"Is it going to rain on my wedding day?" She dropped the bells and they clanged on the marble table.

I almost felt relieved when I heard her concern. Then I realized I actually hadn't checked the weather report in days. Usually I kept a watchful eye on the forecast to know how many white golf umbrellas to put in my trunk, but this week I'd been so preoccupied I hadn't seen it once. I pulled out my phone and clicked the weather app while Kate and Richard did the same.

"Uh oh," Kate said next to me.

Richard put a hand over his eyes. "This is intolerable."

I tried not to panic. The image for the next day was a dark thundercloud with lightning and, if the Weather Channel was accurate, it would last for the entire day and night. This was probably what the captain had been picking up on radar, as well.

"The good news is you have a beautiful ship to get married on," I said. I could have kicked myself for not keeping track of the weather better. I knew I couldn't control it, but it helped not to be completely ambushed by massive thunderstorms. Especially when the wedding was being held on a boat.

"So that's a yes?" Tears sprang to Kristie's eyes. "What about the ceremony on the rooftop? I'm supposed to get married in the open air."

One of the cameramen from the TV crew stepped into the room, cast his eyes over the tense scene, and began filming.

"Not now, buddy." Kate pushed him backward until he was on the other side of the glass doors trying not to stumble down the stairs.

I thought fast. "We can do the ceremony in here. It's the largest room and one hundred fifty guests can definitely fit."

The bride's eyes went to the low ceiling. "But what about the floral canopy?"

"It can still go in here," I said. "It may have to be a bit shorter, but it will still be beautiful."

Kate put an arm around Kristie. "The important thing is getting married, right?"

The girl nodded, then her face darkened as Mrs. Barbery swept into the room from the outside. She wore a pink and purple chiffon creation that could have been a nightgown or an evening gown. When I spotted the pink fur slippers peeking out from under the layers of flowing fabric, I pegged the ensemble as sleepwear. Not any sleepwear I'd ever wear, mind you.

Mrs. Barbery let out a sigh when she saw her stepdaughter. "I hope you're not crying again, Kristie."

"We were discussing the rain plan for tomorrow." I tried to keep my voice upbeat but it came out sounding strained.

Kristie glared at her stepmother. "For your information, it's going to pour all day long."

"Then we'll cover the ship." Mrs. Barbery snapped her fingers at me. "I'm sure you have people who can do that."

"Cover an entire ship? Like with a giant tent?" Richard asked.

"Exactly." Mrs. Barbery put a hand to her red curls. "I'm sure my husband will agree to it."

"But we can't erect a tent over a ship that's in the water," I said, my voice no longer upbeat. "First of all, no tent company has forty-foot side poles. And since the boat is in water, there isn't anything to anchor the poles to."

Mrs. Barbery stamped a foot. "I do not want someone telling me all the ways it can't work, Miss Archer. I need you to tell me how it can work."

"We could tent *parts* of the ship," I said, not sure exactly which parts I meant. "That would give us more covered space."

"Make it happen." Mrs. Barbery shifted her poisonous glare from me, and gave Kristie a sticky smile. "My husband wants this wedding to be perfect for his darling daughter."

Mrs. Barbery flounced out of the room, leaving me feeling like I'd been left standing after a tornado.

"I'm sorry about her. She's been even more awful since we started planning my wedding," Kristie said. "But can you really cover some of the outdoor spaces?"

I leaned down and squeezed her shoulder. "I promise you we will do everything we can, okay?"

My mind raced with all I needed to do if we were going to be holding this wedding in the pouring rain. We already had a tent being erected on the dock next to *Mystic Maven* to be used as the kitchen, but we couldn't put guests under it. Even though the yacht was one hundred and sixty feet long and dwarfed every other boat in the marina, the open spaces it did have were limited, especially covered ones.

"Why don't we go find your fiancé?" Kate began to steer Kristie out of the room. I knew Kate could keep her busy telling her all the things we normally told brides who were blessed with rain on their wedding day. The old standby was rain on your wedding day is good luck, a lie a wedding planner clearly made up to calm down a hysterical bride. Less common and cheesier was only rain brought rainbows. I could never manage to say that one with a straight face.

I mouthed a thank you to Kate and turned to Richard, who also looked a bit panicked. "How did we not see this?" I asked.

He shook his head. "It's been so crazy with all the accidents and then the murder and then the fire. The weather was the last thing on my mind."

"Mine too. But now we'd better figure out what to do. We have over a hundred and fifty guests coming tomorrow and nowhere else to put them except on this ship."

Richard glanced around the main salon, which was filled with furniture. "How are we going to make more space?"

"We'll have to move this furniture out if we're going to jam all the guests in here for the ceremony."

Richard threw his arms in the air. "And where are we going to put all of it? It's not like there's an attic or basement."

I pressed one of the numbers I had preprogrammed into my phone. "I'm calling Davis. If we can get him to add a tent marquee to the wide area at the back of the ship—

"You mean the transom," Richard corrected.

"Yes, the transom. Then we can get at least twenty extra feet. Maybe he can pop up another on the top deck, too."

"Good thinking." Richard began dialing his phone. "Not that

you'd catch me on the top deck of a ship during a thunderstorm. I'm adding staff for tomorrow. If we have to go back and forth between the kitchen tent on the dock and the ship in the pouring rain, I'm going to need more people. Preferably ones with gills."

I left a message for Davis, my go-to tent guy, while Richard talked to his staffing assistant. I made a mental note to put every umbrella I owned in my car and bring a pair of rain boots.

"Annabelle!"

I spun around and saw Leatrice's head at the top of the spiral staircase leading down to the guest rooms. "What are you doing down there?" In all the panic about the rain, I'd forgotten about her. "You were supposed to leave the ship."

"I was exploring," she said. "This place just goes on and on."

"Get up here. You aren't supposed to even be here, much less be wandering all over the place."

Leatrice walked up the stairs and looked around the room. "Isn't this something."

I had to agree with her. It was something all right. The bright orange, turquoise, and yellow that Jeremy had used throughout the room had turned the once-chic beige and cream salon into an assault on the eyes. "It's South Beach meets South of France."

Leatrice nodded, her expression confused. "Was this Richard's idea?"

"Bite your tongue!" Richard said. He slipped his phone into his front suit pocket and walked over to where we stood. "I would never go for something this loud. Everyone knows I'm the soul of understatement."

I decided not to touch that one or bother mentioning that Richard's jacket was lined in hot pink.

"You didn't happen to see Mandy while you were snooping around below, did you?" I asked Leatrice.

She tilted her head to one side. "Mandy?"

"She's the chief stew," I explained. "She's in charge of all the interior staff and could probably help us get this furniture moved out of here."

"Well, if you find her, let me know." Daniel Reese came through the door from the casual dining room. "She's been missing since earlier today."

"Missing?" I asked. First one of the girls who worked under Mandy disappeared and got hit by a car, and now Mandy was missing?

He nodded. "She left the ship at some point in the early morning before anyone was awake and hasn't been seen since."

"Maybe she needed a little break," I said, realizing how ridiculous that sounded in light of all the things going on. "It must be confining to be on board all the time."

"I might agree with you if she'd told anyone she was leaving or got the time off approved," Daniel said. "And her cell phone is turned off so we can't track her."

"So Mandy went AWOL?" Richard asked. "Well, isn't that the cherry on top? It's going to rain buckets, we're stuck on a boat decked out in rustic neon, and now we're down another crew member."

"Did you say Mandy?" Leatrice snapped her fingers. "That's the name of the nice girl who came by looking for you, Annabelle."

My heart sank. I tried not to think of all the reasons why Mandy would have left the ship the day before the wedding and come looking for me. Maybe she got scared because of all the things happening on the ship, including the murder; maybe she'd had enough of Mrs. Barbery; or maybe she ran off because she was somehow involved with all the bad things going on. I didn't really believe the last one though. Mandy had been our one ally on the crew during the entire ordeal, and I couldn't help but worry that something bad had happened to her the way it had to Caren.

"Why do you think she left?" I asked Daniel.

He shrugged. "I don't know, but I don't think it's good."

Richard's voice became shrill. "Of course it's not good. Nothing about this wedding has been good. It's been a disaster from the beginning. I'm telling you, Annabelle, this ship is cursed. Cursed, I say!" He flung himself down on a couch.

I couldn't argue with him. Things were going from bad to worse to catastrophic.

"What else could possibly—" Richard started to say.

I leaned over and clamped a hand over his mouth. "Don't you dare. The second you wonder what else could go wrong, it will."

He made muffled noises into my hand, and I lowered it from his mouth.

"You have got to start using hand cream, Annabelle. Your skin feels like paper-mâché." He dabbed at his mouth. "I have no intention of inviting more trouble. We certainly have all we can handle."

"And then some," I agreed.

Leatrice clapped her hands together. "Are all your weddings this exciting?"

Richard looked at me without smiling. "Kill me now."

CHAPTER 31

"Where are we going?" Richard asked as he followed me up the spiral stairs running from the back deck to the top level of the ship.

"I need to measure the hot tub," I said, pulling my pocket tape measure out of my purse. "If we're moving the ceremony canopy down to the salon, I need to know how big it is. And since it was going to sit over the hot tub on the top deck, I can measure the hot tub to find out."

When we reached the top of the stairs, I looked at the clouds massed in the sky. Even though the storm wasn't predicted to hit until the next day, the sky already looked gray, and I could swear I smelled rain in the air. I brushed the thoughts out of my mind. The key to having so many rain-free weddings had always been a good rain plan. If we planned for rain, it wouldn't happen—so I was a woman on a mission to come up with the world's best plan B.

I glanced at Richard. "Where's Leatrice? I thought she was right behind you."

Richard looked over his shoulder and shrugged. "We'll find her later."

My gut told me it wasn't a good idea to have my eccentric neighbor loose on the ship, although I didn't have time to search for her now. I was on a mission. I had less than ten hours to transform an outdoor wedding into an indoor one, and it wasn't going to be easy. I led the way across the shiny white surface to the elevated hot tub near the middle. We'd had a custom cover made for the hot tub out of the same hard white plastic as the rest of the boat, and it fit so seamlessly you couldn't tell there was water below. I felt a twinge of sadness knowing the ceremony wouldn't be up here on the open deck with the bride and groom elevated above the guests under a magnificent floral canopy. The photos would have been incredible. I shook the image from my head and tried to convince myself the wedding would be just as pretty inside when I knew it wouldn't. Rain plans, no matter how good, were never fabulous.

"Hold this." I gave Richard the end of the tape measure and unrolled it as I walked away from him and up onto the hot tub cover. He held his end down on the edge of the cover, and I bent down and touched the yellow lined ribbon to the other side. I made a mental note of the length then picked up my side and crossed over the cover so I could measure the width. "Okay. That's what I thought. It's a perfect square."

"Is this really what we should be doing now?" Richard let go of his end, and the tape measure snaked across the ground and back up into the metal holder with a snap.

"What do you suggest we do?" I asked. I pulled out my phone and tapped the measurements into the notes section so I wouldn't forget them. "We still have a huge wedding in less than twenty-four hours and a major storm system is coming through."

I started back across the top deck and Richard rushed after me. "Aren't you concerned a crew member has disappeared? And the only one who was helpful at that."

I paused at the top of the stairs leading down. "Of course I am. But I have no idea how to find her or why she ran off. And even if

I did, we'd still have a wedding for one hundred fifty guests to pull off."

"I don't know if I've ever seen you this way."

Richard was right. I'd shifted into Robo Wedding Planner mode. Finding out about the rainstorm and Mandy's disappearance had sent my system into overload, and the only way I could deal with it without falling apart was to focus completely on my work. If I thought too much about everything that had happened on the boat so far, or what it all meant, or how dangerous it was to still be working on board, I might run off screaming. And I couldn't do that with a wedding to run. Luckily, there was plenty to do to switch the wedding over to the rain plan, and it would keep me from worrying about Mandy.

"This is me implementing a rain plan," I said. "What do you think?"

Richard leaned back and put his hands on his hips as he looked at me. "Impressive and terrifying."

I couldn't help but smile. "Finally someone in this business is scared of me. Now, let's go find Jeremy and give him the good news about moving his canopy inside."

We hurried down the stairs and I popped my head into the main salon. No Jeremy Johns.

"He must be with the stepmother." Richard motioned his head at the room. "Now that Mandy's gone, who do we talk to about getting all the furniture moved?"

I gnawed at the edge of my lip. "I don't know. We may have to do it ourselves."

"You must be joking, Annabelle. Might I remind you I am wearing Dolce and Gabbana from head to toe?" He swept his hands up and down his torso. "This suit was not designed for heavy lifting."

I stared at his beige suit, noticing how the pants tapered and the jacket fit snug. "Can you even bend over in that thing?"

He crossed his arms over his chest and looked affronted. "Of course I can. That doesn't mean I intend to work like a pack mule in it. If I'd known you wanted to strap armchairs to my back and work me like a Sherpa, I would have chosen something off-the-rack to wear."

It was my turn to cross my arms. "Like you own anything off-the-rack."

"Of course I do," he said. "I have a Banana Republic suit when I want to dress down. I can be just as plebeian as you when I want to be."

I decided to ignore his backhanded compliment. "We'll find someone to help us move things. But for now, we have to find Jeremy."

We crossed the salon and took the spiral staircase down one level. The master suite took up half a floor facing the bow of the ship. I paused at the large wooden double doors.

"Are you sure you want to do this?" Richard asked.

"We have to." I knocked lightly on the door before I could talk myself out of it. There was no sound from the other side.

"I don't know if anyone heard your butterfly taps," Richard whispered.

"Fine." I drew back my hand to pound on the door when one side glided open.

"*Oui?*" Damian, Mrs. Barbery's stylist from Paris, poked his head out, his dreadlocks swinging around his face. "May I help you?"

His voice was low, so I followed his lead. "We're looking for Jeremy Johns."

"Jeremy?" He drew the name out several extra syllables when he repeated it.

"You know . . ." Richard put a finger on his chin and gave a dead-on impression of Jeremy Johns's haughty look. "This guy."

Damian pointed a finger at Richard and smiled. "Yes. Jeremy. He is not here." He looked behind him and lowered his voice even more. "He go to find someone. I think down."

"Thanks," I said as Damian closed the door with a small wave.

Richard motioned to the stairs leading further down into the ship. "After you, darling."

We twisted our way down another spiral staircase to the floor housing all the guest rooms. The hall was narrower and I felt a twinge of claustrophobia. I shook it off. Now was not the time to add a neurosis to my stress.

"Who do you think he was looking for?" I asked. "The only people staying down here so far are Kristie and Brody."

"And Damian," Richard reminded me. "But maybe Jeremy didn't come to this level. Maybe he went to the crew quarters."

I nodded. "That makes more sense. If he needed help, he'd ask the crew."

We took the twisting staircase down one more level. It felt as if the ship was shrinking. The open, expansive rooms of the top levels had given way to tight corridors and rows of cabins on each side down below. To one side was a small kitchen and eat-in dining area in the same blond wood as upstairs.

"How many people live down here?" Richard asked.

"Well, there are fourteen permanent members of the crew."

Richard shuddered. "I wonder where they keep the slave galley with the oars."

"It's not that bad," I said, more to convince myself than him. "The wood is actually light and pretty."

"I don't see any sign of Jeremy," Richard said. "Let's go back upstairs."

"We've barely looked." I pointed to a door past the kitchen. "What's behind that?"

"The dungeons, a horrible sea monster, a deranged relative locked away for safekeeping. Haven't you learned not to go opening strange doors yet?"

I shook my head at Richard. "Now you're being ridiculous."

Richard rubbed his arms and his eyes darted around the low-ceilinged space. "Being down here gives me the creeps. I'm going back upstairs."

"Wait." I pointed to a door at the end of the hallway. "What's down there?"

Richard hung back as I approached the door. "I'd like to go on the record for saying this is a bad idea."

"Duly noted." I wrenched open the door and found myself standing at the entrance to a huge storage room. Parallel rows of metal shelving reached to the ceiling and were loaded with stacks of paper goods, boxes of dry food, and even enormous sacks of rice and beans.

"This must be the storeroom," I said. "Not a deranged captive in sight."

Richard peeked around my back and gave a low whistle. "They must be able to last a long time on what they have in here."

"Long enough to make an ocean crossing," I said, remembering the captain had said they would be crossing the Atlantic after the wedding. "You can't exactly stop for supplies halfway to Africa."

Richard pointed to a wide metal door at the far end of the room and to the right. "Now that looks like an important door."

The door stood slightly ajar, so I pushed it open and found Leatrice standing next to a crate in the middle of a small room. Guns were attached to the walls on all three sides, everything from handguns to what looked like high-powered automatic weapons.

She beamed when she saw us. "There you are."

"What are you doing here?" I tried not to sound as impatient as I felt. This wasn't the first time I'd found Leatrice somewhere she shouldn't have been. At least this time she wasn't half frozen to death.

"I was just wandering around, checking out the boat. When I found the gun room, I couldn't resist getting a closer look."

"Since we've found Rambo, can we please get out of this

place?" Richard asked. "Being down this deep in the boat makes my skin crawl."

"I've never seen so many guns in real life," Leatrice said as we made our way back to the spiral staircase.

"Apparently, you need a lot of guns when you have as much art and jewelry on board as these people do." I shook my head and started walking again. "Can you please try to avoid any more breaking and entering while you're on board? These people are still my clients for one more day."

"But the door was cracked open," Leatrice said. "I just gave it a push."

"How many times have we heard that before?" Richard said.

He was right. Leatrice claiming to have barely nudged a door open was par for the course.

We reached the top of the stairs and entered the main salon. The entire wedding party stood in the room along with Mr. and Mrs. Barbery, Jeremy Johns, Damian, and Fern. Kristie held a bouquet made out of gift-wrapping ribbons and stood next to the groom. He was the same height as Mr. Barbery but slim with light brown, wavy hair. I'd only met him once, so I gave him a good, hard look to memorize his face. It would be harder to pick him out the next day from a group of groomsmen all dressed the same.

Kate walked over to me with her fakest smile plastered to her face. "Annabelle, we were finishing up the rehearsal so everyone can get to the rehearsal dinner at the Mandarin Hotel."

I shoved Leatrice behind me, and Richard stepped in front of her to complete the human wall. I knew neither of us wanted to explain who she was and why she was here.

"Perfect." I looked at the rows of bridesmaids and groomsmen flanking the bride and groom. "Kate is our rehearsal specialist, so you can feel confident about tomorrow's ceremony. Just remember to relax and not to lock your knees."

Kate raised her eyebrows at me. Technically, we didn't have a rehearsal specialist, but it sounded good. "Ladies," I continued, "don't forget to be on board by eight a.m. to start hair and makeup. Guys, you don't need to be here until noon. Have a great time at dinner."

There was some mumbling about the early start time from the women. Then everyone began to gather their things and make their way out.

Kate had taken on the role of bride's confessor and was talking to her and patting her hand as she walked her outside. I was glad Kristie had bonded with Kate because it freed me up to coordinate the wedding setup the next day. Kate could be by Kristie's side, and I could get things done.

"Let's move away from the stairs," I said to Richard. He nodded and we shuffled over to one side, keeping Leatrice behind us the entire way.

"Don't make a sound," I told her.

"If we back out of the room like this, we can just roll her over the railing," Richard said. I ignored him.

Mr. Barbery stopped in front of us on his way out. "I want to thank you for everything you're doing for Kristie's wedding now that we have a storm bearing down on us. She told me that you're adding tents."

"As many as we can," I said. "It's our job to make things work."

"Well, I appreciate it." He squeezed my shoulder, and I noticed the corner of his eyes crinkle when he smiled. "And if you need anything, you let me know."

"He's quite charming," Richard said as we watched Mr. Barbery walk away. "I still don't understand how he ended up with Cruella De Vil."

I elbowed him as Mrs. Barbery stalked up to us. "Have you made any progress on fixing this storm issue?"

"I'm doing everything I can. Like I told your husband, we're adding as many tents as we can fit on board."

She gave me a critical once-over then her eyes passed over

Richard. "You're both supposed to be the best in the city, you know. I hope you live up to the hype."

I hated threats veiled as compliments. "I can control just about everything on a wedding day except for the weather, Mrs. Barbery." I'd given this line to countless brides and parents over the years. "I promise you the wedding will still be beautiful."

Mrs. Barbery narrowed her eyes at me. "*Diamond Weddings* beautiful?"

"Absolutely," Richard said with more enthusiasm than I could muster.

The bride's stepmother pointed a finger at both of us. "It had better be."

We both let out a breath once she stomped outside, and we stepped away from Leatrice.

"We've got to get you out of here." I leveled a finger at her. "And you can't come back."

"Why would I come back, dear?" Leatrice gave me such an innocent look I felt like strangling her.

"Is this one of your assistants?" Jeremy Johns said, walking over and giving Leatrice a critical once-over. "She seems to fit your team's style."

"We can't all be South of France meets South Blech." Richard waved a hand to indicate the color cacophony of the room.

"Where is South Blech?" Leatrice asked Kate as she returned from walking Kristie off the ship.

A pink flush filled Jeremy's cheeks. "If I were you, I'd watch my step."

"I think it's you who should be afraid of us." I snapped my fingers. "We could ruin you just like that. What will all your fancy clients say when they find out you're a fraud?"

"And have bad taste?" Kate gave him a snarky smile.

Jeremy turned on his heel and stomped down the staircase.

"What was that about?" Fern asked as he joined us.

"We were convincing Jeremy to play nice by threatening to tell the world about his bad taste," Richard said. "And that he has no design background."

Fern put a hand to the peacock blue silk ascot at his throat. "No wonder he's upset."

"Annabelle went straight for the juggler," Kate said.

Richard sighed. "Jugular. Straight for the jugular."

Kate narrowed her eyes at him. "That doesn't sound like a real word."

Richard threw up his hands and spun on his heel. "I'm out."

"Jugglers at a wedding." Leatrice clapped her hands. "You girls always come up with such fun ideas."

"I'm right behind you," I called after Richard.

CHAPTER 32

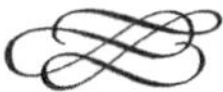

"Where are you?" I screamed into my cell phone as I got out of my car in the District Marina parking lot and started walking down the dock toward *Mystic Maven.* My square metal emergency kit hung over one shoulder, and my canvas Wedding Belles tote bag holding the wedding binder and all the contracts hung from the other. It was still early in the morning and the rain hadn't begun yet, although the wind already made it hard to hear anything. The one good part of the whipping wind was it seemed to have dissipated the fish smell. Nothing like the sweet smell of fish guts blowing through your wedding ceremony.

"I'm in the catering tent," Richard said. "If you're walking to the boat, you can't miss it."

I passed the white box trucks huddled near the entrance to the long dock and got in line with the stream of burly men rolling dollies laden with racks of glasses and silverware. The narrow white tent with solid sidewalls perched at the end of the dock next to the ship and ran about twenty feet from the far end of the dock up to the metal gangway that had been added for staff access. I poked my head in the only open flap in the walls. The narrow makeshift kitchen was lined with tall metal warmers meant to keep food hot and naked banquet tables stacked with trays and metal serving utensils. I knew enough about Richard's catering business to know the food was prepped and cooked off-site and then finished on-site. Luckily, with a cocktail reception that the ship's layout dictated, he didn't need to worry about plating two hundred filet mignons at the same time—so he didn't need as much space as he would have for a seated dinner.

Richard stood in the center of the tent in one of his many dark, tailored suits with a rental order in one hand and his phone in the other.

"When does your staff arrive?" I asked, putting my own phone in the pocket of my black pantsuit and setting my emergency kit and bag on the ground.

He spun around at the sound of my voice inside the tent and put a hand over his heart. "You scared me! I didn't know you could walk so fast."

"The plywood nailed to the dock helped."

Richard shook his head. "Mrs. Barbery had those poor deck-hands nailing sheets of it down at the crack of dawn this morning. She said her guests were not going to have their high heels stuck in the dock."

"Well, for once, she had a good idea." Even though I wasn't wearing heels, the sheets of plywood evened out the bumpy boards of the wooden dock and meant I didn't have to watch every step for a jutting beam.

"It's easy to have good ideas when you don't have to do the work," Richard said. "The ice bar was a great idea until we had to use an industrial crane to get it on board this morning."

"I missed it?" I'd been hoping to see how Richard would manage to get a massive twelve-foot-long slab of ice in the shape of a curved bar onto the ship. "Is it already on the back deck?"

He nodded. "The captain oversaw the process while Mrs. Barbery screamed orders from the top deck. It took every crew member plus me to get it lowered perfectly into place over the catch pans I made for it."

"There are catch pans?" I made a face, imagining black plastic pans usually used to hold melting ice and made a face.

Richard held up a hand. "Before you get your knickers in a twist, I had the pans custom made from clear plastic. You can't even see them, but they'll keep the teak floors on the ship from getting damaged."

"Knickers in a twist?" I said. "I'm assuming you've seen Alexandra already?"

Richard had a habit of picking up phrases from people he was around, and I knew Alexandra had been dropping British slang since she'd arrived.

"She brought the cake on about thirty minutes ago. Said she wanted to get it on before the rain started. She's still on board."

"Good," I said. "I can check that off my list of things to worry about."

"Worry? Why on earth would you worry? We only have some of the wealthiest people in the world flying in for a wedding on a superyacht that looks like the '80s exploded inside it, and it's going to rain so hard we'll all be washed out to sea." Richard's voice got so shrill I was afraid only dogs would be able to hear it. "What's to worry about?"

"I can see you're handling the stress well," I said. "Didn't your doctor tell you to meditate when you felt overwhelmed?"

He put his hands on his hips. "Meditate? And where, pray tell, am I supposed to do that?" He waved an arm at the cramped tent. There was only about a two-foot-long strip of floor going down the middle not covered by a warmer or table. His staff would have to turn sideways and suck in their guts to pass each other. "Shall I hop onto a table or maybe crawl into a warmer?"

"Do you want me to see if Kate can bring you a Xanax?" I tried not to take it personally that my assistant had gotten a prescription for anti-anxiety meds after working with me for a year. I told myself it was the brides and not working for me that pushed her to pharmaceutical relief.

Richard took a deep breath. "No. I'll be fine once Jim gets here. But I told him if he brings his pet flying squirrel, I'll throw it in the Potomac River."

Jim was Richard's long-standing event captain who kept the parties under control when Richard threatened to spin out of it. The only fly in the ointment was his habit of carrying his pet flying squirrel in his coat pocket.

"You've got to stop threatening to throw people in the Potomac. I'm sure he won't bring it," I said. "Anyway, flying squirrels are nocturnal. They're supposed to sleep all day."

"Tell that to Bubbles Flanagan and the Red Hat ladies who came to brunch at her house."

I cringed. "He got out?"

Richard nodded. "And flew from red hat to red hat until Jim finally caught it. By then, all the women were screaming and had nearly beaten each other senseless trying to swat it off each other's heads. The hats were torn to shreds. There was so much red everywhere it looked like a bloodbath."

I put a hand over my mouth to keep from laughing.

Richard pointed a finger at me. "Don't even think about it."

"I'm going to go check on the cake." I grabbed my emergency kit and bag from the floor and ducked out of the tent before I incurred Richard's wrath. I hurried up the gangway using the rope handles for balance. The shoe basket was gone, so I kept my black flats on and pushed open the glass door. The casual dining room had silver trays filled with empty Champagne glasses sitting on the table, and I did a quick count of about a hundred glasses. I continued on into the main salon.

My mouth fell open as I absorbed the South Beach meets South of France concept brought to life. Bright yellow carpet had been put down over the permanent cream carpet. Wide swaths of yellow, orange, and turquoise fabric draped from the center of the ceiling to the walls, creating the illusion of an indoor tent and giving me an instant case of claustrophobia. Massive garden urns painted in Jeremy Johns's garish colors lined the walls and were filled with blue hydrangea.

At the far end of the room stood a garden arch made from what appeared to be curly willow covered with masses of yellow, orange, and turquoise roses. I blinked hard. Roses came in many colors, but turquoise wasn't one of them. I sniffed the air and smelled the faint aroma of paint. Was it the paint from the fire damaged walls or had Jeremy Johns spray painted the roses? I didn't think I wanted to know the answer.

Alexandra stood at the near wall, adjusting the cake she'd placed on the wooden sideboard. The pale blue cake stood about three feet off of the table and had a cascade of lotus blossoms swirling down from the top with one large sugar bloom as a cake topper.

"It's beautiful," I said. It was the only thing in the room that was.

She smiled and stepped back to admire her work. "It did turn out nice. Not that it goes with the rest of the look."

I glanced back at the garish room. The lotus flower cake was like a drop of Zen in a Macy's parade. "Don't worry about it. At least Kristie will have one thing she loves."

"If it looks good to you, I'd love to sneak off the ship before I run into Jeremy."

"Of course." I gave her a quick hug. "I'm going to head downstairs and see if we have any more room to stash extra furniture."

I wound my way down to the lower levels of the ship. At least the downstairs wasn't decorated in Jeremy's gaudy color scheme. I avoided the door to the master suite, popping my head into the small gym down the hall and appraising its available space before checking the one spare bedroom I knew wasn't occupied. I pushed open the door and saw it already had dining room chairs covering the limited space around the bed. I'd have to look elsewhere for a place to stash furniture.

I slipped my emergency kit and bag inside the door to the bride's room without anyone noticing, since the bridesmaids and bride were busy being entertained by Fern and his raunchy stories.

"Let me tell you the secret to curling a man's toes, girls," he said as he unleashed a cloud of hairspray, and all the women leaned in to hear his dubious advice.

I shook my head as I ducked out of the room, and continued down the hall, taking the spiral stairs at the far end leading down to the crew quarters. I knew the crew rooms were even more compact. I also knew Mandy had a private room, and if she wasn't here, maybe I could borrow her space. Considering how helpful she'd been to us, I didn't think she'd mind.

I passed the casual dining area and galley kitchen and edged my way down the narrow hall with the crew's bedrooms. If I remembered what Mandy had told me, hers was one of the first on the left. I tapped on the first door and tried the handle. Locked. I moved to the next and tapped lightly before trying the handle. Not locked. I opened the door and gaped at what I saw. Jeremy Johns was hurriedly closing the door to the built-in closet with one hand while holding a can of lighter fluid in the other.

"What are you doing in here?" A quick scan of the photos on the desk and nightstand told me it was definitely Mandy's room.

Jeremy dropped the lighter fluid, his face flushing scarlet. "I don't answer to you."

I pointed to the can of lighter fluid. "Thinking of setting another fire?"

Jeremy glared at me. "You don't know what you're talking about."

"Maybe you'd like to explain yourself to the security team." I slammed the door and ran down the hall. Daniel and his guys were probably upstairs. My first priority was to find them and tell them I'd found our arsonist.

I scrolled through the saved numbers on my phone as I ran, pressing the one for Daniel Reese before noticing that I didn't have any bars. Of course the cell service was bad in the bowels of the boat. I fought the urge to throw the phone against the wall, instead dropping it in my jacket pocket. Why did technology never work when I needed it the most?

CHAPTER 33

"Why isn't Richard answering his phone?" I listened to the ringing over and over until it finally switched to voicemail. I pressed the screen to end the call. Richard hated listening to voicemail. "I need him to make sure Jeremy doesn't run off the ship and try to get past him on the dock."

"He's probably got his hands full." Kate pointed outside to the fat raindrops beginning to pelt the windows of the ship and splatter into the dark water of the Potomac River.

I'd found her just arriving on board when I'd run back upstairs to the main salon in my hunt for Daniel Reese. The top level of the ship was also the only place I seemed to be able to get cell service, although the weather made my reception fade in and out. So much for communicating with my team using our phones. I refused to walk around a wedding carrying walkie-talkies or wearing headsets. We were coordinating weddings, not directing planes.

"No, no, no." I rubbed my temples. "Not yet. I need a few more hours of dry load-in."

"Well, you aren't going to get it." Kate brushed a few raindrops off her hair. "I barely made it up the gangway before it started. By the way, that metal ramp for the staff is going to be slippery once it gets wet. The TV crew nearly lost a crate of gear coming up."

"Ugh. The TV crew." I wished this wedding day wasn't being filmed.

My rain plan had not included assessing the slipperiness of the gangway that had been set up close to the catering tent, but I knew Kate was right. I stared outside at the heavy gray clouds massed in the sky, blotting out the sun and making it feel as if it was nighttime, and not noon, was approaching. As I watched, the rain changed from heavy drops to drenching sheets blowing sideways and buffeting the ship. No rain plan was good enough to work around this type of storm.

"If Jeremy had motive and opportunity to set the fire, we should tell security," Kate said.

Moments after I'd bumped into her, I'd told Kate what I'd seen down below and my theory about Jeremy. It had been her idea that we tell Richard so he could keep an eye out for Jeremy fleeing the scene. "You can't leave without walking past Richard's catering tent. I should know. I just walked past and he made a comment about my shoes."

"No rain boots?" I asked, glancing at her high heels.

"Not unless they start making boots that can make my legs look this good." She gestured at the considerable amount of leg showing in her snug black evening suit. "Where is Daniel Reese anyway?"

"I haven't seen him yet. I can call him now that I'm up here." I hesitated. "What if he shuts down the wedding?"

"What if he removes Jeremy and we can do this wedding without him on board?" Kate asked.

I snapped my fingers. "I never thought of that. You're a genius. We'll tell Daniel I saw Jeremy with a can of lighter fluid in the crew quarters; he can have Reese take him in for questioning; and we can undo as much of this South Whatever design horror as possible."

I heard a sharp gasp and turned to see Jeremy's head coming up the spiral staircase. His eyes were wide and he looked enraged. He'd clearly heard every word I'd said. His head disappeared as he began to run down the stairs.

"He's trying to get away." I rushed to the stairs and started down them myself, pulling Kate along behind me. "We have to stop him."

"I'm not wearing the right footwear for a chase."

I stole a glance at her high T-strap black shoes and groaned. "Do you even own the right shoes for a chase?"

"So sue me! I didn't know wedding planning would require us to chase down so many violent criminals."

I reached the bottom of the stairs. Kate had slowed me down and distracted me long enough to lose sight of Jeremy. I wasn't sure if he'd gone into a room on this level or kept going down. I knew there was another staircase on the back of the ship connecting all the floors, so my biggest concern was his going up the other stairs and slipping off the boat.

"This way," I pointed down the corridor leading to the guest rooms, the gym, and the other staircase.

Kate sat on the bottom step and rubbed her foot. "Go on without me."

I took off down the corridor and, as I turned to tell Kate to hurry up, one of the guest room doors opened and I ran full-on into it. My hands took the brunt of the impact, and I landed hard on the floor.

"Annabelle!" Fern's head appeared around the door. "What are you doing down there?"

"You opened the door on me! That's what I'm doing down here."

Kate came up behind me and lifted me up from under my

arms. "This is what happens when you run at a wedding. Didn't you tell me never to run?"

"Yes." She was right. One of my hard-and-fast wedding planner rules was "never run." It made you look frantic, and if guests thought you were frantic, they would assume something was wrong. I'd always prided myself on staying cool even if the wedding was burning down around me.

"Why are you running? It's not even noon." Fern held a brush in one hand and a can of hair spray in the other. He probably had begun the bridesmaids' hair before I woke up, but he looked as flawless as ever in a pair of white pants, a white shirt, and a navy and red scarf with an anchor motif tied around his neck. Dressed for the theme, as always.

I brushed cream carpet lint off my jacket. "I'm looking for Jeremy. Have you seen him?"

Fern made a face. "Luckily, no. I've been with Kristie and the girls all morning." He leaned his head back inside the room. "We've been having a good time, haven't we, girls?"

A cacophony of women's voices told me they had. Fern leaned back out into the hall and rolled his eyes. "Tramps."

"Stop that!" I said. Fern loved nothing more than shooting barbs at bridesmaids. To him they were all tramps, hussies, or floozies. And, for some reason, the girls thought it was hilarious. I'd often said if I called a bridesmaid a tramp, I'd be packing my bags. Fern, however, could get away with murder.

"What do you want with Jeremy anyway?" Fern asked. "The less you have to deal with him, the better."

"We found evidence he set the fire," Kate said.

Fern's mouth formed a perfect circle. "I don't know if I want to be trapped below deck with an arsonist running free."

"We were trying to catch him so he could be taken off the ship," I said. "But between Miss Slowpoke and you knocking me down, he got away. I guess now is the time to call Reese."

"Why don't you tell his brother?" Fern pointed over my head with the hair spray. "He's right behind you."

CHAPTER 34

"Daniel?" Kate spun around, pulling away from me and causing me to stumble back a few steps.

Daniel Reese wore black cargo pants and a black Polo-style shirt with his security company's logo stitched in white. He'd clearly gotten the memo stating we wore black to weddings.

"What's this about Jeremy Johns?" he said, looking at each of us in turn.

Kate rested a hand on his bicep and leaned close to him. "We think he's your arsonist."

Daniel raised one dark eyebrow. "Isn't he the one nobody gets along with?"

"We can't stand him," Fern said, lowering his voice and closing the door behind him until it was only open a crack and the sound of laughing girls all but disappeared. "He's a complete diva with questionable taste. Have you seen the colors he combined upstairs? Gauche meets garish."

"But that's not the reason," I said, shooting Fern a look. I wanted Daniel to take us seriously, not think we were basing our accusation on bad taste in colors. "I discovered Jeremy with a can of lighter fluid in the crew quarters. I think he was trying to set another fire."

"That does change things," Daniel said. He pulled a cell phone out of his pants pocket. "I'll tell Mike."

"You don't think he'll need to shut down the wedding, do you?" I asked.

"He'll just want him for questioning. Your wedding can go right ahead as planned." Daniel spoke low into the phone, explaining what we'd discovered about Jeremy. Then he disconnected and slipped the phone back into his pants. "He's in the middle of something. I'm going to bring Jeremy Johns in for him."

I felt relieved we could get Jeremy out of our way without flashing blue lights and cops crawling all over the ship. "There's one small hiccup. We don't know where Jeremy is. He heard us talking about his motive and ran off. Kate and I were chasing him but he got away."

"I knocked her off her feet." Fern winked at me. "She's the only girl who can ever say that."

I rubbed my backside, which still smarted from hitting the floor. "Lucky me."

"So he's hiding somewhere on board?" Daniel asked.

"Unless he got off the ship," I said. "He was running toward the back staircase when we were stopped."

Daniel nodded. "I'll have my guys search the ship."

Voices came from inside the guest room. Fern poked his head inside for a moment then reappeared. "I have to get back to those two-bit hussies." He blew us kisses then disappeared inside the room and closed the door.

"He calls everyone hussies," I explained to Daniel. "Bridesmaids, I mean. Not you. He wouldn't call you a hussy. Or a tramp."

"Annabelle." Kate gave me a pointed look, and I stopped talking.

Daniel grinned, and I was reminded of his brother's expression every time I embarrassed myself. "I'm going to talk to my team. If you see Jeremy Johns, don't try to stop him yourself. Call me."

Kate and I agreed, then he walked off down the corridor. I pulled Kate with me in the other direction. "We need to check on Richard."

"And give him the latest dirt on Jeremy. It will make his day."

Kate was right. Richard would take particular glee in knowing Jeremy was suspect number one. We wound our way up the back staircase, passed by a cameraman setting up a tripod, and walked along the outside of the ship until we reached the narrow metal ramp leading to the dock. The rain was coming down in fast, heavy drops, and I made a mental calculation of how wet we'd get making the dash down the ramp and into the catering tent a few feet away. I put my arms over my head and ran forward, slipping a bit on the slick ramp on the way down and catching the rope railing for balance. I skidded onto the dock and pushed through the plastic flaps of the catering tent. Kate was right behind me and bumped into me when I stopped.

The landscape of the tent had changed since I'd been in it earlier. Instead of just Richard, a pair of pantry cooks, one tall and bald and the other short and round with curly dark hair, stood at the tables. They were loading trays of hors d'oeuvres into the warmers as Richard inspected the food. The savory smells hit me the moment I opened the tent flap, enveloping me and making my stomach growl. I'd had a bottled coffee and a banana on the drive in, but had been too nervous and anxious about the day to eat more—a decision I now regretted.

"There had better not be a drop of water on this food," he said. When he noticed us, he looked up. "Can you believe this? We didn't even get the food unloaded before the rain started."

I saw all the trays were covered with plastic wrap. "It looks fine."

Richard didn't seem mollified. "For the moment. Now I just have to keep it from wilting until it's time to serve."

"That's not our biggest problem," I said. "Have you seen Jeremy?"

"Maybe he ran past the catering tent a little while ago?" Kate asked.

Richard crossed his arms. "We're trying to keep the flaps closed and the rain out. Unless he ran into this tent, I didn't see him. Why?"

I gave Richard the quick rundown. Kate jumped in with an explanation of our low-speed chase through the ship and Fern knocking me off my feet.

"So Daniel is going to take Jeremy in for questioning," I said. "But we don't know where Jeremy ran off to. He could have run off the ship, or he could still be hiding on board."

"He wouldn't leave the ship before the wedding," Richard said. "His ego is too big. He wants to hear everyone say how gorgeous the party is."

"Do you think anyone will actually say that?" Kate asked. "Have you seen the décor?"

For once, I had to agree with Kate. "If he isn't already on the lam, the police or the security team will grab him the second he shows his face."

"Mark my words." Richard wagged a finger at us. "Jeremy Johns is still on board."

A man holding a stack of silver trays wrapped in plastic pushed through the tent flaps behind us.

"Perfect," Richard said. "More trays. Put them down right here."

Kate and I squeezed to the side to let the man get by us.

"We'd better get back inside," I said. "We'll let you know when we're closer to serving time."

"Give me at least a thirty-minute warning. It's going to take me longer to plate up out here."

Kate pulled back the plastic tent flap. The rain had intensified to hard, stinging drops. I wished all of my umbrellas weren't safe and dry in my car trunk. Not that umbrellas were much use when the rain blew sideways like this.

"Run for it!" Kate grabbed a nearby napkin, threw it over her head, and dashed past me up the metal ramp. Just before I started after her, I stopped in my tracks. Through the rain I'd seen a figure appear on the top deck then duck back down. I shook my head. It couldn't be.

Had I really just seen Mandy, the missing chief stew, or were my eyes playing tricks on me?

CHAPTER 35

"Did you see her?" I asked Kate once we'd run through the glass door into the casual dining room. I knew I shouldn't be dripping on the silk carpet, but my pants were soaked and plastered to my legs from the rain flying sideways. I tried to pull them loose so it didn't look like I was wearing black leggings. They flapped back against my wet skin. So much for looking presentable and professional.

"Who?" Kate dropped the soaking orange napkin on the table, then flipped her hair over and shook a cascade of water droplets onto the floor. Her black dress had been formfitting before it got wet. Now it looked like second skin.

I stepped back to avoid the spray of water as I brushed back a strand of hair that had escaped my bun. "I could have sworn I saw Mandy on the top deck."

"Now?" Kate tossed her hair back. "Are you sure?"

I wasn't sure. It had looked just like her when I'd glanced up, although I'd been looking through the rain and the figure had disappeared before I could be certain.

Brody opened the door from the galley kitchen and stepped

into the small room, followed by the captain. Brody smiled when he saw us. The captain just nodded.

"How goes the wedding prep, ladies?" Brody asked.

"Great!" Kate smiled back at him, and I wondered what she was talking about. It was pouring rain, we had an arsonist on the loose, and the missing stew may or may not have just appeared back on board.

"You haven't by any chance seen Jeremy or Mandy recently?" I asked the men.

Brody frowned. "I saw Jeremy this morning, when he was working on the ceremony arch, but not since then. And Mandy? I thought she was missing."

"I've been on the bridge all day monitoring the weather with my first mate," the captain said. "But if you see Mandy, please let me know. I'd like to talk to her."

"Annabelle thought she just saw her on the top deck," Kate said, flipping her hair back and landing a few errant drops of water on my face.

A look of surprise passed over the captain's face, then he frowned. "I'd better get back to the bridge. They're saying this is a hundred-year storm." His *Mystic Maven* slippers padded on the carpet as he crossed the room to the door leading up to the bridge.

The thought of riding out a hundred-year storm during a wedding on a yacht was not a pleasant one. I pushed aside my growing sense of panic and tried to focus.

"Well, I hope for Mandy's sake she's not on board," Brody said once the captain had left. "The captain's not too thrilled about his chief stew going missing. And since she left without notice right before the wedding, my mother might want to kill her."

Brody made a good point. Why would Mandy return after leaving so mysteriously? Especially if there were several people on board who'd be angry with her?

"I'm sure Jeremy is around somewhere," Brody said, winking at us. "Probably with my mother complaining about everything. Do you want me to tell him you're looking for him?"

"Not exactly," I said. "He already knows we're looking for him."

"We chased him through the ship until we lost him," Kate said.

Brody's eyebrows pressed together. "You must really need to talk to him."

"It's not us so much as the security team," I said. "They need to take him in for questioning about the fire."

"Really?" Brody looked surprised.

Kate patted Brody's arm. "It's a long story, but we think Jeremy Johns started it and may have been trying to start another."

"Then the police are coming to take him in?" Brody asked.

I shook my head. "Our security chief will take him in. If he finds him."

"I'll keep a lookout for you." Brody stepped back. "I'd hate for Kristie to find out there's a manhunt on board right before her wedding."

I gave Brody major points for considering his stepsister's panic over his mother's potential hysteria at having her designer dragged off the ship. I hadn't really thought about how Kristie would react, because I'd hoped to have Jeremy off the boat before she got wind of it. If Fern did his job, the ladies would be entertained and scandalized in equal measure downstairs, not even aware if a fleet of Navy Seals came aboard.

"There you are!" Fern's head poked through the door leading to the main salon.

I jumped at the sight of him. "What are you doing up here? Is everything all right with the bride?"

"She's fine," Fern said. "She was a bit stressed earlier, but those bottles of Dom did the trick."

"What bottles of Dom?" I asked, getting a sinking feeling in my gut. "What trick?"

"I needed to relax the girls, so I requisitioned some bottles of

Champagne from the walk-in refrigerator." Fern giggled and I could tell he'd been drinking as well as requisitioning.

"The Champagne for the reception?" I asked. "How many bottles?"

Fern waved a hand at me. "Just a flew. Maybe slix or sleven."

"Slix or sleven?" Kate repeated.

Great. Not only were the bride and bridesmaids probably three sheets to the wind, but also my hairstylist was drunk. I could only imagine what type of styles he was giving these girls. When Fern got tipsy, the hair got big.

I pointed a finger at him. "If you give these girls state fair hair, you are going to be in big trouble."

Fern pressed a hand to his heart. "I would never in a smillion years—"

"I want to see Kristie in the French twist you did at her trial," I said in my best I-mean-business voice. "And make sure the TV cameras do not get footage of our bride acting drunk."

Fern made a pouty face. "Fine. But Kristie and I were thinking of changing to a bouffant."

"No bouffant!" How drunk was the bride to even consider wearing a bouffant hairstyle for her wedding? "Do I need to come down there and supervise?"

Fern looked affronted. "No. I'll do the French twist." His head disappeared then popped back in a moment later. "I almost forgot the reason I came up here. Stepmommie Dearest called all her guests and told them to come early. She wants them on board before the rain really starts."

"Early?" Kate said. "How early?"

Fern glanced at his nonexistent watch. "Now."

"But the ceremony doesn't start for two hours." I looked at Kate in a panic. What would we do with one hundred fifty guests for two hours? That many people on board would fill every open space.

"Can I go down and drink with Fern?" she asked.

I was starting to think getting drunk and ending up with a bouffant wouldn't be the worst thing that could happen.

CHAPTER 36

If one hundred fifty wedding guests would be walking on board two hours early, I needed a plan. And the plan couldn't include me running off the ship and hightailing it to the Mexican border for a life of sunshine and tequila. I glanced out the window at the rain slashing through the air and lashing the ship. The sky was so dark that it felt like nighttime. I had to squint to make out the white catering tent crouched on the dock, the shiny plastic sides trembling as the wind battered them. The wind howled as it whipped torrents of water against the window.

"Fern, can you keep the ladies distracted?" I asked.

Fern raised two fingers to his brow to salute. "You can count on me, Nannabelle." His Champagne breath was not reassuring.

"But no bouffant," I reminded him as he left the room, weaving slightly as he walked. I hoped he would make it down the spiral staircase in one piece.

"Kate," I turned to my assistant, "I need you to go tell Richard we have to move up service. We can't have people drinking for two hours without food."

"He's going to love that," Kate said. We both knew Richard was a stickler with his timing. Telling him to speed things up by two hours would send him into fits. I was glad not to be the one bearing the bad news.

"I'll owe you one," I told Kate, pushing her toward the door.

"You're racking up quite a tab with me," she said. "What will you be doing while I'm throwing myself in the liar's mouth?"

I sighed, not bothering to tell her the word was lion, not liar. "I need to find enough deckhands to escort guests down the dock with umbrellas. Then I need to tell our security team things are about to get more complicated."

"Once all those guests are on the ship, it will be impossible to find anyone," Kate said. "If Jeremy Johns is even still on board."

Kate was right. If Daniel and his team hadn't located Jeremy by now, the chances of finding him once the ship was packed with people were slim. I followed Kate outside, and as she ran down the ramp to the dock, I hurried to the transom. We'd tented the area to give us more space, and right about now I was glad for every square foot. Two blond deckhands in white pants and navy blue *Mystic Maven* shirts stood tightening the ties of the tent's clear sidewalls.

"Hey guys," I called out. "I need you to escort the guests from the end of the dock to the ship. You have *Mystic Maven* umbrellas, right?"

The taller blond nodded, but the other shot a look out at the sheets of rain that made it hard to see if there even was an end to the dock.

"Grab any other crew members you need to help you. The guests will be here two hours earlier than we expected." I left them looking less than thrilled with their assignment and wound my way up the back staircase to the upper deck. The massive ice bar sat under the covered part of the deck, already chilling a dozen bottles of vodka inside, and I was pleased to see the back of the bar had been completely set with glasses. At least guests would be able to drink when they arrived.

I glanced at the glass doors leading into Mr. Barbery's study. We'd never intended to use it for the wedding, but with the rain eliminating all of our outdoor spaces, I wondered if we should open it up for extra standing room.

Through the glass, I caught a glimpse of a person inside the room and I blinked hard. Even though the glass was reflecting back at me, making it difficult to make out the inside of the room clearly, I could have sworn I just saw Mandy again. I rubbed my eyes. Was I starting to see things?

I pulled open the door and ducked inside. The dark wood and beige leather furniture were a stark contrast from the airy décor of the rest of the ship, and I suspected it was the single space the bride's father had been allowed a say in decorating. And since Jeremy hadn't been permitted to unleash his South Beach meets South of France concept on this room, it was now the most tasteful space on board.

My eyes scanned the room. Mandy wasn't anywhere. There wasn't another living soul in the compact room, and there was no back door she could have escaped through. Was I losing my mind or were my eyes playing tricks on me? First, I was convinced I'd spotted Mandy on the top deck, and then I thought I saw her in a salon with only one way in or out. I hoped the stress of the wedding wasn't making me lose it. Even though I joked about brides making me crazy, I didn't want to add literal insanity to my bag of tricks anytime soon.

I let my eyes wander over Mr. Barbery's treasure displayed on the built-in bookshelves. I knew it couldn't be very valuable or it would be kept in a safe, not on exhibit, but I still found the ancient artifacts fascinating. I leaned in close to look at the shimmery coins, the images embossed on them almost too worn away to make out. The clear stand that had held the antique gun was missing entirely, and several books had been pushed over to fill the empty space. Even if the gun had been used to kill the harbormaster, it was probably at the bottom of the Potomac by now.

I tapped my chin as I looked at the shelves. Unless the person who used the gun didn't want to toss it out. Unless it was valuable to him. A keepsake from a lifetime of hunting for treasure. I glanced around the room. But where would Mr. Barbery have hidden the gun if he had, in fact, used it to kill a man? I opened the drawers of his desk. Nothing but papers. I cast my eyes around the room again until they settled on a framed map on a wall in the corner.

I walked over and tugged at the frame and it came away from the wall on one side, exposing a hidden safe. Bingo. I looked behind me to make sure no one was watching me. I didn't have much time before guests began arriving and crowding the vodka bar. I remembered hearing that people usually used birthdays and anniversaries for combinations or passwords. I didn't think Mr. Barbery would be sentimental about his third wedding anniversary, but he would be about his only child's birthday. I thought back to the first time I met Kristie for coffee at Baked and Wired and she'd let it slip that her birthday had been the day before so I'd insisted on getting her a cupcake. It had been the twenty-fifth of June. I twirled the knob of the safe with the numbers of the bride's birthday then tugged. No luck. I swore under my breath. Wait, had she just turned twenty-seven? I tried again with the new birth year and the door swung open.

I stood up on my tiptoes to see into the back of the safe. There, in the back, lay the black gun, its long, encrusted barrel dotted with rust. I reached out to pick it up but stopped when I noticed a couple of gray hairs stuck on the handle, along with something sticky. I felt my heart begin to beat faster. It was one thing to think the gun might have been used to kill the harbormaster; it was another to see the bloody murder weapon. I wondered if the man died right here in this room.

"Calm down," I whispered to myself.

What should I do? My mind raced as I stared at the heavy iron gun blackened from years underwater, then I slammed the door to the safe shut and swung the framed map back in place.

I felt my legs weaken, and I took a few steps so I could sink onto a leather couch. Did this mean Mr. Barbery killed the harbormaster? Was the charming father of the bride behind the accidents and fire, as well? I shook my head. It didn't make any sense. What reason did he have for doing any of it? From what I could see, he had more motivation than anyone to keep the wedding going forward. He wanted a happy daughter and wife, and the accidents, fire, and murder didn't make either woman happy.

I shook my head. No. There must be another explanation. Someone must have used the gun and left it in here to set up Mr. Barbery. If he'd actually killed a man with his own antique gun, he wouldn't be foolish enough to leave it in his own study. Unless he wanted to make it look like he'd been set up. I rubbed my temples. I was going in circles.

I pulled out my phone, searched my call history, and hit redial. I breathed a sigh of relief when I got Reese's voicemail.

"Hey, it's me," I said over the crackling line. "Annabelle. I found something on the ship you need to see. Call me when you get this."

I felt slightly guilty that I hadn't told him that I'd found the murder weapon, but I knew if I did he'd arrive with a forensic unit that would wreak havoc on the wedding. I couldn't deal with Jeremy Johns on the loose plus a police invasion. This way I could get him to come down solo and then hit him with the bombshell.

I glanced over my shoulder at the map as I pushed my way through the glass doors to the outdoor lounge. I peered over the side of the ship and could see a steady stream of black umbrellas approaching from the end of the dock. At least the deckhands had listened to me and were escorting the guests on board.

I looked down one level and saw Kate standing near the

service ramp, waving her arms at me and pointing to the catering tent. I waved back and started down the stairs to join her, even though I dreaded hearing what she might have to say. The catering tent meant Richard, and Richard meant drama, and I'd had about as much drama as I could handle for one lifetime.

CHAPTER 37

"We're going to get killed out here." Kate's voice barely carried over the howling wind and rumbling thunder of the storm.

"Hold on to the rope," I yelled, pushing my wet hair off of my face with one hand and holding an umbrella over us with the other. The rain pelted me from the side and made the umbrella useless, but I still held it up.

"You've got to be kidding," Kate said, as she slid down the metal ramp in front of me, clutching the thin rope railing to keep from falling overboard.

When we reached the dock, we both ran to the catering tent a few feet away and pushed our way through the clear plastic sides.

"Well, it's about time," Richard said, his hands planted on his hips. "I rushed everything for you, and now it's been sitting." Richard's usually perfect hair was curling around his temples the way it did when it rained and he hadn't used enough styling cement.

"We're ready," I said, shaking out my umbrella on the rubber mats covering the floor. "Sorry for the delay."

Richard wagged a finger at me. "Whose idea was it again to hold a wedding on a yacht, Annabelle? This is a disaster."

"It's a superyacht," I corrected him, propping my wet umbrella against the white plastic sidewall of the tent. "And it would have been a perfect idea if it hadn't rained."

"This isn't rain." Kate wrung out the hem of her skirt. "It's a monsoon. Speaking of disasters, Richard, what are you wearing?" Bold words from someone who wore one of the tightest evening suits I'd ever seen. I was surprised she could bend over without the whole thing ripping in half.

Richard glanced at the black trash bags he'd taped around his body with silver strips of duct tape. "If you have a better idea for protecting my Prada suit, I'm all ears."

Kate's mouth fell open. "You're wearing Prada on a night like tonight?"

"You must be out of your mind if you think I'm going to cater a wedding on the most luxurious yacht ever docked at the District Marina and not wear designer."

Richard would never dream of wearing off-the-rack for a six-figure wedding.

"Speaking of designer, did you see the dresses on the women in there? And the jewelry?" Kate nudged me with her elbow. "Do you think it's all real?"

"Of course," Kate said. "The stylist from Paris was telling me how many carats Mrs. Barbery is wearing. PS: It's a lot."

Richard's eyebrows popped up. "All these stylists are really overkill."

"Oh, you think that pushed it over the edge?" Kate ran her fingers through her hair. "Not the cake designer we flew in from Scotland or redecorating the entire ship in the stepmonster's wedding colors?"

Richard made a face at Kate and then turned to me. "Are the waiters getting the drinks through the crowd?"

"Yes. I just wish we didn't have to open the bars before the ceremony, but what can you do when this many people are stuck on a boat during a monsoon?"

"Nothing like cocktails to keep people occupied," Kate said. "And we still have a lot of time to occupy."

"Food or booze," Richard said. "I just hope we have enough food. I know we have enough booze."

A figure draped in a dripping tangerine orange tablecloth burst through the tent sides. "Did someone say booze? Because I don't think I've had enough."

Kate and I jumped back as the tablecloth splattered to the floor and Fern emerged, looking remarkably dry considering the rest of us appeared to have swum to the wedding.

"Where did you get that cloth?" I eyed the orange tablecloth lying in a wet, wadded mound on the floor.

Fern shrugged. "It was lying around and I couldn't find a slumbrella."

"Slumbrella?" Kate asked. "How much Champagne have you had again?"

Fern hiccuped. "Just a few."

Kate eyed him. "Glasses or bottles?"

"Was the tablecloth lying around as in lying over a table to cover it?" I wasn't as concerned about Fern drinking bubbly with the bridesmaids as I was about him snatching a cloth off a table. I didn't remember having extra linens just sitting around and had a horrible vision of the bride catching a glimpse of a now-naked catering table with its knobby metal legs and particle-board top.

"Of course not," Fern said, biting the edge of his lip. "At least I don't think so. But I was in too much of a hurry to notice."

"If those people sent you down here for food, you tell them they'll have to wait . . ." Richard began.

"Is it Kristie?" I swallowed hard remembering how nervous the bride had been about the rain.

"No, no, no." Fern waved his hands around his face as if

shooing off a swarm of mosquitoes. "No one slent me. I came to tell Annabelle before anyone else did."

"Tell me what?" I said, immediately running through the list of possible wedding catastrophes in my head. At least it wasn't the bride; I mentally ticked her off my list. My mind leapt to the next natural problem. "Is it the stepmother? The stylist?"

Fern hesitated. "Maybe you should see for yourself." He snatched my umbrella from where I'd propped it against the tent wall and slipped out between the plastic flaps.

"Great." I grabbed a yellow napkin from a nearby pile and draped it over my head. I'd learned this trick by watching the waitstaff attempt to keep their heads dry while carrying trays onto the boat. If we didn't need to blend in with the formally dressed guests, Kate and I would have worn hooded rain slickers, but I knew that look would never fly with the fashion-conscious stepmother.

"I'm right behind you," Kate said, picking up her own napkin.

Richard threw his oven mitt down on the prep table. "Don't even think about leaving me behind." He turned to one of his chefs. "Get all the platters for the buffet ready, and I'll be back to garnish."

I adjusted my napkin so I could see past the dangling points and pushed my way out of the tent. The rain still beat down wildly, and it stung my cheeks as it blew from the side. I groped the few feet to the ramp and pulled myself up by the rope, my feet slipping on the slick metal. I was surprised we hadn't lost a waiter or two to the dark water below and was grateful when I reached the top. Jumping onto the boat, I ducked in through one of the heavy glass doors, and then held it open for Kate and Richard to follow.

I pulled the sopping wet napkin off of my head and slicked back a dripping strand of hair. I usually wore my auburn hair pulled back in a simple bun, but the rain had ruined my look. Hair kept falling into my eyes, and I could only presume any trace of makeup had run off my face hours ago. I reminded myself I wasn't here to look glamorous and meet men. Surprisingly, I had enough of those in my life already.

"This way." Fern motioned us to follow him across the salon to the marble entrance foyer and gleaming gold staircase that led to the lower decks.

"Where are we going?" Kate asked. "The party isn't down there."

Fern placed a finger over his lips as if all the guests weren't two decks above us putting away vast quantities of vodka. "You'll slee."

I wasn't convinced Fern was sober enough to be leading a posse, but curiosity outweighed the voice of reason in my head.

We formed a silent procession down the twisting staircase to the lower deck with all of the guest bedrooms and the indoor gym. Fern opened a door and I saw deck chairs stacked up to the ceiling.

"Oops," he said. "Wrong one."

He opened the door next to it, and I felt the rush of humidity. The glass door to the steam room hung open across from us and had filled the gym with a warm haze. Like every room on the boat, the gym used space efficiently with one elliptical machine, one treadmill, and one universal weight contraption filling the room.

"I couldn't find the switch to turn it off," Fern explained with a cough. The steam smelled like eucalyptus, and I couldn't resist taking a deep breath.

Kate waved a hand in front of her. "Why is the steam room on during the wedding?"

"Is someone in there?" I narrowed my eyes and could just make out a figure slumped against the tile bench. "And are they fully dressed?"

"All right, buddy." Kate called into the room and clapped her hands. "Party's over. This floor is off-limits."

I felt my skin go cold despite the heat billowing from the steam room. "Oh, no," I said as the body slipped off the bench and rolled onto the floor with a splash and a thud. I could see the water on the floor was tinged pink. "Not again."

Richard jumped back as droplets of warm water hit our legs. "Is that . . . ?"

I splashed over to the limp body and turned him over to feel for a pulse. "Yep."

Kate gave a small scream when she recognized his face. "Is he . . . ?"

"Dead," Fern said. "I checked already."

I pulled my fingers away from the dead man's neck and stepped back. "But what's he doing in here?"

No one had an answer for me, so I rubbed my temples and tried to convince myself this wasn't happening. You'd think it would be easy to avoid dead bodies at weddings, but either I had the worst luck in the world or the universe was telling me I should quit wedding planning and become a coroner.

CHAPTER 38

"Is that really who I think it is?" Kate took a step back and her feet splashed in a puddle, sending droplets of water onto the body.

I took in the wet tuxedo and sandy blond hair sagging limp across the forehead, which had lost its healthy glow. The skin had begun to take on a gray hue underneath the tan, and the blue eyes were wide and unseeing. I fought back a moment of nausea and jerked my eyes away from the body. Luckily, I was running on no food. Otherwise I might have been in serious danger of losing my lunch.

Fern tapped a finger to his chin. "It's Brody all right."

Kate put a hand to her mouth and shook her head. "This is a tragedy."

I looked from Fern to Kate to Richard. "This is bad."

"Dead bodies usually are, Annabelle," Richard said. "I think the heat is getting to you."

I stamped my foot and water splashed around my ankle. "Listen. If Brody is dead, then somebody killed him."

"Do you think it's Jeremy?" Kate asked. "He is on the lam."

"But why would Jeremy want to kill Brody?" Richard asked.

"Maybe Brody cornered him and Jeremy killed him in self-defense." I didn't like the nagging voice in my head reminding me about the bloody gun.

"Brody's a pretty big guy." Kate's voice cracked. "He could definitely take Jeremy."

She had a point. I would have picked Brody to come out ahead of the twitchy designer any day. "But if Jeremy didn't kill him, who did?"

I thought about the gun I'd found in Mr. Barbery's study. The gun that may have killed the harbormaster. And now there was another person killed by a blow to the head.

"Maybe it was Mr. Barbery," I said.

Kate's head snapped toward me. "What? Why?"

I hesitated for a moment. "I found the missing gun in his office safe, and it has blood on it. Unless I'm really wrong, that's what killed the harbormaster. I already knew that Mr. Barbery met with the man in his study on the day of the murder. What if he's behind all this?"

"No way." Kate shook her head. "He's too nice to be a killer. And his own stepson?"

"He spent years as a treasure hunter. I have a feeling that's the kind of job where you have to skirt the law more often than not. He might not be as aboveboard as he'd like us to think."

"But murder?" Kate said. "What's his motive? From the moment we met him he's said making Kristie happy is the most important thing to him. Dropping dead bodies in the middle of her wedding definitely won't make her happy."

I looked down at the inert body then jerked my eyes away. "I know, but the evidence is pointing in his direction."

"Someone else could have killed the harbormaster with his gun," Richard said. "So many people have been off and on this ship over the past week, it could have been anyone."

"Mr. Barbery has always been lovely to me." Fern pressed a

hand to his chest as he stared at Brody. "I can't imagine him doing something like this."

Kate touched Fern's arm. "Agreed."

Richard rolled his eyes. "Well, now that these two have exonerated all the suspects who are charming, can we get back to the matter at hand?" He gestured to the body. "Can we tell how long he's been dead? That would help us determine who might have done this."

"Not long," Kate said. "We just saw him about fifteen minutes ago with the captain. Should I go find Daniel and let him know?"

I grabbed her arm. "Wait a second. As soon as the police know there's been a murder on board, they'll stop the wedding. This will become one big floating crime scene. I already called Reese to tell him about the murder weapon. I'd rather be able to talk to him before calling in the cavalry."

Richard gaped at me. "Are you suggesting we don't tell anyone the bride's stepbrother got steamed to death?"

"As soon as we do, the ship will be locked down. What harm would it do to wait until Reese calls me back?" I glanced at the clock on my phone. "We could move up the ceremony and be done in thirty minutes."

"The girls are all ready." Fern gave a small hiccup. "I can have them lined up in five."

Richard pretended to put his fingers in his ears. "I am not hearing this. Won't Kristie notice Brody's missing?"

"She's a bride. She'll be easily distracted by all the hoopla," I said. "And with the ceremony jammed into the main salon, it will be too crowded to notice who's there or not. He's not in the wedding party. And besides, once she finds out she'll be devastated. I'd rather her have a few happy memories of her wedding day before she finds out."

"At least she'll get her ceremony and be married. Once they find out Brody is dead, who knows when they'd even consider a wedding? Annabelle's right. It's the nicest thing we could do for Kristie considering how close she was to him. The longer we can go without destroying this day for her, the better." Kate's voice sounded wooden as her eyes stayed locked on Brody. "The string quartet is already set up in the main salon. I can start moving guests down."

I pulled one of Richard's fingers away from his ear. "It's not like he's going to get more dead in half an hour. This way the bride gets her ceremony. If Reese hasn't called me back by then, I'll tell Daniel."

"What about my reception?" Richard said. "No one will remember my crab puffs and Gruyère beggar's purses if you upstage me with a dead body."

Kate eyed him. "So you don't have a problem with hiding a death, but you have a problem with your food taking second billing to the murder?"

Richard made a face at her. "You make me sound so catty when you put it like that."

"So how will we keep Daniel from finding the body before the ceremony is over?" I asked. "And we can't let the TV cameras from *Diamond Weddings* anywhere near this."

We all looked down at the wet corpse lying in the steam room.

"Once Kristie walks down the aisle, I can come down here and guard the door," Fern said.

I hesitated for a second wondering how Fern would explain prowling around the corridor in front of the gym. Then I remembered he managed to get away with more than the rest of us ever could with his combination of moxie and charm.

"Okay. And once the ceremony is over, we'll let Daniel find the body."

Richard cleared his throat.

"Fine," I said. "Once cocktails are over. Now let's go get this bride down the aisle."

CHAPTER 39

"If you'll proceed downstairs to the main salon, the ceremony will begin shortly." I directed a group of guests toward the staircase, trying to sound as pleasant as possible as I yelled over the rain pounding on the roof of the ship. I'd already circulated through the crowd once, but only a handful of people had made their way to the stairs. At this rate, I'd lose my voice before I got the crowd to the ceremony.

It usually took three passes through a room for people to actually follow directions and, as I had done at many weddings before, I longed for a tiny cattle prod. Although I was pretty sure it would be illegal, I was also sure guests would move faster once they were zapped with a hundred volts.

"The bar will reopen after the ceremony," I reassured a cluster of women in long glittery gowns who stood in line to refill their vodka glasses. They ignored me and didn't budge. Either they couldn't hear me over the downpour or they were well on their way to getting soused.

I glanced at an ornate clock hanging on the wall above the ice bar. At this point Kate had probably gotten the groomsmen in place and reviewed the cues with the string quartet while Fern moved Kristie and her attendants upstairs. I had to get these guests down so we could start the ceremony. I walked up to the bartender behind the ice bar, putting my hand on the slick freezing surface for a moment for balance. Then I pulled it away and wiped it on my wet pants. Not much help there.

"We need to close the bar so we can get these lushes downstairs for the ceremony," I said, keeping my voice low so the nearby cameraman wouldn't hear me and film me trying to close the bar. That was not how I envisioned my network debut.

"Good luck," he said, shaking his head. "I've never seen people go through straight vodka like this. You might start a riot."

I sighed. There was only one thing to do. I dragged a black rubber busing bin out from the bottom of the back bar, then pulled the bottles of vodka one by one out of the ice and put them in the bin. I bent down into a squat and heaved the bin up. "Problem solved."

I angled the bin with vodka so guests couldn't see it as I pushed my way through the glass door to Mr. Barbery's study. I placed the bin behind one of the leather sofas and pulled the sofa forward to hide them completely. I wiped my wet hand on the front of my pantsuit.

Through the glass door I could see the bartender gesturing the bar was closed and pointing toward the stairs. Like magic, the guests began moving downstairs. It was true that when you moved the booze, you moved the people.

I smoothed down my wet suit jacket, and my hand felt a bump in the front pocket. I dipped my hand inside and found the gummy bears I'd stashed earlier in the day and forgotten about.

"Annabelle."

I jumped when I heard my name whispered and looked around the room to see where it had come from. I could have sworn I was alone in the room.

"Over here." The voice came from a crack in the wall of books I'd never noticed before. It looked like one panel of the bookcase was actually hinged like a door. Did *Mystic Maven* have hidden rooms and passageways?

I stepped back. "Who's there?"

"It's me, Mandy. Hurry in here before someone sees."

I was too startled to ask any more questions before she grabbed my wrist and pulled me behind the bookcase. As Mandy slid the panel back into place, I looked around me. We stood on the dimly lit landing of yet another spiral staircase that appeared to go down into the ship. "What is this?"

"It's a secret passageway leading to the master suite and then down below to the storerooms. It's how Mr. Barbery gets around the ship."

That explained why we rarely saw the bride's father when we were on board. I turned to Mandy and pulled my wrist out of her grasp. She no longer wore her *Mystic Maven* uniform. Instead she was in jeans and a dark blue fleece zipped up to her neck. Her hair looked dry, so I knew she must have arrived before the storm. "What's going on? Why did you disappear and why are you hiding in secret passageways?"

"Didn't you get my message?"

I shook my head. "What message?"

Mandy chewed the edge of her thumbnail. "Then you don't know what's going on?"

I grabbed her by the shoulders. "What are you talking about?"

"Kate said you've solved crimes before," she said. "I figured you would know what to do with the evidence."

I knew Kate's offhanded comment when we first met Mandy would come back to bite me. I needed to have a serious talk with Kate about her over sharing problem. "What evidence?"

"An envelope that was dropped off at your apartment the other night."

I let my head drop. "That was from you?"

"Yes. Do you still have it?"

As I waited for more explanation, I could hear the sounds of prelude music reverberating through the walls. "Yes, but I don't understand. Why bring it to me?"

Mandy waved a hand. "We have a bigger problem. The information belongs to the captain and he knows it's missing."

I didn't like the idea of having something that belonged to the captain. He didn't seem like the type to let stealing slide.

"Are you sure he cares? I mean it's just an envelope of receipts and arrest records for people I've never heard of."

"So you saw what was inside?" Mandy started chewing her thumbnail again. "Trust me, he cares."

"Okay," I said. "But what is it? Does it have something to do with the murder or the accidents or the fire?"

"I don't know," Mandy said. "I didn't know what to think when I found out so I ran."

"Found out what?" I asked. This girl was not making sense.

Mandy wouldn't meet my eyes. "Those arrest records are all for members of our crew."

I swallowed hard. This really was the Ship of the Damned.

CHAPTER 40

"So, let me get this straight," I said, my voice echoing in the closed stairwell. "You discovered that half the crew was replaced with criminals. How?"

Mandy gave a small wave of her hand. "Snooping in the captain's office."

I studied her as I dug a gummy bear out of the mini cellophane packet in my suit pocket and popped it in my mouth. It was a little sticky from the rain, but I didn't care as long as I got the sugar rush. "Does that mean you have a criminal record, too?"

"No, but I don't think I was supposed to be here. My name is Amanda Fraser and there is an arrest record for an Amanda Frasier. I must have been hired by accident."

"I don't get it," I said. "Why hire a crew you can't trust to work on a ship filled with valuable art?"

Mandy shrugged one shoulder. "You've got me. Maybe he keeps the files in case he needs leverage on us. But I got freaked out when I saw them, so I ran. I had no idea everyone I was working with was a criminal."

The muffled prelude music grew louder. It sounded like the string ensemble was playing and from the muffled notes I could tell it was the song for the parents' entrance. I couldn't stay hidden in this secret staircase much longer.

"Why did you come back on board?" I asked.

"Curiosity, I guess. Once I left I started thinking about why the captain would hire all of us and keep files. Something isn't right about this."

I took the crumpled bag of gummy bears from my pocket and held it out to Mandy. She shook her head. "That's an understatement," I said. "Do you think this could be connected to the murders?"

"It must be." Mandy paused. "Did you say murders?"

"Can you promise to keep a secret?" I tucked the cellophane candy bag back into my pocket after taking out a pair of slightly damp orange bears.

She gestured to the cramped landing. "I'm hiding in a secret passageway. Who am I going to tell?"

She had a good point. "There's been another murder on board."

Mandy put a hand over her mouth. "Who? When? I haven't seen anything on the news about it."

"It just happened," I said. The string ensemble switched to the music for the bridal party's entrance, and I felt relieved Kate was going forward with the ceremony. "Fern found the body about a half hour ago."

"Are the police here?" Mandy looked nervous.

"Not yet," I admitted. "They don't know about the second murder."

Mandy looked a little confused. "You didn't tell the police you found a dead body?"

"We're definitely going to," I said quickly. "Just as soon as the ceremony is over. And maybe part of the cocktail hour. From the sounds of the music below, the ceremony should be over in about twenty minutes."

Mandy's eyes widened. "Do you think what I found out about the captain and crew is related to this?"

I popped another gummy bear. At this rate, I would need to invest in family-sized bags for future weddings. "It must be, although I can't figure out how the second dead body is connected to any of it."

"Who is it?"

"Brody."

Mandy paled. "What? Are you sure?"

"Pretty sure. He's lying in the steam room without a pulse."

Mandy hitched in her breath and gave a jerky shake of her head. "I can't believe it. Who could have killed him?"

"Well, I saw Jeremy Johns trying to set another fire in your quarters. He overheard me saying we were going to turn him over to the cops and took off running. Maybe Brody found him and confronted him and got the worse end of it." I thought about the bloody gun in the father's safe. "Or maybe it was someone else."

The muffled notes of the bride's processional came up through the staircase, and I imagined Fern doing his usual primping of the veil and dress at the back of the aisle, which, in this case, was the doorway into the main salon from the casual dining room. I felt a twinge of guilt about missing the processional, but I knew Kate and Fern could get a bridal party down the aisle in their sleep.

"That designer overpowered Brody?" Mandy asked. "I don't know."

"I agree, but if it's not Jeremy, then who could it be?"

Mandy shook her head. "I have no idea. But it doesn't look good for me to be on board again, does it?"

"Now that you mention it, showing up right as another person is murdered probably doesn't look so good."

"Do you think I could slip off without being seen?" she asked.

"Maybe, but do you have anything to hide? I'm sure if you explain everything, the police will understand. It's not like you had a motive to kill anyone."

She stopped biting her nail. "It's not the police I'm worried about. What if the killer wants to get rid of me too?"

"Why would they want to do that?"

"What if it all has to do with the crew and the criminal records? What if I saw something I saw in those files that points to the real killer? Those files were originals."

"Wait." I grabbed her arm. "So the only copy of those papers is —?" I didn't want to hear the answer to my question.

CHAPTER 41

"No one knows where the papers are, though, do they?" I asked Mandy. Even though Leatrice drove me crazy, I couldn't stand the thought of her in danger.

"Not unless they followed me when I delivered them."

That was only slightly reassuring. I listened, but the only sound was the unrelenting rainfall on the fiberglass hull, made even louder in the enclosed stairwell. That meant the ceremony was taking place, but the recessional hadn't started yet. I took Mandy's hand. "If you're going to get off the ship, you should do it now while everyone is occupied at the ceremony. Once the security team finds the body, no one will be able to leave."

She nodded and reached to push open the hidden doorway. "I'll slip out through the back stairs and send you a message once I'm safe. Or if I think of anything that could help you find the killer."

I peered down the staircase that wound narrowly down into the lower levels of the ship. "Where did you say this leads?"

"There's a secret exit on each floor. First, the master suite—"

I stopped her. "That's perfect. The Barberys won't be there since they're at the ceremony. It should be deserted."

We exchanged a quick hug, then Mandy slipped through the hinged panel of books and I started down the twisting staircase. I wanted to make sure the security team was far away from the steam room.

I reached another narrow landing with a door. I pushed it just enough to open a crack. I could see I'd reached the master suite, and the room seemed empty and silent. I pushed the door far enough so I could slip out and I pulled the door closed behind me. In this room the secret door was part of a shelving unit to the side of the king-sized bed. To the left of the bed was a doorway leading into a sprawling closet, and beyond that a short set of curved stairs that led up to a large Jacuzzi tub. I couldn't help gaping. The master suite took up as much space as all the rest of the bedrooms put together.

I'd never ventured inside the room because Mrs. Barbery was usually holed up inside with Jeremy Johns. Now I understood why the stepmother spent all her time here. It was stunning. Cream silk covered the walls and the bed. A modern painting of deep blue waves hung over the bed along with a crystal chandelier. Glass walls took up the entire front of the room and looked out over the bow of the ship. I imagined the view was incredible when the ship was at sea. Right now all I could see were gray skies and sheets of rain.

I sat down on the bed and pulled out my phone. With Mrs. Barbery and everyone else upstairs at the ceremony, this was probably the best time and place to make an urgent call.

"Leatrice?" I said when she answered the phone.

"Annabelle?" She wasn't used to me calling her, and the connection wasn't the best because of the storm. "Isn't the wedding today?"

"I'm at the wedding," I said. "Do you remember the envelope you gave me? The one Mandy dropped off?"

"Yes, dear." She said, her voice going in and out. "I almost forgot. Such . . . nice girl. Is . . . important?" Leatrice asked. "I can bring . . . to you."

"No!" I said. The last thing I needed to add to the mix was Leatrice. "It's fine. People are looking for that envelope. Can you just make sure no one goes in my apartment?"

The phone cut out. At least I knew the potential evidence was safe and sound in Georgetown. Well, as safe as anything could be with Leatrice watching over it. I dropped the phone into my pocket and tiptoed over to the door, peeking my head outside. The hallway was empty, so I darted out and closed the door silently. I hurried to the staircase at the end of the hall and wound my way down to the level below.

"Annabelle! There you are!" Fern's voice made me skid down the last two stairs, and I clutched the handrail to keep from falling.

I stared at him. "What are you wearing?" He appeared to have on nothing but a large beige towel wrapped around his chest with a matching towel wrapped around his head as a turban.

"I'm a diversion."

"You certainly are," I said.

"You told me to keep the security team away from the steam room. That's what I'm doing. If anyone comes down, I'll say I'm about to take a steam."

"In the middle of a wedding?" I asked. "Doesn't that strike you as an odd thing to do?"

Fern waved a hand and giggled. "Like a slecurity officer would know."

I wondered just how much Champagne Fern had ingested to make him think running around a wedding in a towel was a good idea.

"But you'll be happy to know Kristie and all her hussy bridesmaids got down the aisle."

"Were any of them sober?" I asked.

Fern shrugged.

I glanced at my watch. "We probably only have ten minutes before the ceremony ends. That means we only have to keep the murder secret for about another hour at most."

Fern readjusted his towel turban and hiccuped. "Easy pleasy."

CHAPTER 42

"There you are," I said as I dashed into the kitchen tent where Richard stood garnishing a platter of hors d'oeuvres with fresh flowers. I wiped the water off my face as I breathed in the savory smell of rosemary filling the small space. I noticed a second tray of lamb skewers threaded with fresh sprigs of the herb and wondered if I could distract Richard and steal a few. The gummy bears were not filling.

Richard looked up at me and the clear plastic shower cap he wore slipped down on his forehead. "There *I* am? Where have *you* been? The ceremony ended twenty minutes ago."

I tried to ignore the shower cap and the obvious question of where he got it. "I've been busy."

Richard tapped his foot. "Well, while you've been gallivanting around, I've been slaving away out here on the docks."

I doubted if anyone had ever claimed to be "slaving away on the docks" while wearing a designer suit. I looked at the metal framework holding the tent together, the bars rattling as the wind shook them, and I couldn't help but notice the walls of the tent groaning as the rain pummeled them. I said a quick prayer the tent would not be lifted up and blown away, taking Richard and several hundred hors d'oeuvres with it.

"I haven't been gallivanting around," I said. "I've been trying to do some damage control. And figure out what's going on."

"What's going on is these guests are eating and drinking like they were just rescued from a desert island." He snapped a white rose head from a long stem and placed it at the top of a tray of mini lobster rolls. "If they keep up this pace, I don't know if I have enough food to last all night."

"It won't have to last all night," I said. "Just until the police discover the second dead body and shut us down."

"I thought the plan was to tell the security team once my cocktail party was over." Richard looked at his watch. "It's almost time for the first dance."

I held up my hands. "Okay, okay. Since our plan was going so well, I hoped I could buy a little more time to try to figure things out."

"Going so well?" Richard's eyes widened and he snatched up a rose. "Which part of this night seems to be going well to you?" He ripped a bruised petal off the bloom. "The monsoon?" Rip. "The dead body?" Rip, rip. "The fact that some of us may be going to jail for obstruction of justice?" Rip, rip, rip. The rose fell apart and he threw the petals to the ground.

"Well, obviously not those things."

Richard pointed to his head. "For heaven's sake, Annabelle, I've resorted to wearing a shower cap. A shower cap! Me!" His voice cracked. "It's almost too much to bear."

I tried not to stare at the thin, crinkled plastic covering his hair and put a hand over my mouth to stifle my urge to giggle. "Where on earth did you even get a shower cap?"

He pointed to his head and I noticed faint lettering on the plastic.

"Does it say *Mystic Maven* on your head?" I asked.

Richard nodded. "I found them in the gym bathroom. You have to hand it to them. These people know how to brand."

Why was I surprised the ship had its own imprinted shower caps?

"If you breathe a word of this to anyone, I'll deny it until my last dying breath." Richard shook a finger at me. "And if those TV cameras come anywhere near this tent and film me like this, they'll regret it."

"Your secret is safe with me. I, for one, do not have a death wish."

Richard bobbled his head at me. "You don't seem to have a problem running around a ship with a killer on board. Sounds like a death wish to me."

"All right," I said. "I'll find Daniel Reese and tell him everything. Up until the part about us not telling him for the past hour so we could go ahead with the ceremony. I might leave that part out."

"Good thinking. And, if asked, I was here in the kitchen tent the entire night."

"Stay here then. I'll come get you once I've spilled the beans." I shot a look at his head. "It's not like you want anyone to see you in this state anyway."

He leveled a finger at me. "Don't even dream of posting a photo. And if I end up in a 'snap' or a 'chat' or a 'story' . . . " He made air quotes. "Heads will roll."

"Believe me, a monsoon does not Instagram well."

I pulled back the flap of the tent. The rain had changed to steady, fat drops bouncing off the waterlogged sheets of plywood covering the dock. I eyed the metal ramp a few feet away and, just as I was about to make a dash for it, noticed a small figure in a bright yellow rain coat and rain hat disappearing through the ship's glass door at the top of the ramp.

I blinked and then blinked again. The only person I knew with an ensemble like that was Leatrice, but I had specifically told her to stay away.

And, of course, I knew she wouldn't listen to me. I steeled myself for the rain then hurried up the ramp to the boat, pushing open the glass door and preparing to give Leatrice a thorough scolding.

The room was empty aside from trays of Champagne glasses and used hors d'oeuvre trays stacked to go back down to the kitchen tent. She must be nearby, I told myself as I shook the rain off my clothes. I peeked into the main salon. It was still packed with guests, and there wasn't a bright yellow rain jacket in sight. I made for the galley kitchen where Richard's headwaiter was opening a bottle of Champagne.

"Jim!" I clutched the tall man's arm. "Have you seen a little old lady in a yellow rain coat?"

He jerked his head toward the door on the other side of the galley. "She went that way looking for you. Do you want me to go after her?"

"No, I've got it. You just keep the guests drunk so they won't notice when the police arrive."

Jim stared at me, his mouth falling open a bit, but I left before he could do anything more than look confused. The door from the galley led to a back spiral staircase. I paused for a moment then decided to go down. I wound down the stairs, holding tightly on the rail so I wouldn't slide all the way down, and paused when I reached the next floor. Down the hallway I could see Fern still wearing his fluffy beige towel ensemble. Leatrice stood next to him.

"Aha," I said, striding down the hall.

Leatrice turned and beamed at me from under her oversized yellow rain hat. "I've been looking for you, dear."

"That's my line," I said. "And what are you doing here? I told you not to come down."

"You did?" Leatrice looked confused. "I didn't hear you say

that. But, then, we did have a bad connection." She looked at Fern. "If I'd known this was a toga party, I would have dressed accordingly."

"This isn't a toga party," I said. "Fern's being a distraction."

"Isn't he always?"

Fern batted his eyelashes at me and shifted the towel on his head so it wasn't so crooked. Leatrice had a point.

I grabbed Leatrice's arm. "I need to get you off the ship. It isn't safe here."

"But I brought you this." She held up a manila envelope. "The envelope you asked me about over the phone. The one I delivered to you the other day."

I gave her a pointed look. "The one in my apartment?" Not that I was the least bit shocked Leatrice had let herself into my apartment.

She patted my hand. "Yes, dear. You're welcome."

I took the envelope from her. "You still can't be here. Things are about to get unpleasant, and I don't want you caught in the middle of it."

Leatrice's face brightened as she looked past me down the hall. "You look familiar."

CHAPTER 43

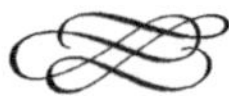

I spun around then let out a breath when I saw it was Mandy and not Daniel Reese. "You startled me. I thought you were headed off the ship"

"I was, but I wanted to grab a heavier coat from my room." Mandy let her eyes linger on Fern's towel-turbaned head, which he patted.

I didn't even bother to explain because the explanation would sound ridiculous. I looked over my shoulder to the stairs. At least no one else was a witness, even though I could hear the low hum of the guests one floor above us. If all was going according to plan, they were being plied with enough food and drink to keep them from entertaining any notion of exploring the ship.

"You've come by our building before, haven't you?" Leatrice asked.

Mandy nodded, her eyes fixed on the manila envelope. "I thought it was at your place, Annabelle."

"We had a bit of a mix-up. Leatrice thought I wanted her to bring it to me on board."

Mandy's eyes darted up and down the narrow hallway. "That's the only evidence we have showing something fishy is going on."

"Leatrice," I said, "we have to get you and that envelope off the ship. It isn't safe here."

Her face fell. "But I just got here and it took me forever to drive here in this rain."

"You drove in this storm?" Mandy gaped at her and then sighed. "You can't send her out in this weather."

"Fine," I said, my sigh matching Mandy's. "But we have to keep you out of the way."

"She can hide out in my room until the rain slacks off a bit," Mandy offered. "No one will look for her there."

"Are you sure?" I asked. I could only imagine what kind of trouble Mandy would get into if anyone discovered my nutty old neighbor had crashed the wedding and was hiding out in her bedroom. Then again, Mandy was already in hot water, so what was a little more?

"Of course. I was on my way there anyway."

Leatrice and Mandy headed down the hall to the spiral staircase that led down to the crew quarters. I trailed behind, still not comfortable with the idea of Leatrice hiding on the ship with the wedding going on above us and a dead body yet to be discovered just steps away.

"What are you doing?" I said to Fern when I noticed he was following me. I started walking faster.

"This is exciting. I've always wanted to go into hiding," Fern said in a low voice as we wound our way down the staircase. "This is just like being in the witness relocation program."

"This is nothing like that," I said when we reached the lower level. "Leatrice is hiding out until we can get her safely off the ship. That's all."

"Why are you trying to take this away from me, Annabelle?" Fern pushed me back as he sped up and passed me in the narrow hallway, almost bumping into Leatrice and Mandy when they stopped in front of a doorway.

Mandy opened the door and waved Leatrice inside the small windowless room.

"Make yourself at home." She took a couple of steps over to the closet. "I need to find my *Mystic Maven* raincoat or I'll get drenched out there."

Leatrice took a seat at the blond wood desk and put the envelope in front of her, pushing the crystal *Mystic Maven* paperweight out of her way.

"Did you open it?" I asked Leatrice.

She looked affronted. "Of course not, dear. I would never pry."

I restrained myself from mentioning the many ways she'd pried in my life, from trying to set me up with the pizza delivery boys to leaving open cookbooks on my kitchen counter to slipping flyers for cleaning services under my door. I picked up the envelope and ripped open the back flap.

"What are those?" Leatrice asked.

"Arrest records. I flipped through the files. "Half the people on this ship seem to have some sort of criminal record.

"Except me," Mandy said, pulling a black coat from the closet. "But I think that was because of a spelling mistake."

"I like the fabric," Fern said to Mandy, appraising the black nylon rain coat she'd slipped on. "But the cut doesn't do your figure any favors, honey."

Leatrice rubbed her hands together. "Oooh. It's like a pirate ship. How exciting."

"I don't think many pirates were into petty shoplifting and bouncing checks." I scanned the records quickly then set them aside and turned to the receipts.

"Is it normal to buy so many guns?" Leatrice asked, staring over my shoulder at the paperwork.

"What's that?" Mandy asked, straining to look while Fern held her back and adjusted her coat.

"Those receipts are from dark net gun suppliers," Leatrice said, "All small orders but lots of them."

I looked at her. "How do you know?"

"I recognized the names from my time on the dark net with Boots and Dagger Dan."

I tried to forget Leatrice's time hanging out with online hackers. It did not make me feel better to know that she was familiar with the seedier side of the internet.

"Why does a luxury yacht need to purchase so many guns under the radar?" I wondered aloud.

"Why do they make raincoats so boxy? Life is full of mysteries." Fern pointed at Mandy. "What you need is a belt to cinch your waist."

I glanced back at Fern pawing through the closet while Mandy looked helpless beside him. I mouthed an apology to her then turned back to the papers. "I can't imagine a private yacht needing this kind of an arsenal. I wonder if the harbormaster somehow saw the guns and questioned them."

"That gun room had crates filled with automatic weapons," Leatrice said. "Those must be what they bought under the table."

"Of course those crates were filled with guns," I said, thinking back to seeing them when we found Leatrice. I hadn't focused on that at the time, but now it seemed obvious.

"If I stumbled across the crates of guns, someone else could have," Leatrice said. "I'll bet the harbormaster has to check the cargo of every ship."

"And these orders were in the captain's files," I said.

"You think he's behind everything?" Leatrice asked.

"Maybe," I said. "But I doubt he could pull this off on his own." I wondered how much Kristie's father knew. Being a treasure hunter wasn't that far from being a smuggler, and if my hunch was correct, the guns below deck were not bought to protect the artwork. Was the personable Mr. Barbery really a gun runner? And had he killed the harbormaster to protect his secret?

Fern stood up with a white terry cloth sash from a robe in one hand. "We could use this to shape the waist."

Mandy waved him off. "I think I'll be fine."

Fern made a face then shrugged. "Suit yourself." He looked down at the sash. "What am I talking about? This towel isn't doing my figure any favors either." He tied the sash around his own waist then appraised himself in the mirror on the inside of the closet door and nodded his approval.

I put the papers back in the envelope and pulled my cell phone from my pocket, hitting the speed dial for Reese. "Crap. No service. It must be the storm. Fern, can you stay here with Leatrice and guard these papers? I need to go find our security team and tell them everything."

Fern gave me a salute, and I tried not to worry that my first line of defense was decked out in terry cloth from head to toe, now with a cinched waist.

"Good luck sneaking off the ship," I said to Mandy as I opened the door to the hall.

"Look at all the dresses you have in the back," Fern said as he resumed pawing through Mandy's closet. "I'll bet some of these would look amazing on me."

"I'm right behind you," Mandy said. I hoped for her sake she'd be able to escape from Fern and Leatrice, but I didn't give her great odds.

CHAPTER 44

I took the spiral staircase, stopping at each level and peering down the hall to look for the black-clad security officers. Either they were all upstairs with the guests or they were better at being unobtrusive than I'd given them credit for. I paused before reaching the top level and took a breath. My mind felt like a jumble of information and clues that didn't connect. I knew I had almost all the pieces of the puzzle, although the answer still eluded me.

First, there were the accidents and the fire. Clearly those were done to get the wedding off the ship. But the two murders seemed unconnected to those things and to each other. Who would want both the harbormaster and Brody dead? What did they have in common? If the huge stash of guns was the reason the harbormaster was killed, how could Brody be connected to the guns as well? Nothing I came up with seemed likely, but who knew at this point?

I stepped into the galley kitchen where Jim, the catering captain, stood opening and closing the wooden cabinets while making a soft cooing noise.

"Looking for something?" I asked.

He spun around and slammed a cabinet door shut. "What? No. I mean, I'm sure I'll find . . ." Jim put a hand over his heart. "You startled me is all."

"I've spent a decent amount of time on board the ship, so I can probably help you find whatever it is you're looking for."

His eyes darted around the narrow kitchen. "Probably not."

I stared hard at him. "Jim?"

He ran a hand over his bald head. "Fine. Just promise me you won't tell Richard."

"Okay." I had no desire to get Richard even more worked up than he already was, so it was an easy promise to make. "Tell me."

Jim slumped against the counter. "I brought Rocky with me even though Richard told me not to. I was just so worried he'd be scared alone in the storm. And now he's run off."

"Rocky?" My mouth fell open as I recalled the name. "You brought your pet flying squirrel to the wedding and now you can't find him?"

Jim nodded without meeting my eyes.

I took a deep breath to calm myself. One more thing to add to my list of disasters waiting to happen. "If I see Rocky, I'll stick him in my pocket, okay?"

Jim didn't look comforted.

I passed through the next room and into the main salon, scanning the crowd for Daniel Reese. The low-hanging swaths of bright fabric nearly touched people's heads, making the room feel even tighter, but I finally spotted him at the far end of the room. I tried to catch his eye by waving my hands over my head, but his attention was focused in the other direction. I'd have to work my way through the crowd.

"Excuse me, pardon me," I said as I pushed through the tuxedo-clad men and bejeweled women standing elbow to elbow. Some tried to move aside for me, some stared at my wet hair and clothes, but most ignored me. I stubbed my toe on one of Jeremy Johns's ridiculous neon urns and cursed. By the time I reached

Daniel, Champagne had been spilled on me twice and one smoked salmon and caviar croustade had been dropped on my shoe.

I grasped his arm. "I finally found you." I had to scream to be heard over the din of the guests.

He flinched when I grabbed him then relaxed when he recognized me. "I take it you've been outside?"

I put a hand to my bun, which was soaking wet. "Listen, I need to talk to you."

He motioned to the staircase in the middle of the salon a few feet away. We pushed our way through and I led the way down. When we reached the floor with the gym, I stopped and waited for Daniel to catch up.

"What's up?" he said.

"Three things. Maybe four. Three major ones, really."

He folded his arms over his chest. "Start with any of them."

"Okay, first, there's a dead body in the steam room. Mrs. Barbery's son Brody. And second, I found a bloody gun in the father's safe. I think it was used to kill the harbormaster. And three, I think I have the evidence showing some pretty illegal stuff taking place on this ship."

Daniel's arms fell to his sides. "Are you serious?"

I didn't bother answering. I motioned him to the door to the gym and he followed me in. I pointed to the steam room. "See for yourself."

I hung back while he walked over to the steam room and poked his head inside. I tried not to look too closely but could still make out the form of Brody on the tile floor.

Daniel backed out and let the door close. He turned to me, his face grim. "I need to call this in to Mike."

"Of course," I said. "I would never want to stand in the way of justice. I tried to call just now and couldn't get a signal." I hoped it would never come out how long I'd been sitting on this information. "The antique gun is still in the safe upstairs, but let me give you the evidence about the other guns and crew. My friends are guarding it for me."

I led the way down to Mandy's room and knocked on the door as I pushed it open. Daniel Reese looked past me into the empty room.

"They're gone." I hurried into the room and opened the door to the small closet, then my eyes went to the desk. Nothing. No Fern. No Leatrice. No envelope. "They promised me they would stay right here." My gut told me Leatrice and Fern hadn't just wandered off. But where were they?

My eyes caught the corner of a shoe poking out from under a blanket on the floor in the far corner. I pulled the blanket off, and my hand flew to my mouth.

"Oh no."

It was Mandy. And from the blood on her forehead, it was clear she wasn't napping.

CHAPTER 45

After Daniel found a pulse on Mandy, he'd called the paramedics and his brother. Now Detective Reese was on his way along with probably half of the DC Police Department. I felt a small rush of excitement that I'd see him soon coupled with a twinge of anxiety that he'd be less than thrilled I'd found another dead body. Not to mention the murder weapon. At least I could point to my earlier voice mail, which he'd never returned, as my attempt to loop him in.

"Who did this?" I sank onto the bed as I realized the wedding and all my attempts to save it were about to come to a screeching halt. I avoided looking at Mandy's motionless form on the floor and felt guilt wash over me. If I'd gotten Daniel involved earlier, none of this would have happened. Then again, my bride wouldn't have had a ceremony—so I had at least one mark in the win column.

I reflexively reached for the gummy bear bag in my pocket. If there was ever a moment I needed a hit of the sugary sweet candy, this was it. I felt the empty bag and slumped even further onto the bed.

"Weren't your friends with her?" Daniel asked. "They would be the most likely suspects."

I thought of tiny Leatrice and Fern wrapped up in towels. "You wouldn't think that if you'd seen them lately."

"Then you think they left the room and someone else came in and knocked this woman unconscious?" Daniel asked.

"Maybe," I said, but I knew that didn't make much sense. I'd specifically told them to stay put. And Mandy had been on her way off the ship. None of this made any sense. "Or they were taken by whoever did this."

Daniel scanned the room. "I don't see any object that could've been used to leave a bump like that." He jerked a thumb in Mandy's direction.

I agreed. The room was spare. The furniture was built into the walls and the cream-shaded lamp was secured to the desk. It made sense not to have knickknacks scattered about if the boat got in heavy swells. But it made the bump on Mandy's head even more difficult to explain.

"I need to find Leatrice and Fern," I said. "They'll be able to tell us what happened. And if the same person who killed Brody and the harbormaster did this to Mandy, those two may be in danger."

Daniel looked unconvinced. "I don't like the idea of any more people running loose on the ship. We haven't been able to locate Jeremy even though we found the stash of lighter fluid and confiscated it."

I'd almost forgotten about Jeremy and my suspicions about him as the arsonist. Brody's murder had eclipsed that, though I knew everything had to be connected somehow. The thought that awful Jeremy Johns might be connected to Leatrice's and Fern's disappearance made my stomach twist into knots.

"There are already one hundred fifty guests running loose on the ship," I told him. "I'm the least of your worries."

Daniel gave me a crooked grin that was an exact copy of his brother's. "From what Mike tells me, I tend to doubt that."

I didn't have time to ask him what his brother had told him

about me. And I wasn't so sure I wanted to know. The last time we'd seen each other we'd argued over my involvement on the ship. And now he was being called in for another murder on board plus a potential attempted murder. I knew he would be less than thrilled with me, and I hated to admit he'd been right about everything.

"Let me help you out and ask if any of my guys have seen them first." Daniel held up his walkie-talkie. "What were they wearing?"

I took a breath. He asked for it. "One is wearing nothing but beige towels, and the other is in a yellow rain coat and matching hat."

He raised an eyebrow. "Which is which?"

"Fern is in the towels, and Leatrice is the one who looks like a pint-sized whaler."

Daniel relayed the information to his team then turned back to me. "I really think you should wait here until Mike arrives."

Being at the scene of another crime was the last place I wanted to be when Detective Reese arrived. "I promise to come right back here after I have a look around. I just want to make sure they're okay and aren't being held hostage by a murderer."

"Fine." Daniel waved a hand at me. "Go. But don't leave the ship."

"I don't think I can unless I'm willing to swim away." I stood up and edged past him out the narrow doorway. "I won't be long."

I rushed down the hall and took the spiral stairs two at a time. When I reached the main salon, I scanned the crowd. No towel turban or yellow rain hat, but the guests did seem to be drunker. The servers probably couldn't get the hors d'oeuvres through the crowd although I noticed every person had a drink in hand.

I pushed through the crowd into the casual dining room and then poked my head into the galley kitchen. No luck. I glanced at the open door in the corner leading up to the bridge. No chance they were there.

I stopped to think for a moment. If a killer had them, where would he or she take them? Or where would the two of them go with evidence they knew they had to guard? And if they'd escaped from the person who'd knocked out Mandy, where would they go to hide? And, most important, where would Fern dare to go dressed in nothing but towels? He'd never let himself be seen wearing a fabric like terry cloth by all those society women. That meant they were probably still below deck.

"There you are." Kate's head appeared in the doorway from the main salon and she pushed the swinging door open. "I've been looking everywhere for you." She flopped onto the banquette ringing the wall of the casual dining room and kicked off her *Mystic Maven* slippers.

"Since when did you put those on?" I asked.

She held up a foot and let the slipper dangle from her toes. "Since the ramp to the dock became a slip and slide."

I joined her on the banquette and nudged a silver tray aside so I could rest my arms on the table. "I've been with Daniel Reese downstairs. I told him about Brody."

"Well, that's a relief. Can we shut down this party and go home?" Kate pushed a damp strand of hair off her forehead. This was one of the few days I'd seen her hair lose its bounce.

Not that any of us looked like our usual selves having to work in near monsoon conditions. I was soaked all the way to my underwear, the one saving grace being I hadn't worn Spanx. I imagined soaking wet Spanx would be the modern world's version of a torture device. My bun was a sopping knot of hair that, if squeezed, ran a stream of water down my back, and any trace of makeup had washed off my face hours ago. I knew I looked as beaten down as I felt.

Aside from Kate's wet hair, she didn't look half bad. She wore considerably more makeup than I did to begin with, but she'd managed to keep most of it on her face, and it appeared her lipstick had been recently reapplied. I gave her an A for effort and an A plus for vanity.

"The party may be shutting down, although I doubt we can leave anytime soon," I said. "Detective Reese is on his way along with the paramedics."

Kate raised an eyebrow. "At this point, I think Brody is beyond the paramedics' help."

"Not for him. For Mandy."

Kate sat up. "Mandy?"

"We found her knocked out downstairs. Leatrice and Fern were supposed to be with her, but they're gone."

Kate held up her hands. "Whoa there. Since when is Leatrice on board?"

"Long story," I said. "Basically, she brought some evidence Mandy dropped off at my apartment to keep safe so I stashed her and Fern in Mandy's room so no one would see her. But when I took Daniel Reese down to check out the evidence, Mandy was knocked out and Leatrice and Fern were gone."

"What kind of evidence?"

"It proves some of the crew have criminal records and this ship is packing more guns than an NRA convention," I said. "Criminal records and printouts of dark net transactions. And I think the father and captain are running a gun smuggling operation."

"Are you kidding me?" Kate said.

"The captain and father have to be part of it," I continued. "If the harbormaster discovered the guns, it may have been why he was killed."

"But how does Jeremy fit into all this?"

"No idea. We all know it doesn't seem likely he overpowered Brody, but Brody is dead and Jeremy is gone. And now Leatrice and Fern are missing. I don't know what to think anymore, but some of the crew must be in on it."

The captain stepped out of the open doorway in the corner. "Would you mind joining us on the bridge, ladies?"

Why hadn't it occurred to me that if the bridge was right behind this room, then so was the captain?

CHAPTER 46

As the captain stepped into the room, I made a mental note of his broad shoulders and muscled arms. This was not someone I would want to meet in a dark alley.

"I didn't know you were there."

"I'm sure he knows that," Kate said under her breath. "Otherwise you wouldn't have been talking sh—Ouch!"

I pinched her leg under the table to shut her up.

"Let's go, ladies." The captain jerked a hand toward the doorway. "You can come with me willingly or I can drag you."

"Sweet-talker," Kate mumbled as she moved forward.

I hesitated. I knew there were two entrances to the bridge. One led to the casual dining room we were in, and one led to the other side of the main salon. The bridge itself was a half moon shape curved across the front of the deck and was filled with sophisticated computers used for tracking weather and navigating. It was removed from the rest of the ship to give privacy, and I knew very well no one would hear us or know to look for us on the bridge since it was tucked away.

"Please." The captain lifted me up by one arm. "I insist."

"Okay," I said, as my feet left the ground. I hoped Kate would make a run for it, but the captain grabbed her by the arm and pushed both of us up the short flight of stairs to the bridge.

Glass ran floor to ceiling across three sides of the bridge so we could see the rain continuing to lash against the boat. The intensity of the storm made it impossible to see more than a few feet past the glass. I recognized the first mate in his white uniform sitting at a terminal and another posted by the opposite door. So much for escaping out the other exit.

"How can we help you?" I asked once the captain had released us.

"You can give me back the stolen paperwork, for one." He crossed to the far end of the room.

"We didn't steal it," Kate said. "Mandy took it and gave it to Annabelle. So it really isn't our fault."

I glared at her. So much for deniability. "Thanks, Kate."

"Mandy didn't take them." The captain chuckled. "Caren did. I sent Mandy to get them back."

Wait, what? Kate and I exchanged a look. Mandy wasn't one of the good guys? Then why had she told me so much about her cohorts? I wondered if maybe she'd switched sides without the captain knowing.

"Well, it doesn't matter who took them. I don't have them anymore," I said.

"That's a problem." The captain paced in front of us, the soaked hem of his pants legs flapping against his leg. "It's also a problem you saw the documents."

Kate waved her hand. "To be clear, I didn't see them. I'm just going off what Annabelle told me."

The captain stopped in front of me. "How many other people have you told?"

I looked into his dark, hard eyes and stopped breathing for a moment as the gravity of the situation hit home. He and at least part of the crew were in on the plan, whatever it was. That included Mandy, who up until a few minutes ago was our only ally on the ship. I had a growing feeling he wouldn't let anyone leave the ship who knew the truth and could disrupt their scheme. Suddenly, I wondered if Caren's death really was accidental. I felt dizzy at the thought.

"Well, Daniel Reese knows," Kate said.

"The head of that security team?" The captain turned to the first mate at the console. "Go find him, and bring him here."

The man left the room. I would have kicked Kate, but I still felt light headed and didn't want to fall over in the process.

She winked at me. "I got your blackjack."

"No, you don't," I said, feeling my dizziness passing and my composure crumbling. "And it's 'I got your back, Jack,' not 'blackjack.'"

"That's what I said."

The captain cleared his throat to get our attention. I ignored him.

"No." I pointed a finger at her. "You said blackjack, like the casino game."

"So?" She shrugged. "What did you say?"

"That's it." I threw my arms up in the air. Out of the corner of my eye I saw two more crew in white uniforms come onto the bridge, but I didn't care. The wedding stress coupled with the dead bodies topped with my nutty associates had finally done it to me. I was losing my wedding planner cool. I pulled my hair out of its bun and shook it out around my shoulders. "I've had it. I can't do this one more second. I quit. I'm leaving."

Kate gaped at me as I started striding toward the stairs.

"I don't think so." The captain opened a nearby drawer and pulled out a gun.

That stopped me. Before I could process being held at gunpoint, Kate yelped and I turned to her. Something flew from her head to mine, and I couldn't stop myself from shrieking and swatting at it. What was happening? Did the ship have rats capable of flight? The creature leapt from my head onto the captain's, and he dropped the gun as he beat himself about the face.

"What the . . . ?" he yelled as tiny feet skittered around his hair and slipped down his forehead.

I was finally able to focus enough to see the flying rat was actually Jim's flying squirrel, Rocky. I felt a moment of satisfaction I'd found him before I registered Kate's voice screaming at me.

"Grab the gun, Annabelle!"

I scanned the floor and saw where the gun had landed. By then, the captain had dislodged Rocky, who'd jumped onto Kate's arm and scampered up to perch on her shoulder. I dropped to my hands and knees and fumbled for the gun as the captain kicked at my hands. He managed to kick the gun out of my reach and bent down to retrieve it while I nursed my bruised fingers.

"Not so fast, punk," said a voice from the far door.

"Drop it or we'll pump you so full of lead you'll look like a piece of Battenberg lace."

Now that wasn't something you heard every day. I turned around to look at the crew members in white uniforms with semiautomatic weapons trained on the captain. He left the gun on the floor as he straightened up, his hands in the air.

My mouth dropped open. "Leatrice? Fern?"

CHAPTER 47

"What are you doing here?" I ran over to Leatrice and Fern, making sure to keep out of the path of any potential gunfire. "And where did you find uniforms?"

"'Where did you find one small enough?' is a better question." Kate followed behind me, Rocky still balanced on her shoulder, eyeing Leatrice's pint-sized white uniform with *Mystic Maven* embroidered on the chest.

Leatrice smiled without taking her eyes off the captain, who had scratches on his forehead beginning to bleed. "Fern hemmed mine with fashion tape."

Fern shrugged. "I had some left over from my towel ensemble."

"Did you raid my emergency kit?" I asked. I'd left the boxy metal kit in the bride's room with strict instructions not to let the bridesmaids tear into it.

Fern squeezed my hand. "Sweetie, if there's ever been a real wedding emergency, this is it."

"Fair enough." I made a mental note to buy more fashion tape before our next wedding.

A crack of lightning lit up the sky and the bridge, reminding me of an old-fashioned camera flash. I jumped and clutched Fern as a boom of thunder followed. Only when I saw my hand resting on Fern's arm did I realize my hands were shaking. I forced myself to take a slow breath to steady my racing heart.

"Once we took out Mandy, we searched for another room where we could hide and found a storeroom with extra uniforms," Leatrice said. "Then I remembered where I saw all those crates of machine guns, so we decided to arm ourselves and get a confession out of the crew."

The captain took a step and Leatrice jabbed her gun in his direction. "Not another inch, buster, or we'll let the rat have another go at you." The captain's eyes darted to Rocky, then his hand went to his bloody forehead.

Since when had Leatrice morphed into Dirty Harry?

"Just FYI, it's not a rat," I whispered to her. "It's a flying squirrel."

"Really, dear?" she whispered back. "But don't you think it sounds better to tell him it's a flying attack rat?"

Fair enough. "Go back a second," I said. "How did you know about Mandy?"

"Ask the captain." Leatrice jerked the end of her gun toward the man, who stood glaring at us with his hands halfway up. "They were all in it together."

The captain pressed his lips together, and I doubted we were going to get any confessions out of him.

"But how did you know?" I asked.

"Easy." Fern hoisted his semi-automatic rifle a bit higher. "When you left to get security, Mandy panicked and tried to sweet-talk the papers out of us. She said she'd hide them for us."

"Because she wasn't the one who took them off the ship," I said.

"Very good, Annabelle." Fern gave me a wink. "It was one of the girls who works under her. Caren, right? Leatrice realized it once she got a good look at Mandy in the light, didn't you, dear?"

Leatrice hitched her pants up on one side. "I knew I recognized her, but it was from her coming by the building looking for you and trying to get in your apartment. She wasn't the one who dropped off the envelope, though in the uniforms and with their hair pulled back, they looked similar."

"The captain here told us Mandy left the ship because she was out trying to track down the girl and the missing papers." I thought about the young crew member who'd been killed running in front of a car not too far from my apartment in Georgetown. It wasn't difficult to imagine why she'd been chased into oncoming traffic now that I knew she'd been the one to steal the evidence. "And she told you all of this?"

"She thought she had us cornered, so she got chatty." Fern nudged Leatrice. "The old girl has a real talent for getting people to spill their guts."

Leatrice giggled. "Once she got to talking she didn't want to stop. She bragged about how smart she was to put two and two together and figure out Caren had taken the papers to you. She figured out where the girl had been coming from since the evidence wasn't on her when she was hit by the car."

Fern wrinkled his nose. "All that bragging was not the prettiest look on her."

Leatrice frowned. "I should have known something was up when she stopped by and asked me to let her wait in your apartment for you. Of course, I respected your privacy and told her no."

"Of course." I guessed there was a first time for everything. "So how did you turn the tables on her? When Daniel and I found her, she was out cold."

Leatrice grinned. "When Fern dropped his towels, I hit Mandy with the paperweight from the desk."

I felt like smacking myself on the head. The *Mystic Maven* crystal paperweight. Every desk on the ship had one, and they were heavy enough to stay put in rough weather or do some damage to someone's head. I should have noticed the one from Mandy's desk was missing.

"You dropped your towels?" Kate nodded her approval to Fern as Rocky walked back and forth across her shoulders. "Nice one."

"What can I say?" Fern wiggled his eyebrows up and down. "I'm full of impressive surprises."

"Did she mention Jeremy Johns being involved?" I asked.

The captain gave a derisive laugh. "The only crime he's capable of is stealing your payments."

"I beg your pardon?" Kate said.

"I gave the designer the money for everyone's wedding payment balances, and now he's done a runner."

I felt my stomach drop. "What do you mean everyone?"

The captain grinned. "All of you. Everyone on board who was hired for the wedding. Seems like a bit of poetic justice to me."

Kate gasped and staggered a few feet to lean against the console. "But that's hundreds of thousands of dollars we're supposed to distribute."

"After years avoiding government entanglement, Mr. Barbery only deals in cash so it can't be traced," the captain said.

"That's why Jeremy ran." I rubbed my temples as the realization we weren't going to be paid sank in. "Not because he was afraid of having the fire pinned on him."

"The fire?" The captain shook his head. "Jeremy didn't have anything to do with the fire."

"But I saw him with lighter fluid in Mandy's . . ." I smacked myself on the forehead with my free hand. "That was Mandy's lighter fluid, wasn't it? And she was able to call in the fire before it spread because she was the one who started it."

The captain shrugged. "We didn't want to seriously damage the ship. Just get everyone off it. If Mandy were smart, she wouldn't have left the evidence sitting around for nosy Jeremy to find. That man has been a thorn in our side since he arrived."

"Tell us about it," Kate said.

"It seems he was as suspicious as you were about the accidents," the captain said. "And neither of you could keep from poking into things that didn't concern you."

I brushed off the unpleasant comparison to the loathsome designer as I envisioned Jeremy fleeing with our money. Then I felt sick. All our work and all the stress of the past week had been for nothing. I hoped for Jeremy's sake he'd run far away because if I ever found him, I would kill him myself.

"What's going on here?" Mrs. Barbery stormed onto the bridge in her ivory sequined gown with the first mate close on her heels.

For the first time since I'd met her, I felt a bit of relief at seeing Mrs. Barbery. "We discovered that some of your crew, including the captain, are involved in gun smuggling."

"What?" She spun on the captain. "Isn't this exactly what I didn't want to happen? I told you not to let things get out of hand, didn't I?"

I exchanged a confused look with Kate then gaped at the stepmother. "You knew?"

Mrs. Barbery flicked a hand in my direction. "When you're the third wife and you signed an airtight prenup, you need to get creative. Luckily, Captain Hammer was amenable to my ideas for alternative revenue streams since he'd been working for my husband for years but never gotten part of the bounty. His bitterness was my gain."

"So Mr. Barbery isn't involved? It's you?"

The stepmother tossed her red curls off her shoulder. "Surprised I'm more than just a pretty face?"

Kate pumped her fist. "I knew the dad was too nice to be involved."

I shook my head. "And Brody? I thought he was too hot to be a bad guy?"

"We don't know he was involved," Kate said. "He could have been killed because he was trying to expose the crime ring."

Mrs. Barbery's face went white. "Did you say Brody was killed?"

I swallowed hard. She hadn't known her son was dead. At least not until Kate had spilled the beans. "Someone hit him on the head and left him in the steam room."

Mrs. Barbery's face regained its color then reddened, and she slapped her beaded clutch against her leg as she advanced on the captain. "Did you do this?"

He shook his head.

I looked down at the captain's wet pants legs. "Then why is the hem of your pants wet?" I pointed to the still-damp bottom few inches of his pants. "His pants legs are wet even though nothing else is, which means he hasn't been outside in the rain, but probably splashed around on a wet floor."

Fern snapped his fingers. "Like the steam room."

"Exactly," I said, staring straight at the captain. "Brody must have decided to double-cross you, or maybe he got cold feet. Either way, you hit him over the head hard enough to kill him and shoved him in the steam room."

"Brody was never a part of this." Mrs. Barbery's voice cracked.

The captain looked fearful as the stepmother advanced on him. "You know he had a soft spot for Kristie. He got too suspicious. He wouldn't look the other way."

"I'm guessing you had to do whatever it took to make sure she didn't honeymoon on board this ship because that would mean that she would see whatever gun delivery you had planned," I said. "That's what all the accidents and fire were about, right? Scaring her off? But it wasn't working and Brody figured out what was going on. He was afraid you'd hurt her. After all, the harbormaster had been killed."

Mrs. Barbery stood inches away from the captain. "Did you kill my son?"

"I'm sure forensics will find evidence to link him to the

murder," I said. "Like traces of eucalyptus in the water on his pants that could only come from the steam room?"

"It was an accident. If he'd just kept his mouth shut everything would have been fine. I told him we'd cut him in." He looked over Mrs. Barbery's head, and his eyes flashed anger. I felt glad to have the guns and attack squirrel on our side.

Mrs. Barbery pulled a revolver out of her beaded clutch and let the bag drop to the floor. Before I could say a word, she fired straight at the captain's chest and he staggered backward, falling onto one of the computer consoles. She took a step closer and fired again as he sagged to the floor like a puppet with no strings. The first mate lunged for her gun and she spun around, firing off a round that caught him in the shoulder. He flew back to the floor and lay still.

All movement on the bridge stopped as Mrs. Barbery released the gun from her hand and it bounced on the carpet. She wiped her hands on the front of her gown and pulled herself up to her full height. "I believe I'd like to go see my son."

"Should someone go after her?" Kate asked after Mrs. Barbery had walked off the bridge.

"Let's leave that to the cops," I said, a wave of exhaustion course through me.

I noticed a flash of blue lights in the distance. Detective Reese and the paramedics must have arrived. I knew it was a long walk from the parking lot to the end of the dock where *Mystic Maven* was tied up, and I hoped the boat hadn't risen so high it was impossible to climb up the metal ramps to reach the ship.

Suddenly, I remembered the kitchen tent on the dock. Richard! He was still in the catering kitchen, and I'd promised to come get him once I'd told Daniel. I could only pray the police didn't make him their first stop on the way to the ship. If he got taken in for questioning in a shower cap, he'd never forgive me.

CHAPTER 48

"Up here." I waved my arms at the top of the metal ramp leading down to the dock. I could make out the faint shapes of men in dark rain coats blending with the night as they approached the dock and the catering tent. I assumed they were cops. They passed the tent and followed my voice to the ramp. Richard owed me one.

"Be careful. It's slick," I yelled over the pouring rain and rumbling thunder. I cast my eyes to the sky, and could see nothing but torrents of water through the blackness. There seemed to be no end in sight to this storm.

I watched the men clutch the thin ropes on either side of the ramp for balance as they climbed up the ramp. I held out my hand as the first man reached the top. He stepped on board and pulled off his hood. It was Detective Reese.

"I'm surprised you've only had one fatality so far if people have been using that thing," he said, breathing heavily. He held out an arm and hoisted up the man behind him.

"About that one fatality," I said.

He looked me up and down and then shook his head. "How is it you always manage to make wedding planning so deadly?"

I gestured to the storm. "Are you saying this is my fault?"

"Not the rain," he said. "That's an added bonus this time."

I led the way through the glass door to the casual dining room where trays still covered most surfaces. "But the homicidal maniacs?"

"Have you ever considered revisiting the way you select your clients?" He ran a hand through his dark hair, sending a few drops of rain onto the floor.

"They're weddings. If I eliminated everyone who was emotionally imbalanced or homicidal, I wouldn't have any clients."

The corner of his mouth turned up in a smile. I couldn't help but notice the hazel of his eyes deepening into green. I knew he enjoyed provoking me, and I fought the urge to stick my tongue out at him. "Why don't I take you to one of this wedding's homicidal maniacs?"

He swept a hand in front of me. "Lead the way."

We walked up the few stairs to the bridge. Reese did a noticeable double take once we were on the bridge.

Leatrice and Fern stood to the far side of the room holding their guns trained on Mrs. Barbery. She sat facing away from us in one of the console chairs with her arms tied behind her back. Even though the lighting was dim, it looked like she was tied up with control-top pantyhose. Kate stood near the first mate holding a gun with both hands and Rocky balanced on her shoulder. The captain's body lay crumpled on the floor, blood seeping onto the carpet. One of Daniel's security officers sat next to the first mate, applying pressure to his shoulder with a cloth while another black-clad officer stood guard over the stepmother.

Reese looked at me. "I don't even know where to begin."

I summed up what we knew for sure and what we'd guessed while the captain was zipped into a body bag and taken out and the first mate was loaded onto a stretcher by the paramedics. "Your brother apprehended Mrs. Barbery when she went down to see her son's body but he brought her up here so he could preserve the other crime scene. Leatrice tied her up. And one of Daniel's guards is with Mandy."

Reese looked up from the notepad where he was writing down what I was saying. "And she's the one Leatrice hit with the paperweight?"

"That's right," Leatrice said. "I hope she's all right, though. Aside from being a smuggler with a criminal record, she seemed like a nice girl."

"And what happened to the evidence she was after?" Reese asked.

I turned to Leatrice and Fern as I realized that I'd completely forgotten about the envelope I'd been so concerned with them guarding. "Did you hide it somewhere?"

Leatrice reached one hand into the front of her uniform and produced the manila envelope. "I didn't think anyone would look for it there."

Fern smoothed his hands down his chest. "I would have hidden it but the extra padding made my waist look too thick."

Reese accepted the envelope with a grin, then began giving orders for his men to question the crew and escort guests off the ship.

"Can you run down and tell Richard what's going on?" I asked Fern once Reese was busy with his men. "I don't want him to start sending up dessert and late-night bites, although I could go for some mini Swiss burgers and sweet potato fries right about now."

Fern nodded but shook a finger at me. "A moment on the lips, Annabelle."

"And whatever you do, don't tell him about Jeremy John getting away with all of our payments," I added as he headed for the door. "We'll tell him later, when he's far away from knives."

"What's that?" Reese asked.

"Do you remember that designer we all despised? Well, he managed to steal all the cash that was meant to pay the wedding vendors and disappear."

"So you won't get paid for all your work?"

"None of us will." I took a breath and tried to shake it off. "So, did the paramedics already take Mandy away?"

He punched in a number on his cell phone. "Let me ask my brother."

I hadn't seen Daniel Reese since I'd left him down below with an injured Mandy. Then it struck me he didn't know Mandy was involved in the crimes. I hadn't found out until Leatrice told me on the bridge, so as far as Daniel knew, Mandy was another victim.

Daniel clicked off his phone. "She's on her way to the hospital. She regained consciousness and Daniel says she'll be fine."

"You may want to let the hospital know she's a suspect," I said.

"I'm sure Daniel sent a cop with her."

I cringed. "Not if he didn't know Mandy was one of the bad guys."

Reese groaned.

"I'm sorry," I said. "There was a lot going on. I was held at gunpoint, attacked by a flying squirrel, and saved by Leatrice and Fern, who were armed with semi-automatic weapons. It's been a busy night."

"Okay, okay." The detective held up a hand and got on his phone to his brother again. "I need you to send one of your guys to the hospital to keep an eye on Mandy. Our vic is now a suspect. I'll explain later."

Leatrice gave my hand a squeeze. "I'm sure it will be fine, dear. I gave her quite a wallop on the head. I doubt she'll be running off anytime soon."

"What happened to that paperweight anyway?" I asked.

Leatrice tapped her chin. "I left it in the storeroom when we changed. Do you think they'll let me keep it as a souvenir?" She lowered her voice. "I'm definitely keeping the uniform."

Fabulous, I thought. I'd have a walking reminder of the most disastrous wedding in history.

I heard raised voices from outside the bridge. Who was making so much noise? I hurried down the stairs to the dining area where a pair of Daniel's security officers were holding Mr. Barbery.

"I want to see my wife." He strained against their grasp. "This has to be a mistake."

Kate ran in the room from the salon on the other side and as the door swung shut behind her, I saw Kristie in her white wedding gown sobbing against her husband's shoulder. I felt a sob catch in my own throat.

"Mr. Barbery." I walked over to him and put a hand on his arm. "I'm so sorry."

I'd never meant the words more in my life. I was sorry that I'd suspected him, sorry that I hadn't suspected the captain or how desperate he was, and desperately sorry that Brody had been killed. I felt tears burn my eyes and I blinked them back.

He met my eyes and his face went slack. "So it's true? About Brody? My wife? Captain Hammer? All of it?"

I nodded, unable to speak as I watched his face crumple. The security guards loosened their grip as his shoulders sagged and all the fight went out of him. Kate put an arm around his shoulders and led him to sit at the banquette where he put his head in his hands and quietly sobbed. I turned away so I wouldn't start crying myself.

Kate slipped her hand into mine and squeezed it. "Let's go home."

CHAPTER 49

"It feels good to get out of those wet clothes." Kate padded down the hall of my apartment wearing my white terry cloth bathrobe with the Willard Hotel insignia on the front. "I thought I was so soaked I'd never dry out."

"It would take more than a change of clothes to dry that one out," Richard said under his breath as he reclined on my sofa, still wearing his Prada suit sans the jacket, which hung on a hook by my front door. Once he'd removed the garbage bags, duct tape, and shower cap, he'd been completely unscathed by the rain. I, however, had looked as if I'd been swimming in my clothes. I didn't know if my favorite black pantsuit would ever fully recover.

"I heard that," Kate said, as she ducked into my kitchen and opened the refrigerator.

"I may not have anything in there," I said. I sat cross-legged on the couch beside Richard, wearing a pair of black yoga pants and a white Wedding Belles T-shirt. I'd toweled off my hair, but drops of water still snaked down my back. Getting off the ship had improved my mood, but I still felt an ache in my chest.

Richard tilted his head at me "May not? When have you ever had anything edible in there?"

I made a face at him, feeling some comfort in the familiar patter. "When you've cooked for me."

"I'd be happy to cook for you if I could afford the supplies." Richard had not taken the news of nonpayment well, and I expected to hear about it for years to come.

Leatrice sat in the overstuffed chair across from the couch, still wearing the *Mystic Maven* uniform. She'd walked off the ship in it and either the police didn't know she wasn't actually part of the crew or didn't care. Either way, I knew I'd be seeing a lot of that uniform in the future.

"At least we all got deposits." Kate emerged from the kitchen with a box of Wheat Thins and a mostly intact rectangle of precut cheddar cheese and set them down on the coffee table.

Richard spluttered for a moment before going red in the face and throwing his arms in the air.

"Allow me to translate," I said. "What I think Richard means is, the deposits weren't big enough to make up for all our effort."

"Do you think there's any chance of tracking down Jeremy Johns?" Kate asked, perched on the arm of my sofa with her legs crossed.

Fern came out of the kitchen holding the unfinished bottle of Champagne from the other night. "That boy is long gone."

"That's probably flat," I said. I'd put a stopper in it, but I knew from experience Champagne didn't keep well.

Fern poured a bit into a glass and swigged it. "Very flat. Who else wants some?"

"Well, I want to eat and go to sleep," I said. "And forget this wedding day ever happened."

"It wasn't a total loss," Kate said. "We did get the bride and groom married. Isn't that what you say always matters in the end?"

I supposed Kate was right or, to be more accurate, I was right.

We'd managed to get Kristie down the aisle and she'd had her first dance before the police swarmed the boat. And we'd sent the couple off to a suite at the Mandarin Hotel before they could see the stepbrother's body being taken off the ship. So maybe a partial victory, although it didn't feel like one.

Leatrice jumped at the sound of a knock on the door.

"We're saved," Fern said. "It must be the Thai food we ordered."

Kate got up from her perch on the arm of the couch and opened the door.

"Even better," Fern said when Detective Reese stepped inside.

"I thought I might find you all here," he said. Drops of rain clung to his long, black rain coat, but his hair was dry and I noticed an open umbrella resting in the hallway outside my door.

"Can we offer you some cheese?" Fern made a sweeping gesture toward the sliced cheddar. "Or flat Champagne?"

Reese grinned as he shook his head. "No thanks. I just came by to update you all on the case."

I stood up and walked over to him. "Did Mrs. Barbery confess?"

"She's not talking, but we're pretty sure the captain killed her son. He had blood spatter on his wrist and the inside of his sleeve from bashing the guy over the head. We're running tests on the gun that you left in the safe but it looks like any prints were wiped clean. What I want to know is why the gun wasn't tossed overboard?"

"I thought the same thing," I said. "I think Mr. Barbery was being set up to take the fall. Maybe by the captain. Maybe by his wife. They must have put the gun in there planning to reveal it to the cops if they needed to. Mandy told me she saw the harbor-master in his office, and I'd be willing to bet more of the crew would have come forward as witnesses. Anything Mandy told me was misinformation meant to send me down the wrong path so it makes sense that she told me about Mr. Barbery and the harbor-master to plant the seed of suspicion."

Kate made a tsking noise. "Talk about someone who's having a bad day. Stepson murdered. Wife running an international smuggling ring out of your yacht. And on top of all that, he almost gets framed for murder. Usually the worst thing that happens to the dad is having to write all the checks."

"Do not mention checks." Richard flopped his head back on the couch and draped an arm over his eyes.

Reese raised an eyebrow.

"He's pretty upset that Jeremy Johns ran off with all the cash payments for the wedding," I whispered.

Reese dropped his voice to match mine. "No word on Jeremy. But we did arrest Mandy as she was trying to sneak out of the hospital."

"So she recovered?" Leatrice leaned forward, her superhuman hearing clearly intact. "Because I hit her pretty hard. I even had to stand up on the desk chair to do it."

"She recovered enough to be hanging halfway out of a hospital window," Reese said. "Pretty impressive if she had a concussion."

"It's my fault she wasn't arrested on the ship," I said. "I forgot to tell your brother she was a suspect."

He put a hand on my bare arm, and I was aware of the heat of his skin against mine. "Don't beat yourself up too much. Despite what you might think of your investigating skills, you aren't a trained detective. Anyway, we got her."

"I know, but . . ."

He squeezed my arm. "Be glad you didn't get shot," he whispered as he motioned to Fern and Leatrice. "With those two armed with semi-automatic weapons, we're lucky there weren't more fatalities."

I couldn't help smiling. "Thanks." He was right. I should be grateful my friends were all safe, and we'd survived another wedding. Even if we hadn't gotten our final payment, the reception had been shut down, and two people had left in body bags.

"There is one thing I need to give you. It's from Mr. Barbery."

"The bride's father gave you something for me?" I asked.

The corner of his mouth turned up into a smile. "I might have mentioned what happened with Jeremy Johns and all the payments."

Kate sat forward. "When did you mention this?"

"While I was getting his statement." Reese pulled a fat envelope out of his blazer pocket. "He felt pretty bad about it and thought he should make up for it after all you did trying to save his daughter's wedding."

I took the envelope and felt the heaviness in my hand. "Is this what I think it is?"

Reese grinned. "It should all be there."

The room fell silent while I opened the envelope and flipped through the thick stack of hundred dollar bills. I felt tears sting the back of my eyes as I held up the money for everyone to see. "We got paid after all."

Richard leapt to his feet and rushed over to Reese, pushing me aside and throwing his arms around the detective. "You saved us!"

"Out of my way." Fern pushed Richard aside and planted a loud kiss on both of Reese's cheeks, then winked at me. "I've always wanted to do that."

Reese blinked, seemingly too stunned to speak. Kate made a move toward him but I knocked her back onto the couch.

"Can we please not terrify the poor man after what he just did for us?" I handed the cash to Kate. "Why don't you start counting it out?"

Reese cleared his throat. "I'd better go. I still have a pile of paperwork to fill out from tonight."

He gestured for me to follow him outside to the hallway. I pulled the door closed, even though I knew everyone inside my apartment probably had their ears pressed to the door within seconds of my shutting it.

"You'll have to forgive my friends," I said. "They really are very grateful."

"I could tell," Reese said. "Now about our date that got interrupted."

"I know, I know. I'm sorry. This wedding made me so crazy–"

Reese put a finger to my lips to stop me. "Don't apologize. I get it. It's your job. I have a demanding job, too, remember?" He wrapped an arm around my waist and leaned in close. "But I did have an idea about how we could make up for lost time."

My throat felt too dry to speak so I just nodded as his lips met mine, sending ripples of pleasure down my spine and making my knees go weak. He pulled me closer and kissed me deeper, and I forgot all about my friends whispering on the other side of the door, the dead bodies, and Jeremy Johns getting away with a pile of cash. For one brief moment, everything felt right.

THE END

FREE DOWNLOAD!

A GLAMOROUS BRIDAL SHOW.
A CLEVER JEWELRY HEIST.

CAN ANNABELLE TRACK DOWN THE BAUBLES AND NAB A BURGLAR?

amazon kindle

nook

kobo

iBooks

Get your free copy of the novella "Dead Ringer" when you sign up to the author's mailing list.

Get started here:

deadringer.lauradurham.com

For a preview of the next Annabelle Archer book, turn the page!

PREVIEW OF "NIGHT OF THE LIVING WED"—ANNABELLE ARCHER BOOK #6

Chapter One

"I can't believe we're finally going to a hotel where we don't have a wedding." I rolled down my car window, sweeping my auburn hair up into a ponytail so it wouldn't blow in my face. I breathed in the cool mountain air, pausing at an empty intersection before making a left to follow the sign to the Omni Bedford Springs Resort. Even if the lack of traffic hadn't been a tip-off, the heady scent of pine trees and the cacophony of birds and croaking frogs would have told me we weren't in DC anymore.

My assistant, Kate, leaned her blond head back on the passenger headrest with her legs stretched in front of her, barely covered by her short wool kilt. Despite the cloud cover, she wore oversized sunglasses, and I suspected her eyes were closed behind them. "I can't believe we finally have a weekend off."

"You know, most couples don't pick Halloween weekend unless they're the kind of people who like costume weddings or orange flowers." I took a sip from the Venti Mocha Frappuccino

I'd gotten at a Starbucks a hundred miles ago and sucked up mostly whipped cream that had melted in the bottom of the plastic cup.

For us, the wedding season stretched from April until mid-November, but we rarely had Halloween weddings. Not that we wouldn't take them. As the owner of Wedding Belles, one of DC's top wedding planning companies, I'd made it company policy not to take weddings over Thanksgiving or Christmas or on Easter Sunday, but all other holidays were fair game.

"Well, I can't believe we took your car, Annabelle," Richard said from the back seat. "Your Volvo sedan isn't exactly my idea of arriving in style."

I glanced in my rearview mirror to see the owner of Richard Gerard Catering and my best friend for the past six years with his arms crossed and his short dark hair sculpted into perfect spikes. "Do I need to remind you that we don't all fit in your Mercedes convertible?"

"I don't mind riding in a mom car." Fern popped his head in the space between the two front seats, his brown hair drawn back into a tight man bun. "More room for my bags."

As Washington's wedding hair guru, Fern never went anywhere without plenty of designer hair products and styling tools.

"Speaking of bags." Richard pushed the Louis Vuitton duffel bag next to him closer to Fern. "What is in all of them? You know we're only going for the weekend, right?"

"None of you packed light," I said, remembering that we'd barely been able to close my trunk due to the number of bags Kate, Richard, and Fern had brought. Hence the duffel bag in the back seat.

"I even had to put Hermès on the floor," Richard said, motioning to the black leather cross-body bag he usually wore.

"To be clear, the bag is on the floor," I said. "Not the dog."

The brown-and-black Yorkie nudged Fern's head out of the way and hopped to the front seat, his tiny pink tongue hanging out of his mouth as he sniffed the air. Technically, the dog belonged to Richard's partner and was named Butterscotch, but Richard had taken to bringing the pint-sized pup everywhere and calling him Hermès. Richard believed everything he owned should be designer.

"Small consolation," Richard said.

Even though the Pennsylvania resort was only three hours from Washington, the unhurried roads and rolling hills felt like they were a universe away from the hustle and bustle of the capitol city. Since we'd exited the highway, the sounds of passing cars had given way to the quiet of the rural area, and we could now drink in the crisp air without also sucking down exhaust fumes. I closed my eyes for a moment to enjoy the cool wind on my face.

"There it is," Kate said, snapping me out of my momentary bliss.

As the car drove around a bend, the resort came into view. Stretched out across an expanse of green lawn, the three-level building dotted with peaked roofs was dominated by the white wraparound porch on each floor that ran the length of the resort. The center section of the hotel—red brick fronted with a series of tall, white columns—boasted a covered portico jutting out from the building. Rocking chairs lined the porches and overlooked a manicured garden across from the main entrance. The resort looked so tranquil and idyllic, I felt my breath begin to slow in response.

"How do Debbie and Darla know about this place again?" Kate slipped her sunglasses down her nose to get a better look.

Debbie and Darla were the mother-daughter duo who had given us the weekend away as a thank you for all the hard work we'd done for Darla's blowout wedding to Turner Grant the

Third. Usually our tips came in the form of cash or gift cards, but Debbie and Darla wanted to send their wedding team to their favorite weekend getaway resort. Considering the fact that we'd planned the wedding for nearly two years, we graciously accepted. Due to everyone's packed schedules since their wedding, we'd only now been able to coordinate a weekend we were all available.

"They come here all the time," I said as I pulled the car up under the covered portico. "Debbie raves about the spa."

"Don't you mean bar?" Richard said. "We never saw them sober."

"You don't think they'll be here this weekend, do you?" Kate's eyes darted around like she expected them to pop out of the nearby bushes and surprise us.

"I doubt it," I said.

"That wouldn't be so bad," Fern said. "They were entertaining."

Richard opened his car door. "Because they were always drunk."

"Their wedding was fun." Fern unfolded himself from the car and stretched. "Although the suit I wore still smells like bourbon."

No surprise, since we'd had two bourbon bars and passed mint juleps at the reception.

"That seersucker suit?" Richard rolled his eyes. "Is that a great loss?"

Fern sucked in his breath. "I was dressing to the occasion. And that wedding was Southern through and through."

Fern took great pains to dress to the theme of the wedding, which had resulted in him doing wedding hair in everything from an Indian sari to a Japanese kimono to a hula skirt.

"I suppose we should be happy he didn't dress in an antebellum gown with a hoop skirt," Kate said to me under her breath.

I opened my car door and stepped out, glad to stretch my legs. Hermès jumped out behind me and began inspecting a nearby shrub.

A valet rushed up to me. "Checking in? Name?"

I nodded, handing him my keys. "Annabelle Archer."

I reached inside the car to pop the truck and straightened as I heard the roar of motorcycles behind me. A pair of black Harleys pulled up behind us and two immense leather-clad men stepped off them, removing their helmets and revealing bald heads, goatees, and multiple piercings.

"Will you look at this place?" Mack, the Harley rider with the red goatee, leaned back to look up at the resort.

"It was almost worth all those hours of floral meetings with Debbie and Darla to get a payoff like this," Buster said in his deep, booming voice, running a hand down his dark goatee.

Buster and Mack were the owners of Lush and our favorite floral design team. They were also members of a Christian biker gang and didn't abide cursing. I'd often thought it was a good thing their paths didn't cross often with Fern's on a wedding day, since he had a habit of calling the bridesmaids all sorts of colorful names.

I grabbed my purse from the floor of the passenger's seat. "Should we check in?"

Richard slung his black messenger bag across his chest, scooping up Hermès and dropping him inside. "Let's go."

"There's a cocktail with my name on it," Kate said as she took long strides toward the front door.

Fern hitched his Louis Vuitton duffel onto his shoulder, glass clinking from the travel-sized bottles of booze he told us he'd packed in case the bars closed early or the minibar didn't have his brands. "I'm right behind you, sister."

I followed Kate through the black double doors to the lobby. High ceilings gave the space an airy feel with hardwood floors and classic upholstered furniture gathered around multiple crackling fireplaces. I inhaled the scent of the burning logs mixed with the lush fresh flowers displayed on a nearby mahogany side table.

"You made it!" A tall, good-looking man with slightly receding close-cropped brown hair rushed over to us, and I recognized him right away as the Bedford Springs director of catering I'd gotten to know at a party at the Washington Omni a few months prior. We'd hit it off as friends—connecting over our shared love of fountain soda and '80s music—and had kept in touch over email since then. He'd even come down to DC for another weekend, and we'd met up for drinks and wedding war stories. I'd been excited to tell him that I was coming to his resort for the weekend, and he'd been equally excited to host us, and I knew he'd scheduled a few activities for us so he could show off the hotel.

"Hi, Stuart," I said, returning his air kiss. "Kate, you remember . . ."

"Of course I do." Kate gave him a kiss on the cheek that was more lips than air.

Why did I think Kate would ever forget an attractive man? I made introductions all around as Kate kept a firm grip on Stuart's arm.

"I tried to put all your rooms together," Stuart said as he walked us toward the registration desk at the far end of the lobby. "But that meant I had to put you on the second floor."

"That's fine," I said.

Stuart let out a breath. "Oh, good. I'm glad you don't mind."

"Why would we mind?" Richard asked.

"Some people are funny about staying near the haunted section."

Kate's hand dropped from Stuart's arm. "Excuse me?"

Hermès yipped, and Richard gave him a pat on the head. "Are any of the ghosts brides?"

The catering director cocked his head. "I beg your pardon?"

Fern nudged him. "You know. Ghosts wandering the halls in wedding gowns? Jilted brides who killed themselves in despair? That kind of thing."

"Not that I know of." Stuart's expression told me that my group was not exactly what he'd expected.

Kate linked her arm through his and fluttered her eyelashes at him. "Then bring on the ghosts."

***

To continue reading, turn the page and order *Night of the Living Wed.*

ALSO BY LAURA DURHAM

Better Off Wed

For Better or Hearse

Dead Ringer

Review To A Kill

Death on the Aisle

Night of the Living Wed

Eat, Prey, Love

Groomed for Murder

Wed or Alive

To Love and To Perish

To get notices whenever I release a new book, follow me on BookBub:

https://www.bookbub.com/profile/laura-durham

Did you enjoy this book? You can make a big difference!

I'm very lucky to have a loyal bunch of readers, and honest reviews are the best way to help bring my books to the attention of new readers.

If you enjoyed *Death on the Aisle,* I would be very grateful if you could spend just five minutes leaving a review (it can be as short as you like) on Goodreads, Bookbub, or your favorite retailer.

Thanks for reading and reviewing!

This book is dedicated to all of the amazing wedding assistants who worked with me over the years. Kate is a compilation of little bits of many of you (plus a good deal of fiction). Thanks for braving it through all the crazy weddings with me! It wouldn't have been nearly as much fun without you all by my side! xoxo

ACKNOWLEDGMENTS

This book would not have happened without the amazing help and inspired feedback from my advanced reading team. Thank you for catching my goofs and typos, and thank you for the spot-on editing suggestions. You all rock!

This book was inspired by one of my past weddings that took place on a superyacht during a massive rainstorm. All the characters are different but the setting is inspired by one of the craziest days in my wedding planning career. For everyone who was there that day with me, I hope you enjoy this fictionalized retelling. I've always thought it was the perfect setting for a murder!

A huge thank you to all my readers. It's always wonderful hearing from you so keep those emails, tweets, and messages coming!

ABOUT THE AUTHOR

Laura Durham has been writing for as long as she can remember and has been plotting murders since she began planning weddings over twenty years ago. Her first novel, BETTER OFF WED, won the Agatha Award for Best First Novel.

When she isn't writing or wrangling brides, Laura loves traveling with her family, standup paddling, perfecting the perfect brownie recipe, and reading obsessively.

She loves hearing from readers and she would love to hear from you! Send an email or connect on Facebook or Twitter or Instagram (links below) .

Find me on:

www.lauradurham.com

laura@lauradurham.com

Cover Design by Alchemy Book Covers